THRILLED TO DEATH

Books by L.J. Sellers

THRILLED TO DEATH

A DETECTIVE JACKSON MYSTERY

L.J. SELLERS

THOMAS & MERCER

Published by Thomas & Mercer
P.O. Box 400818
Las Vegas, NV 89140

ISBN-13: 9781612186184
ISBN-10: 1612186181

Library of Congress Control Number: 2012943266

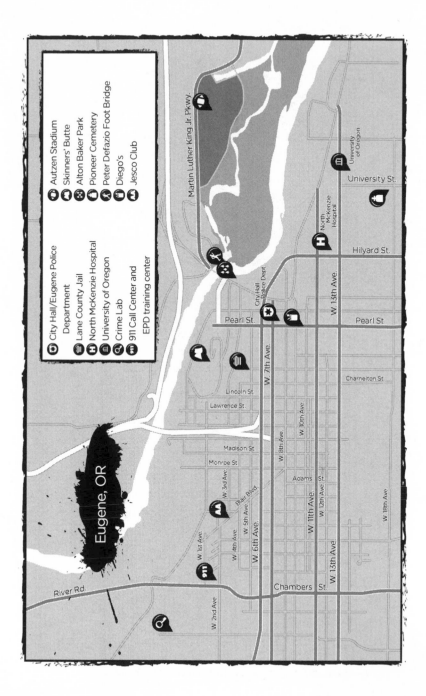

Cast of Characters

Wade Jackson: veteran detective/violent crimes unit
Kera Kollmorgan: Jackson's girlfriend/nurse
Danette Blake: Kera's ex-daughter-in-law
Michah: Danette's baby son/Kera's grandson
Katie Jackson: Jackson's daughter
Rob Schakowski (Schak): detective/task force member
Ed McCray: veteran detective/task force member
Lara Evans: detective/task force member
Michael Quince: detective/task force member
Robert Zapata: missing persons detective
Denise Lammers: Jackson's supervisor/sergeant
Sophie Speranza: news reporter
Rich Gunderson: medical examiner/attends crime scenes
Jasmine Parker: evidence technician
Joe Berloni: evidence technician
Rudolph Konrad: pathologist/performs autopsies
Victor Slonecker: district attorney
Jim Trang: assistant district attorney
Courtney Durham: rich young woman who disappears
Elle Durham: rich widow/Courtney's mother
Brett Fenton: Courtney's boyfriend
Brooke Durham: Courtney's sister
Stella Callahan: Courtney's psychiatrist
Elias Goodbe: founder of Young Mother's Outreach Center
Seth Valder: owner of strip club
Zoran Mircovitch: owner of Thrillseekers
Eddie Lucas (D.J.): owner of Dirty Jobs

THRILLED TO DEATH

CHAPTER 1

"I want to give my baby away." The words nearly tripped over each other in their rush to leave her mouth.

Dr. Callahan's eyes widened briefly. "How much thought have you given this?"

"I don't know." Danette squirmed in her chair. This was why she was in the psychiatrist's office, to verbalize some of the horrible things she'd been feeling. "I've been thinking about it for weeks, but without really admitting to myself that's what I want. I'm overwhelmed and depressed all the time. I don't think I love this baby as much as someone else would."

Dr. Callahan scribbled something on a pad. "Are you talking about giving him up for adoption?"

"Micah's grandmother would love to raise him."

Her shrink looked at the clock. "We're past our time, and I have another patient waiting." She handed Danette a slip of paper.

"This is a prescription for Lexapro. Start on it right away. I don't think the Paxil is working for you. Please don't do anything rash until we've had a chance to talk some more. You'll be back on Thursday, correct?"

Danette nodded. Thursday was her regular day, but she had called Dr. Callahan last night, crying and begging to come in because her life felt out of control and she no longer trusted herself with little Micah. Luckily there had been a cancellation for this morning.

Danette bolted from the office, feeling ashamed. What was wrong with her that she didn't want her own baby? Dr. Callahan clearly disapproved. Danette pulled up the hood of her sweatshirt, wishing she could hide her face as well. She pounded down the stairs and out of the building. Maybe she should leave Micah with Kera until she worked through this. The baby would be better off. Maybe she could go somewhere and clear her head for a while. As Danette crossed the parking lot, she pulled on sunglasses without really noticing the morning sun and bright-blue sky. She glanced at the beat-up cargo van parked next to her Toyota. It hadn't been there when she arrived.

As Danette turned the key in her car lock, she heard the van door slide open.

CHAPTER 2

Kera looked at the clock: 11:32 a.m. *Where was Danette?* She called her cell phone again but Danette still didn't answer. This time Kera left a message: "I'm a little worried because you said you'd be back by ten fifteen. I'm supposed to be at work in half an hour. Please call me."

After a few more minutes of vacillating, Kera called the Planned Parenthood clinic where she worked and told them her situation. She felt guilty about missing her shift because she only worked part-time. She and her ex-husband had used the life-insurance money from their son's death in Iraq to pay off the house, so her finances were more flexible now. Benefitting from Nathan's death made her so uncomfortable, Kera atoned for it by volunteering to care for disabled Iraq veterans. It never felt like enough.

She lifted three-month-old Micah out of his playpen. He grabbed her copper-colored braid and stuck it in his mouth. Kera gently extracted her hair and carried him out to the back deck, where the view of the city helped her relax. She was far more worried about her daughter-in-law than her job.

Legally, Danette was not her relative. Danette and her son, Nathan, had never married. In fact, they had barely known each other before he shipped out. Still, Nathan had left Danette pregnant and now they had Micah. Referring to Danette as her daughter-in-law was easier than saying *mother of her grandchild* or *dead son's girlfriend.*

Kera pushed Nathan from her mind. There was no point in compounding her worry with grief. She walked around the deck, showing Micah the petunias and geraniums blooming in big stone pots, but that only used five minutes. Kera debated whether to call Jackson. He would probably drop everything and start to investigate, but what if Danette was just out shopping, stealing a few minutes of free time away from the baby?

Kera tried to think of the name of the doctor Danette had gone to see. Carlson? Davison? Danette had called last night and asked if she could bring Micah by in the morning. Kera had been curious about the last-minute doctor's appointment and wondered why Danette didn't want to take the baby with her, but she hadn't asked. When she had been a new mother all those years ago, she hadn't let Nathan out of her sight until he was a year old.

Danette was a different kind of mother. She left Micah with anyone and everyone who would watch him. Kera worried Danette was not particularly bonded to her baby. She had only met the young woman last fall, but she sensed Danette was unhappy. Her recent move to Eugene, in hopes of attending nursing school, would make it easier on all of them.

Where was Danette now?

Kera remembered the doctor's last name: Callahan. She put Micah in his playpen and danced his little elephant up and down until he stopped fussing. She brought her laptop into the living room and got on the internet.

The online directory revealed two Dr. Callahans in the Eugene/Springfield area. One was a cardiac surgeon named Charles, and the other was a psychiatrist named Stella. The worry in her stomach tightened a notch. Was Danette seeing a mental-health professional? Yesterday, Kera would have considered that good news. Now that Danette was AWOL, it confirmed her worst fears.

Had Danette run off and abandoned her baby? Kera pictured a tearstained postcard arriving in the mail next week, explaining how it was all for the best. Despite her worry, a little part of Kera's heart leapt with joy at the idea she would get to keep Micah right here with her. She looked over at the boy as he kicked his feet and giggled at the bird mobile above his head. He looked so much like Nathan.

Kera tried calling Danette again. No answer.

She dialed Dr. Callahan and left a message: "This is Kera Kollmorgan, mother-in-law of Danette Blake. I believe Danette had an appointment with you this morning. She was supposed to return hours ago to pick up her child but hasn't shown up. I can't reach her by phone and I'm very worried. Please call me."

That was waste of time, Kera thought, clicking the phone closed. Psychiatrists and counselors were notoriously hard to reach, rarely returned phone calls, and wouldn't talk about their patients under any circumstances. At least she had done something. It wasn't in her nature to sit and wait.

Kera pressed speed dial #2 and hoped Jackson would pick up.

* * *

Jackson sat on the paper-covered table in the exam room, thinking he was wasting his time.

Dr. Murtz announced, "I believe you're still constipated. I'll write you a prescription for a laxative. That should take care of your bowel pain."

"What about the tightness in my chest?"

"That's just stress. Your heart sounds fine. Maybe you need a vacation."

"Maybe." Jackson hopped off the table and pulled on his clothes as Murtz left the room. Maybe he needed a new doctor. If the police department didn't make him get a physical once a year, he wouldn't even have a doctor. At six feet tall and right around two hundred pounds, he was healthy enough. He ate right, at least half the time, and now that he was involved with Kera, a fitness fanatic, he was running three days a week too.

Jackson tossed the prescription in the trash on his way out. He'd already been through one prescription, and he wasn't subjecting himself to it again. Maybe the pain in his gut was stress related too. Summer was coming; maybe he would take a real vacation this year. Take his daughter, Katie, to Magic Mountain, or better yet, surfing in Hawaii. He almost laughed at the thought of himself on a surfboard. He was the opposite of blond and tan, and not quite good-looking either, he mused.

On the way to his city-issued cruiser, Jackson remembered to take his phone off vibrate mode and saw Kera had called. As he started the car, he listened to her message: "It's Kera. I'm worried about Danette. Can you come over? It's official police business."

Her tone made him squeal the tires a little as he pulled into the street. He'd only known Kera for eight months, but he was crazy about her in a way he'd never experienced before. Or maybe he'd once felt this way about his ex-wife, before she'd started drinking, but he didn't remember it. His reality now was that he never had enough time with Kera, and he had to find a way to change that.

The trip to Kera's took ten minutes. Eugene, Oregon was a small college city and you could get from point A to point B in twenty-five minutes or less, even on a bicycle. As a police officer who had lived here his whole life, it often took him less.

Kera answered the door with a bundle of baby on her shoulder. She was tall, striking, and moved like an athlete. Jackson felt a little giddy every time he saw her. Kera gave him a forced smile. "I'm sorry to bother you with this, but I don't know what else to do."

"What's going on?" Jackson felt a stab of worry. Kera was more upset than he'd realized. He kissed her forehead. "Let's go sit down."

Jackson followed Kera into the kitchen, where she poured herself a glass of water and eased down to the table without jostling the baby. "Danette was supposed to pick up Micah two hours ago," Kera reported. "She had an appointment with a doctor, but she hasn't come back and she doesn't answer her phone."

Jackson gave her a gentle smile. "It's too soon to worry." He didn't want to dismiss her fears, just ease them. "Anything could have happened. A flat tire, a change of plans. Or maybe Danette ran into a friend and started talking."

"Why wouldn't she call or answer her phone?"

"Maybe she left her cell phone at the doctor's or in her car." Jackson poured himself some coffee. "You want some?"

Kera shook her head.

"We can try calling places where she might be."

"I already did." Kera pressed her lips together and looked as if she might cry. "Something is wrong. I just know it. Either something dreadful happened to Danette or she has abandoned her baby."

"What makes you think she might abandon Micah?"

"The doctor she saw this morning, Stella Callahan, is a psychiatrist. I know Danette has been depressed." Kera patted the baby's back as she talked. "Sometimes new mothers experience emotional and hormonal upheaval after the birth of a child, and they feel and act irrational. For some it's just postpartum depression; for others it goes way beyond."

Jackson reached for the little blue-eyed bundle. The boy smiled and Jackson felt a warm hand touch his heart. *Who could ditch this little guy?* "Have you called the hospitals?"

"Yes. I'm sorry to burden you with this."

"Don't be. I'm glad for something to focus on. Sergeant Lammers keeps giving me little bullshit cases."

"Oh, that's right. You had another doctor's appointment. What did he say?"

"He said I'm constipated."

Kera rolled her eyes. "Murtz is a moron. You need to go to the hospital and get a CAT scan or an MRI. The doctors in the ER will be able to diagnose this thing. It could be some kind of abnormal growth."

Jackson knew what she meant. "Next time the pain gets bad, I will."

"Promise me?"

"I will." Jackson stood. "I need two addresses: Danette's and the doctor she went to see. After I check out Danette's apartment, I'll drive over to the psychiatrist's and see if Danette kept her appointment or left her cell phone there. It makes sense for you to wait here in case she shows up."

As Jackson headed down Chambers, he called Sergeant Lammers and left her a message, telling her he was looking into a possible missing-person situation and would be in to the department later. The assault case he'd been assigned last week was going nowhere. Jackson had visited the woman in the hospital and she'd denied her boyfriend had attacked her. There was no point in looking for the *dark-haired man with a tattoo* she claimed had barged into her home and beaten her for no apparent reason. He didn't exist. Jackson worried that her boyfriend would eventually kill Cheri, but then at least he would be able to build a case against him.

The duplex where Danette lived, courtesy of taxpayer-funded Section Eight housing, was just off River Road and Sunny Street. The low-rent cul-de-sac housed a group of duplexes, each a little shabbier than the next. Two little girls rode tricycles in the asphalt center area. No parents seemed to be watching them. Danette's side of the building was dark and her car was not in the driveway. Jackson pounded on the door anyway. After a few minutes, he checked the knob, but it was locked. Out of thoroughness, he checked the side door under the carport and found it locked too. If this were a homicide investigation, he would pound on the neighbors' doors as well, but it was too early to assume Danette was missing. Jackson expected Kera to call any minute and tell him the young mother had turned up with some lame excuse for her behavior. He'd heard it all.

As he turned around, a woman stepped out of the home across the way and watched him until he got into the Impala. Jackson was glad someone was paying attention to the stranger in close proximity to the little girls. He would talk to that neighbor first if he had to come back.

It was a quick drive to the psychiatrist's office on Lincoln Street, on the edge of the downtown area. The small, two-story cinderblock building had a parking area in the back and was surrounded by private homes. Jackson scanned the lot but didn't see Danette's blue Toyota Corolla. It seemed unlikely she would still be here or that she would leave her car. He moved past the insurance agency on the first floor and slowly took the stairs to the offices on the second floor. The pain in his gut had receded to a dull background noise, and he wanted to keep it that way.

The shrink's office was at the end of the hallway. The door opened into a small lobby. A moment later, a voice came over an intercom: "This is Dr. Callahan. I'll be out to see you in ten minutes." He glanced up at the corner nearest the inner door and found the camera. *Interesting setup,* he thought. *Certainly cheaper than paying a receptionist to read magazines all day.* While he waited, he brainstormed his next moves. First, he would issue an attempt-to-locate on the Toyota, then he would go back to Danette's apartment and let himself in to look around.

At five minutes to one, a middle-aged man emerged from the inner office, glanced at Jackson, then scurried into the hall. The doctor appeared moments later. She did not approach him or offer her hand. "I'm Dr. Callahan. How can I help you?" She had a big face with a square jaw and was a little thick in the middle. The doctor still managed to be attractive.

"I'm Detective Wade Jackson. I'd like to ask you about Danette Blake." Jackson stood to be on her level. "I know about doctor-client confidentiality, but Danette seems to be unaccounted for at the moment and her mother-in-law is very worried. I'm hoping you'll humor me and answer a few questions."

Callahan's jaw tightened. "Unlikely. I won't discuss Danette's sessions or her treatment."

"For now, I just need to know if she kept her appointment this morning."

"She did."

"When was she here?"

"From nine o'clock to nine fifty-five."

"Did she say anything about where she was going when she left?"

"I couldn't tell you if she did."

"Danette is not answering her cell phone. Did she leave it here?"

A flicker of fear shot through Callahan's eyes. "Where is her baby?"

"Micah is with Kera, his grandmother." Jackson stepped toward the doctor. "Can we sit down and talk for a moment?"

She didn't budge. "I don't have anything else to say."

"Why are you worried about the baby?"

"I'm not."

"Will you check your office for Danette's phone?"

"Sure." Callahan pivoted and strode back through the door.

Jackson followed closely so she couldn't shut him out. Once inside, Callahan gave a cursory look around the small, plush office. "It's not here."

The room held two pieces of padded furniture where a patient might get comfortable. He checked the chair and the couch, running his hands along the seams to see if the phone had slipped out of sight. No luck.

"Satisfied?"

He scanned the floor and turned to Callahan, who stood with arms folded across her chest. "If Danette contacts you for any reason, please call me." Jackson handed her a business card. "I don't want to waste the department's time and resources looking for someone who isn't missing or doesn't want to be found."

"Fair enough."

"Would Danette abandon her baby?"

"I can't answer that."

"Thanks for your time."

Jackson gave another glance around the office but didn't see a young woman's coat or purse. He called Kera as he took the stairs down.

She was slow to answer. "What did you find out?"

"Danette had a session with the doctor, but she didn't leave her cell phone. Her car isn't in the parking lot, so I assume she drove away. Sorry, that's all I know so far." Jackson stopped in front of the insurance office. "What was Danette wearing when she dropped off Micah?"

"Faded blue jeans, a short-sleeved pink sweater, and a navy-blue zip-front sweatshirt with a hood. Why are you asking? Should I be worried?"

"I'm just gathering information that may be useful. Are you doing okay?"

"Yes and no. If she would only call. Even if she's not coming back. I just need to know."

"Try not to focus on it." Jackson was trying to be more empathetic. The females in his life had requested it. "I'll call the department and issue an attempt-to-locate. If we have every officer in town looking for her car or someone matching her description, we should find her soon."

"Thanks, Jackson. Call me if you learn anything at all."

When they had first gotten together, Kera had called him Wade, even though no one else did. He missed that. Still standing in the building's lobby, Jackson called the department and gave the desk officer the information.

"Is this a new missing-persons case?"

"Not officially yet. She's a friend of the family."

"How old is Danette?"

"Twenty."

The desk officer hesitated. "Unless you have reason to believe she's in danger, the attempt-to-locate isn't exactly protocol for someone that age."

"Humor me, please. My gut feeling is that this might be serious." Jackson's intestines were relatively quiet at the moment, but it wouldn't last. He hung up and walked into the insurance office. A thirty-something woman at the front desk looked up. "Welcome to Barnell's Insurance. How can I help meet your insurance needs today?"

Jackson wondered how many times a day the poor woman had to say that. He introduced himself. "I'm looking for a young woman who was in the building this morning. She's five-eight, dark haired, brown skinned, and wearing jeans and a dark-blue zip-up sweatshirt. Have you seen her?"

The receptionist shook her head. "Not this morning. I've been busy, so I haven't spent much time looking into the lobby."

"Had you seen her before today?"

"I saw her last week. She was headed upstairs." The woman flushed a little, looking sheepish. "I try not to pay attention to the psychiatrist's patients out of respect for their privacy."

"Did you notice anything unusual about this woman or her behavior?"

She thought for a moment. "I remember thinking she wasn't typical of Dr. Callahan's patients. Most of them are middle-aged, well-off, and white. I think that's why I noticed this young woman. Or maybe it was the creepy guy with her."

Jackson felt a little shimmer up his spine. "Describe him."

"Tall, six foot or more, dark hair pulled back into a short ponytail, dark clothes, and a little patch of facial hair." She pointed to the middle of her chin.

"He went with her upstairs?"

"No. He came into the lobby, then went back outside."

Jackson handed her a card. "If you think of anything, let me know."

In the parking lot, Jackson glanced around. A dark-green Scion and a maroon minivan were still in the far corner—probably employees—and a white midsize truck had pulled in while he was in the building. Still no blue Toyota. Jackson climbed into his Impala and sat for a moment, thinking. *Where would I go if I were twenty and had a chance to escape my responsibilities? Even for a few hours?*

The mall, of course. Valley River Center, with its clothing shops, jewelry stores, and sevenplex movie theater. Jackson called information and chose to be connected to the mall's business center. From there, he asked for the security department, described Danette, and asked them to watch for her.

"Is she dangerous?"

"No."

"I'll get word to the uniforms out there."

Jackson made a similar call to Gateway Mall in Springfield, Eugene's adjoining sister city, then headed back to Danette's apartment. Driving out River Road, the April sun heated up the car, so he rolled down the window. The fresh air felt great. Eugene in the springtime was a glorious place. The sky was often brilliant blue, the green canopy was back on the trees, and purple azaleas bloomed everywhere. He hoped the weather would hold until Saturday and that Saturday would still be a day off when it rolled around. Maybe he and Kera and Katie would hike up Spencer Butte and have a picnic.

He thought about calling Kera, but he had nothing new to report. He didn't want to hear the worry and disappointment in her voice. It was way too soon in their relationship to disappoint her. That would come in time. Right now, he wanted to be her knight in shining armor, to come to her rescue again. Just as he had when the crazy lady had poisoned Kera because she worked at Planned Parenthood. They'd met during that bizarre case last fall.

As he pulled into Danette's cul-de-sac, Jackson had the sinking feeling this situation would not turn out well. He checked his watch: 3:05. Danette had been missing for five hours. The idea that she was hanging out at the mall didn't hold together unless the young woman's mental-health problems were more complicated than Kera realized.

The skinny neighbor who had watched him earlier came out and pretended to search for something in her car. Jackson decided to approach her before she called the police. Her little girl came running out and the woman sent her back inside with a look.

Jackson introduced himself. "The young woman who lives across from you, Danette Blake, is a friend of the family and she's been missing for five hours. Have you seen her?"

"Not since early this morning. What do you mean by missing?"

"She didn't show up when she was supposed to."

"She could be with her boyfriend."

"What's his name?"

"I think I heard her call him Chad. I don't know his last name."

"What does he look like?"

"He's tall and has dark hair. He looks Indian."

"What kind of car does he drive?"

"I've never seen him in a car. I think he rides a bike." She made a face. "He probably lost his license."

"Do you know where I might find him?"

"I don't know anything about him. I barely know Danette. She just moved here a month ago."

"Thanks."

Jackson headed across the asphalt. He used a credit card to open the cheap lock and shook his head at people's failure to protect themselves with decent locks.

The scent of baby powder, wet diapers, and mashed bananas permeated the air and triggered a series of flashbacks. Katie as a baby in her little swing, bouncing to the music. Katie throwing mashed carrots at his face and laughing with delight. Jackson smiled. His daughter had grown up to be a lovely young woman of fourteen, who had come to share his passion for restoring and modifying vehicles. They were currently building a three-wheeled motorcycle together and were almost finished. He was a lucky man.

Jackson tucked away his memories and looked around. The place was messy with toys and clothes scattered around, but it was clean under the surface. Most important, there was no sign of upheaval or struggle, nothing to indicate Danette had left against her will. He headed for her bathroom to see if her stuff was still there. A woman might leave town with just the clothes on her back, but she wouldn't willingly leave behind her makeup and moisturizer.

The countertop was almost bare, and Jackson couldn't find any makeup in the drawers. He looked in the shower. Shampoo, conditioner, and razor were still in the white metal basket. Inconclusive, he decided. It was possible Danette simply didn't wear cosmetics. He headed into her bedroom and opened a small closet. It held plenty of clothing, much of it in bright shades of red, orange, and pink. The dresser was also full. If Danette had gone on the run, she had packed lightly.

A search of her living room revealed little. She had course catalogs for Lane Community College and the University of Oregon, magazines about baby care, a makeshift bookshelf full of sci-fi paperbacks, and a few unopened bills that had been forwarded to the new address. Danette hadn't lived here long enough to accumulate any real clutter. Jackson tried, and failed, to find an address book with contact information. He headed into the kitchen and spotted an open laptop on the table. The temptation to turn it on and snoop through her e-mails was overwhelming.

Yet he refrained. Danette had not even been gone long enough to justify filing a missing-persons report. He was only here because of Kera. If anyone else had asked the department to investigate this situation, they would have gotten a quick word of sympathy and a suggestion to come back later if she was still missing. He had no business violating Danette's personal space. Jackson abruptly left the house, locking it from the inside and pulling the door closed.

"I've done everything I can for now." Jackson stood in Kera's big, bright living room, feeling guilty. She looked so troubled. "Patrol units are on the lookout for Danette. Security guards at both malls are looking for her. I checked her apartment and I talked to her shrink. I'm sorry." He pulled Kera into his arms and held her for a moment. Micah was sleeping in his playpen.

"What now?" Kera pressed her lips together and fought back tears.

"In the morning, you go in to the department and file a missing-persons report."

"Why wait?"

"Adults aren't considered missing until they've been gone at least twenty-four hours."

Kera looked alarmed. "So much could happen between now and then. What if Danette's been kidnapped or assaulted?"

"This may not be reassuring, but I've already done more than anyone else will do. Except put her into the national database."

Kera tried to smile. "Thanks, Jackson. I'm glad to know you."

"I have to get into the department and file some paperwork on another case. Is there someone you can call to keep you company?"

"Don't worry. I'll be fine. I've got Micah to keep me occupied."

Jackson kissed her and left while she was still upbeat. He feared Kera still had a long way to go in dealing with this situation. Danette could turn out to be one of those never-ending cases in which a young woman simply vanishes and her family is left to wonder: *Did she run away? Is she dead and buried somewhere?* The fact that Danette's car was gone made Jackson lean toward runaway.

Kera had the strength to survive this; she'd been tested many times. Jackson had to unclench his fists to grab the wheel. Some people's lives seemed so blessed, while others took hit after hit. He thought God was out there somewhere, but didn't seem all that involved in personal lives. Jackson accepted that. He'd taken his share of hits too.

CHAPTER 3

DJ wished he'd remembered to put his CD collection back in the van. It was a long drive out to his client's house. He'd just passed through Veneta and still had five miles to go. He thought the girl might enjoy some music too. She had seemed terrorized when he'd grabbed her this morning. Even with the chloroform, she had managed to nail him in the ribs with an elbow before she went out. He hadn't expected it. This was only his second pickup of a live person, and he'd thought it would be easy. He'd snatched a few pets for people in the middle of nasty divorces, and once he'd picked up the corpse of an old man who'd died while banging his male lover and moved the geezer to save the family embarrassment. His one live-person snatch had been a high-on-heroin, fifteen-year-old girl whom he'd taken home to her parents. This was a new experience, and in his opinion, a pretty fucked-up situation.

He glanced in the rearview mirror, which was aimed down at the floor in the back of the van. The girl was almost completely conscious now and looked terrified. He was surprised. He'd expected the chloroform to last longer.

He reached for his radio and found a country-rock station. DJ sang along for a while, feeling pleased with himself for his morning's work. Even with the long drive out and back, per hour it was a sweet deal. Since he'd handled it so well, maybe his client would give him more contracts like it. It was so much better than crawling under houses to fetch dead animals.

He passed the five-mile marker and watched for the private driveway on the left. He'd only been here once before and the road was easy to miss. He slowed, turned between the two poplar trees, and stopped in front of the plain black gate with the camera mounted high in the center. After a moment, the gate opened and he entered the property.

* * *

Danette forced herself to breathe through her nose in long counts of ten. The bandanna not only made it hard to take in air, it cut into the corners of her mouth and made her eyes water, wetting the cloth that blindfolded her. Her head ached from the after-effect of whatever he'd used to knock her out.

She lay on her side, her hands bound in front by handcuffs and her ankles bound by thin nylon rope. She pulled her knees up next to her chin and tried to work the knots on her ankles. The handcuffs gave her just enough flex to maneuver. If he had used rope on her wrists instead…

Still, she made little progress, and her fingers soon ached. Danette rested for a moment and tried not to think about what was waiting for her.

The steady hum of tires told her they were traveling along a well-maintained road. She had no idea how long she'd been unconscious, so it was impossible to guess how long she'd been in the van. It felt like hours. *What do they want with me?* This wasn't about money, because she and her mother didn't have any, which meant it had to be about sex. *Oh dear god.* Danette prayed she wouldn't be raped.

Why me? Is God punishing me for not loving my baby? For wanting to give Micah away?

The hum of the tires changed pitch, and she realized the van was slowing. Her heart pounded as she frantically pulled at the nylon around her ankles, hindered by her inability to see what she was doing. She felt the van make a sharp left, then stop. What was next? Was she strong enough to take it? Her fingers found a loop and something gave. She pulled on the piece of rope that had a bit of slack. The van rolled forward again.

* * *

Instinctively, DJ glanced back at the girl. Everything was as it should be. She was still bound, gagged, and blindfolded. *Was she breathing? Shit.* He felt a stir of adrenaline as he stopped the van and stared at the girl's chest. She was breathing. He was just being paranoid. He let off the brake and rolled forward. It would all turn out okay. He would carry her into the house and his client would hand him a stack of cash. Then he would go back to his little Dirty Jobs business, which had earned him the nickname DJ, a much more manly name than what his mother had called him. The three thousand would get him caught up on the trailer-park rent and let him live a little on the wild side for a month or so. It was a no-risk deal he'd been promised.

After a quarter mile, the trees opened into a clearing and the big custom home came into view. Floor-to-ceiling windows in the foyer caught the midmorning sun. He pulled up in front of the attached three-car garage and waited. In a moment, the overhead door closest to the house opened and he pulled in. Was he supposed to wait or would his client come into the garage? This was new to him.

He decided the situation called for confidence. He climbed out of the van, scooted around to the side door, and opened it. The girl was on her knees, waiting. She lunged forward, head butting him in the chest. The blow knocked him back against the silver Mercedes. The girl fell forward and ended up straddling the opening, with her face against the concrete floor and her bound feet sticking up into the van.

She hadn't thought that through very well. He squatted, lifted her up on his shoulder, and carried her toward the house.

CHAPTER 4

Kera couldn't stop thinking about Danette. As she paced the house, she could feel her back muscles tense and her pulse accelerate. She knew this level of anxiety was unhealthy and unproductive, so she forced herself to sit down and take deep breaths. Little Micah needed her to be calm and happy. He was sleeping now, but when he woke he would pick up on her mood.

Kera moved to her computer in the office at the back of the house. She glanced at her wonderful view and remembered to thank the universe for being good to her. Financially anyway. She lived in a wonderful home and rarely worried about money. On a global scale, she was very fortunate. Before her son had been born, she'd spent a few years in Uganda working in a Red Cross medical center. The experience had given her a worldview she never let herself forget.

Her computer was still on from that morning, so she opened her Facebook page. She'd created the page at the urging of one of her coworkers, feeling a little silly about it at the time, then let it sit for a month or so. Recently, she'd been using the site, making friends, and communicating with people, including Danette. Kera hoped Danette's page might give her a clue.

She typed Danette's name into the search bar, and when her page came up, the first thing Kera checked was her last status update. At 10:15 the night before, Danette had posted: *This baby won't go to sleep and it's making me crazy.* The previous post at 2:06 yesterday afternoon said: *Micah is napping and I get to be a person for a few minutes!!!*

Kera scrolled down through a few more posts and got distracted by pictures of Micah. He looked so much like Nathan as a baby. Kera wondered if her grandson would still look like his father as he got older. If he did, would it be joyful or painful for her? Sometimes it was hard to tell the difference. Kera forced herself back to the task.

Danette's picture jumped out from the top left corner. She was striking, with prominent wide cheekbones, irises so dark you couldn't tell where the pupils stopped, and a full mouth that needed no lipstick. Few people would call her cute, but no one could walk past Danette without noticing her. Jackson had commented once that Danette was a darker-toned version of herself, and that was probably why Nathan had been attracted to her.

She moved down the page and clicked open Danette's friend list, hoping to find a dark-haired young man named Chad. He was not in the list of ninety-seven. She clicked open the pages of the last four friends who had commented on Danette's page and posted the same message: *Have you seen or heard from Danette today? Do you know where she is? If so, please e-mail my FB page.* Kera would have liked to hear from them in person, but she didn't dare post her phone number on an open internet page.

The baby cried out, making her jump out of her chair. Kera rushed to the living room. Micah was still on his blanket in the playpen and hadn't been awake long enough to work up a good wail. She picked him up and headed straight for the diaper bag. How long before she had to go out and buy baby supplies?

Kera fixed a bottle of formula and carried Micah into her office. It was tricky with the baby in her lap, but she managed to check her Facebook e-mail and was pleased to see she had already heard from a young woman named Melissa. Unfortunately, Melissa had nothing to add to the situation but panic (*OMG!*). Kera spent a few minutes responding and soothing the woman's fears. That was the dilemma. By asking around, she was spreading the worry. If Danette waltzed in an hour later, safe and sound, Kera would feel guilty about getting everyone stirred up over nothing.

This wasn't *nothing*. Jackson sensed it too or he wouldn't have made all the effort this afternoon.

Kera called Danette's mother again. "Margaret, it's Kera. Have you heard anything?"

"I called everyone I could remember Danette has hung out with in the last year. No one has seen her or heard from her." Mrs. Blake sounded as distressed as Kera felt.

"Unless you think Danette will show up at your house, you're welcome to come to Eugene and stay with me while we figure this out." Margaret lived in Corvallis, another college town about thirty miles away. "I know how hard it is to be alone when you're worried about your child."

"Thank you. That's very kind. If I can arrange for some time off work, I might do that."

After they hung up, Kera started thinking about Danette's computer and what she might learn by checking her e-mail. Jackson had already been inside the house, so it must be easy to get in. Kera called him, but he didn't pick up, so she left a message. He was probably home by now, having dinner with Katie. Kera suppressed a little pang of jealousy. Jackson needed alone time with his daughter. That's what made him a great guy.

CHAPTER 5

Jackson entered Sergeant Lammers' office and braced himself for an argument. The big woman smiled. "Jackson, how are you feeling?"

"Okay." Her niceness worried him.

"What did your doctor say?"

"He thinks I'm constipated."

"He says you're full of shit?" She burst out laughing.

Jackson returned the grin. "Aren't we all?"

The sergeant got control, smiled again. Denise Lammers was two hundred pounds of muscle and ambition. Even when she looked happy, she was still intimidating. "Do you have the doctor's report?"

"The office faxed it over. It was addressed to you."

"I haven't seen it, but if you say you're ready to take on big cases, I'll send them your way. You still have the best homicide-clearance rate in the department."

"Thank you. Is that all?"

"Actually, I have a request."

Jackson's bowels churned. "What is it?"

"I want you to do an interview with a reporter. Take her around with you for a day and show her what the job is like."

Now he understood the smile and hated her for it. "Why me? Why not Evans or Quince? They both like that kind of thing."

"She asked for you."

Oh shit. A squeezing pain unlike anything he'd ever experienced shot through his left kidney. "Why is this necessary?"

"It will be great PR for us. An in-depth story about how our department solves homicide cases. The reporter may even turn it into a book."

"We don't need that kind of publicity."

Lammers slammed her meaty fist against the desk. "Yes we do! We are in a funding crisis like never before. The county releases criminals from the jail as fast as we arrest them, and the public is fed up. But the damn taxpayers won't approve bonds to increase the budget. The best thing this department has going for it is our homicide-clearance rate. We might as well showcase the part we get right." She whacked the desk again, a little less vigorously. "It's an interview, Jackson. She earned the right. Just fucking do it."

"Yes, ma'am." Jackson left the room. As he strode down the hall, his chest tightened. He forced himself to breathe deeply. Even more than he hated the idea of spending a day with Sophie Speranza, reporter for the *Willamette News*, he hated being ordered to do so. This was not in his job description.

He felt the other detectives in the crowded room watching him as he strode toward his desk. It was that point in the late afternoon when they had people from both shifts milling about. He didn't meet anyone's eyes. He needed a moment to process. Burying his face in his computer screen so no one would come up to him, Jackson tried to work his mind around the situation. Sophie had broken open a case in February by interviewing assault victims and finding the link between them, so he owed her something. This would be a chance to pay her back. The slate would be clean and he wouldn't have to take her calls anymore.

"Jackson, are you okay?" Evans' voice was suddenly there. Jackson opened his eyes, not realizing he'd even closed them.

"I'm fine."

From the look on Evans' face, she didn't believe him. "What did the doctor say?"

How the hell did everyone know he'd been to the doctor? "I'm fine." He stared hard, hoping she would back off. She was the newest detective in the unit and had been assigned to work with him a year ago as a training experience. Evans had quickly proved to be a resourceful investigator. As a bonus, her heart-shaped face, bright-blue eyes, and tight body were a nice change of pace from looking at Schakowski. "How's your case going?"

"Don't change the subject. The doctor said you're fine, now what did Lammers want? You looked so pissed coming out of there, it has to be major."

"She wants me to give Sophie Speranza an interview, take her around with me for a day."

Evans started to laugh, then stopped. "I'm sorry. It won't be that bad. Let me know if I can help."

"Thanks. I think I'll call Sophie now and set it up. Might as well get it over with while I don't have a big case hanging."

"I thought you were working on a missing-persons case."

Crap. Just because he'd been to see his doctor twice in the last ten days didn't mean everyone had to know his every movement. He was fine! Out loud he said, "Danette dropped her baby off with Kera this morning and never came back. We have no idea what's going on."

"That's pretty weird. Her baby's only a few months old."

"Danette may be just taking a break. It's tough being a single mom."

"Again, let me know if I can help. I'm still interviewing witnesses in the bar shooting, but I have a confession so the hard work is over."

"Thanks."

Evans went back to her work space, about six feet away. The big open room was crammed full of desks, and the workstations were grouped by unit: burglary/theft, violent crimes, and special investigations. Narrow walkways lined with filing cabinets separated the clusters. The only bright spot was a bank of windows along the outside wall, but the vertical wooden beams surrounding the building ruined the view.

After staring at his phone for a full minute, Jackson called Sophie.

She sounded surprised to hear from him. "Thanks, Jackson. I'm so excited about this opportunity."

"Can we do it tomorrow? I happen to have some free time, and who knows when it will happen again."

"Sure. I can arrange that. How early can I come in? I'd like to spend most of the day."

"Be here at ten o'clock, and we'll see how it goes."

"See you then."

Jackson dreaded the interview most of all. He hated answering questions. He could ask them all day, but it was not in his nature to respond to probing. He shut off his computer, filed his paperwork from the assault case, and headed out.

On his way to pick up Katie from drill-team practice, the pain flamed near his kidney again. This time it was so bad he had to pull off into a store parking lot. He waited ten minutes for the burning to subside, then called his ex-wife.

"Renee? I need you to do me a favor and pick up Katie and take her to your place."

"Are you working a homicide?"

"I'm going to the emergency room."

"Seriously? In the sixteen years we were married, you never saw a doctor except for your annual physical."

"Maybe I should have. Tell Katie I'm fine. I just need to get an MRI, so I know what's going on."

"Are you in pain?"

Jackson realized he'd never told Katie or Renee about his flare-ups. Only Kera and Sergeant Lammers knew the specifics. "I've had this pain in my lower abdomen off and on for months." He decided to keep the chest-tightening symptom to himself. "Don't worry. My doctor thinks it's nothing."

"Please keep us posted. Katie will worry if you don't call."

Jackson started his cruiser and headed across the downtown area to North McKenzie. He'd spent plenty of time at the hospital over the years, usually waiting to question a victim or a witness, but he'd never been a patient. This morning when Kera had said he might have a growth, it had been a wake-up call. *What if this was cancer?* It felt like it had invaded his kidneys. Nobody survived kidney cancer. What if he had waited too long?

Jackson thought about his last will and testament, which hadn't been updated in a long time. As a patrol cop, he'd been encouraged to keep his affairs in order. The first responders to a situation were always more at risk. *Oh, damn.* Was Renee still his beneficiary? He would have to change that and ensure his life-insurance money went into a trust for Katie.

The downtown hospital was only a block from the University of Oregon, and the side-by-side institutions were major employers and life forces in the community. North McKenzie was building a new hospital on the outskirts of Springfield, so the dynamic would change and not for the better. Jackson found a parking space on the first floor of the parking garage across the street. Grateful for the short walk, he tried not to hold his gut or wince as he hobbled in.

The glass-walled waiting area in the ER was moderately quiet. Jackson only counted three people who looked miserable enough to be checked in for services: a young man with a bloody towel wrapped around his hand, an older woman who kept putting her head in her lap, and a little boy with fever-pink cheeks who slept against his mother. The others waiting in the hard plastic chairs were keeping company.

Jackson sat in one of the little cubicles at the check-in counter. A thirty-something woman in purple scrubs with deadpan delivery asked him twenty-seven questions: *When was your last bowel movement? Are you here because you want pain medication? Have you ever been tested for HIV?*

He was glad he wasn't bleeding, because she was in no hurry to get him back to see a doctor. After fifteen minutes with the questioner, he took a seat near the dizzy old woman. Jackson knew he should call Kera, but he hesitated. She was already worried about Danette, and he hated to add to her stress. Yet his cell phone was in his hand and he felt an overwhelming need to hear her voice.

"Hi Kera. Any news?"

"Not yet. I even got on Facebook and contacted some of Danette's friends. It's almost seven o'clock. This is not a case of a young woman stealing a few hours of free time."

He could hear her effort not to sound panicked. "You're probably right, but it could still be a case of a young woman escaping the responsibilities of parenthood. There's no reason to assume she's in danger."

"I want to get inside her house and get on her computer. I need to find Chad's last name so you can run a background check."

Jackson lowered his voice. "It's not a good idea. What if Danette *is* in trouble? What if the perpetrators come to her house looking for something? You could be in danger."

A pause. "I hadn't thought about that. What could Danette be involved in?"

"Drugs come to mind."

"She's not a user. I would know."

"She does need money, and there's money in running drugs."

"I don't believe it." In the background, Micah started to wail. Kera said, "I've got to go. Call me later." She got off the phone.

Jackson wanted to wail too. The hot-knife pain that used to come and go was now constant and nailing him on both sides. *If both kidneys hurt, it probably wasn't cancer.*

Jackson looked around to see if anyone had been called back while he was on the phone. The young man with the bloody hand was gone. Had he grown tired of waiting?

Two hours later, he climbed on a table and closed his eyes as they slid him into a big square machine with a round hole in the middle. The ER doctor, a thin man with an Indian accent, had ordered a CAT scan. When Jackson had mentioned his primary-care physician's theory about constipation, Dr. Malik looked alarmed. "That is nonsense."

Two hours after that, Dr. Malik came into the little exam room where Jackson was stretched out on the narrow table trying to nap. He sat up, pulling the thin blanket with him. The doctor looked distressed. Jackson's heart missed a beat. "Mr. Jackson, I think I know what's going on."

"Yeah?" His heart slammed so hard he expected the doctor to hear it. "What have I got?"

Dr. Malik pulled up a rolling stool and sat close to the exam table. He held out CAT scan images for Jackson to view. "Do you see these white swirls here?"

All Jackson saw was a big black-and-white mess, but he nodded. They'd given him a painkiller earlier. It hadn't done much for the hot-knife feeling, but his brain was a little fuzzy.

"We're looking down from your skull into your abdomen. The round area in the middle is your aorta, and the white swirls are a fibrotic growth. I consulted with a local urologist and we believe it's retroperitoneal fibrosis. You've probably had it a long time."

Jackson's hand went to his heart. It wasn't cancer, but it sounded serious. He swallowed the lump in his throat. "Is it going to get me?"

"That's hard to say. It's very thick around your aorta, but it doesn't seem to be growing over your heart."

"Why do my kidneys hurt?"

"Because this growth goes around your aorta all the way down to the top of your legs. See here?" The doctor held up another black-and-white image and pointed at something. "These are your ureters. The fibrosis is strangling them and preventing your kidneys from draining properly. You're lucky, because I've seen this disease before even though it's very rare. Most ER doctors wouldn't have any idea what this is."

Jackson tried to feel lucky. "What do we do now?"

"Step one. We put stents into your ureters to open them up." The doctor used his fingers and his clipped Indian accent to outline the plan. "Step two. You make an appointment to see a urologist and a cardiologist."

"Can you give me a clue? Is this thing reversible?"

"The growth can often be controlled with steroids, but you will likely need surgery to free the ureters from the fibrosis."

"There's no cure?"

"No, but you may be able to live with it for quite some time."
Dr. Malik gave him a grim smile. "Sometimes, but not often, it
goes into remission."

"Will I be functional and able to work?"

"Most likely."

Jackson reached for his pants. He'd heard all he could process
in one sitting.

"You're not going home yet."

"No?"

"We have to put stents in right now or you'll lose your
kidneys."

Jackson tried to imagine how they would get stents into his
urinary channels. *Oh god.* Nauseated, he lay back down.

"We can give you general anesthesia so you're unconscious,
but it's really not necessary. It's a very simple procedure."

Right. Why would he want to be unconscious while they
shoved little plastic tubes into his penis? Jackson suppressed a
moan. The anesthesia would take too much time before and after.
He needed to get this over with and get going. He had a missing
person to find.

"You can give me something though, can't you? Maybe a mild
tranquilizer?"

"Of course. The room is ready now if you are."

CHAPTER 6

Tuesday, April 7, 8:16 a.m.

When the doorbell rang early the next morning, Kera nearly dropped the coffee she was carrying. She set the cup on the desk and ran for the front door. It had to be Danette. Thank god, this would be over.

Margaret Blake stood on the front step, her expression grim, her black clothes giving off the vibe she was already in mourning.

"Margaret, come in."

"Call me Maggie, please. We're family now whether we like it or not." Danette's mother came in, pulling a small suitcase behind her. Mrs. Blake was shorter, heavier, and paler than her daughter. Kera often wondered about Mr. Blake, because Danette looked nothing like her mother.

"I'm glad you're here."

"What else could I do? I was going crazy sitting at home."

"Would you like some coffee?" Kera led her toward the kitchen.

"Sure. How's the baby?"

"He's fine. He's sleeping in his daybed in my bedroom. He was up half the night and just went back to sleep. I feel like I haven't slept."

"Me neither."

Kera noticed Maggie did not ask to see Micah. In the kitchen, Kera poured coffee and Maggie said, "I didn't want Danette to have this baby. I was so afraid it would ruin her life. I raised a child alone, so I know how difficult it is. Now something terrible has happened to her." Maggie began to cry.

Kera instinctively put a hand on her shoulder. It was good to have Maggie here. Now she had a reason to stay strong and not give in to her own emotions. "We don't know that she's in danger. In fact, I think she may have taken off with a new boyfriend."

"Without the baby?"

"Danette's appointment yesterday was with a psychiatrist. I think she's been depressed."

Maggie's eyes widened. "I didn't know. Danette and I haven't been close lately. We argued so much about her decision to keep the baby it caused a strain. I feel terrible."

"Whatever is going on with Danette is not your fault. Post-partum depression is caused by brain chemistry and hormones."

"What are we going to do?"

"I'll file a missing-persons report with the police, then go over to Danette's house and, if I can get in, I'll go through her e-mail to see what I can find." Kera finished her coffee, which had gone cold. "Would you mind staying here and taking care of Micah? I think one of us needs to be here in case Danette shows up."

"Sounds like a good plan."

As she drove downtown to city hall, Kera wanted to call Jackson and see how he was doing, but she didn't want to wake him this early after his long ordeal at the hospital the night before. He'd called her around nine o'clock and told her about his RF diagnosis. Her instinct had been to drive straight to the hospital, but Jackson had convinced her to stay home with the baby. She felt guilty about not being with him during his procedure, but she suspected that's what Jackson wanted. He wasn't ready to let her see him in a hospital gown. She understood he associated medical issues with weakness. As a person with a chronic disease, he would have to get over that.

Until she'd researched it online the night before, she hadn't known much about retroperitoneal fibrosis. Now she knew it was fickle. Some people lived long, relatively normal lives, and others had surgery after surgery and still died young.

By the time she found a place to park on Pearl Street, the sun had burned through the clouds and was shining brightly on the new leaves sprouting everywhere. Climbing the stairs to the white brick building, Kera felt a glimmer of optimism. Spring was a time of rebirth. Jackson would be one of the lucky ones, and Danette would be fine too. Maybe she had simply taken a day to clear her head.

Once inside police headquarters, Kera stated her business to the woman behind the plexiglass, then was escorted back into the bowels of the department. They passed a large open area crammed with desks. She wondered which one was Jackson's. This was the first time she'd been past the barrier.

In a small office down the hall, the desk clerk dropped her off. "This is Detective Zapata. He handles most of our missing people." The detective stood and smiled broadly, white teeth gleaming under his mustache. Kera liked him instantly.

"Please have a seat," he said. "How can I help you?"

She eased onto the hard chair, purse in her lap, knot in her stomach. Kera wondered how many others had sat here, worried sick about someone they loved. She took a breath and told him everything that had happened since yesterday morning.

"What was she seeing the doctor about?" Detective Zapata got right to the heart of it.

"Dr. Callahan is a psychiatrist. I suspect, but do not know for sure, that Danette has postpartum depression."

"Have you tried contacting the father of the baby?"

"My son is the father. He died in Iraq before Micah was born." She could say it now without losing control.

"I'm sorry to hear that." The detective gave her a sincere look of sympathy. After a moment, he said, "Does Danette use drugs?"

"No."

"Does she have a boyfriend?"

"She was seeing a guy named Chad. Tall and dark with a soul patch. That's all I know. Detective Jackson may have found out more by now."

Zapata raised his thick dark eyebrows. "Jackson is already investigating?"

"He looked into a few things yesterday."

The detective gave her a look she couldn't read. "Have you considered the possibility that Danette doesn't want to be found?"

"Of course, but what if something happened to her? I want you to investigate."

"We'll do everything we can. Do you have a photo of Danette?"

Kera handed him a disk with a JPEG file. "Her mother said this was taken last year."

"Great." Zapata slid the disk into his computer. "If you can get the boyfriend's last name, it would help us."

"I'll try."

After another ten minutes of answering questions, Kera left the little office and headed toward the front of the building. A feeling that the report would be filed and forgotten settled into the pit of her stomach. Thank god she knew Jackson. He would follow up, even if he had to do it on his own time.

In the lobby, an attractive young woman with short red hair stood in front of the window and swore. "Damn! Detective Jackson said to meet him here at ten o'clock."

"I can try to locate him for you," the desk officer said, her voice muffled behind the protective shield.

"I think I can help." Kera turned toward the petite woman with the oversized red leather bag. "I'm Kera Kollmorgan, a friend of Jackson's. He's out sick this morning. I'm sure he's sorry to have missed your appointment and you'll hear from him soon."

"Sophie Speranza, *Willamette News*." She offered her hand and gave Kera a quick sizing up.

The infamous Sophie? Kera found it hard to believe Jackson had planned an interview with her. "It's good to meet you. I've read your news stories."

Something clicked in Sophie's eyes. "You're the nurse from Planned Parenthood who was almost killed last fall."

"Still alive and well." Kera suddenly realized she had an opportunity here. "Would you like to have coffee, Sophie? I have a story you might be interested in."

They walked over to Full City Coffee, ordered tall house blends, and found a small table in the back of the crowded little pastry house.

"Is that how you know Jackson?" Sophie asked. "From the Planned Parenthood bombing?"

"It's how we met. We're dating now."

"Interesting." Sophie dug around in her big bag for a notepad and pen. "What's really going on with Jackson? I can't imagine him calling in sick."

"It's the truth and that's all I can tell you."

"Okay. What's your story?" Sophie clicked her pen, signaling her readiness.

"My daughter-in-law is missing. She dropped off her baby with me yesterday morning to take care of for an hour and never came back. No one has seen her since she left the doctor's yesterday around ten o'clock."

"No kidding?" Sophie looked up from her scribbling. "What about the baby's father?"

"My son was killed in Iraq. He and Danette were never married."

"Do you think she abandoned her baby?"

"Why do you assume that's what happened?"

Sophie held up her hands. "It was just a question."

"Sorry I snapped. I'm curious about why that was the first thing you thought." Kera believed Detective Zapata had come to the same conclusion. "Why not assume something happened to prevent her from coming back?"

"I'm not sure." Sophie put her pen in her mouth and pondered. "It's the baby factor. A young single mother, likely overwhelmed. She doesn't seem like a target for a kidnapper. What else is there? If she had been in a car accident, you would have heard by now."

Kera struggled to control her emotions. "I know. I've been through a hundred scenarios in my mind. Danette's car is gone but her clothes are not." Kera took a sip of her coffee. "What if someone did grab her? What if she fell and hit her head and now has amnesia? I'd like to get Danette's picture in the paper and on the network news. It's the least we can do."

"Tell me everything. I'll do what I can."

CHAPTER 7

Jackson woke with a burning need to pee. He felt as if he'd consumed a twelve-pack of diet soda, then promptly passed out. He charged into the bathroom and relieved himself.

A few minutes later while getting dressed for work, his bladder signaled him again. He headed back to the bathroom. *How much fluid had they given him at the hospital?*

Apparently, not that much. The need to pee was there, but the urine was not. Jackson remembered the ER doctor casually mentioning the stents might produce a slight discomfort. Oh joy. Nothing like walking around with a full-bladder sensation. His ex-wife had complained about the feeling for the last month of her pregnancy. Now he understood.

At least his kidneys were still working, Jackson reminded himself as he made coffee. So far, no intense pain like before. The disease was livable for most patients, the doctor had said. Jackson tried to put the diagnosis and impending surgery out of his head.

Obsessing about it wouldn't change his reality. He had a young woman to find.

Again, all eyes were on him as he entered the crowded space. The wooden slats outside the windows gave the room a jail-like quality. For a while, they'd had hope the voters would approve a bond for new headquarters, but the economic meltdown had crushed it. Jackson moved a little slower than usual, the stents exerting a constant mild pressure. He hoped no one noticed. His coworkers were giving him the once-over, this being the first time he'd called in sick in recent memory. He nodded at Schakowski to let him know information would be forthcoming and ignored everyone else.

Jackson checked his voice mail and found two calls from Cheri, his hospitalized assault victim. In the first, she said she wanted to change her statement and press charges against her boyfriend. In the second, she did a 180 and said never mind. Disgusted, Jackson hung up and listened to his third message. It was from Sergeant Lammers.

"I can't believe you called in sick just to get out of an interview with a reporter!" Lammers yelled the minute the door closed behind him. She was standing, her giant frame almost eyeball to eyeball with his. "Shit, Jackson. That really sets my ulcer on fire."

"I was at the hospital until about two this morning. I honestly forgot about Sophie Speranza."

"The hospital?" Lammers looked skeptical, but she sat down.

"The pain got pretty bad, so I went to the ER. They did a CAT scan and found a growth."

"A tumor?"

"No, a fibrous growth. It's not malignant like cancer, but right now it's interfering with my kidneys, so I need surgery. I'll be fine."

"Shit, Jackson. That sounds serious." Lammers almost looked sympathetic.

He pulled his shoulders back. "Not really. I'll just need to take steroids."

"Should you be at work?"

"No reason not to." Jackson kept it casual. "I'll need some time off after the surgery, but that's it." He refused to think about or mention that the nasty stuff was growing around his aorta too. This could be his last month on the job for all he knew, but the mode around here was *Show no fear*.

"Hmph." Lammers tapped the desk with her pen. "When is your surgery?"

"I don't know yet. I have an appointment with a urologist on Wednesday."

"Keep me posted. If you need time off, let me know."

"Thanks."

He turned to leave, and Lammers said, "Call that reporter and reschedule your interview ASAP."

Crap! He left Lammers' office, thinking her lack of curiosity about his condition was both welcome and unsurprising. He would not get so lucky with the other detectives. He decided to circumvent answering questions all day by sending out a group e-mail. It would spare his fellow tough guys the uncomfortable social encounter in which they had to express concern while not openly feeling sorry for him. Instead, they could shoot back an e-mail that said, *Tough break. Take it easy.*

Jackson decided to call Sophie and get the interview over with today if he could. He hated having it hanging over him for Lammers to nag him about. Sophie picked up on the first ring. "Hey, Jackson. Thanks for calling. Are you okay?"

"Sort of. We can still do the interview if you're up for it. I'm working on a missing-persons case and you can sit in on some of the process."

"Great. I'm on my way."

When they were in the privacy of the soft-interview room, Sophie said, "I met your girlfriend this morning. I like her. She's a feisty, take-charge kind of woman."

Jackson recoiled. He hated the thought of Sophie chatting up Kera. "How did you meet Kera?"

"Right here, out in the lobby. She had just filed a missing-persons report, and I was here to meet you. She told me about Danette. I'm hoping to get a story and photo into the paper."

"Great. This is one kind of case that needs publicity." *Unlike all the others you hound me about.* "Let's get this rolling."

Sophie looked at her list of questions. "What made you decide to be a cop?"

Jackson decided to share a memory from when he was a kid, hoping it would make the reporter happy so they could move on. "When I was ten, my older brother Derrick and I had a yard service. Once, being lazy kids, we dumped leaves in the trash can of the crazy old woman next door and she called the police. When the cop showed up at our house wanting to talk to us, I was scared. But he was a good man, gentle, and he listened to us. In the end, he complimented Derrick and me for having our own business. I was captivated by his uniform, his gun, his authority, and his compassion. At that moment, I decided to become a cop when I grew up."

"Is this the only job you've ever had?"

"Since I was twenty-two."

"Any regrets?"

"None. I love my work. The only downside is sometimes during the first few days of a homicide I have to leave my daughter with her aunt or her mother, but I try to make up for it." Jackson stood. "Let's go down to missing persons so you can see how we work a case."

In the expanded cubicle area that served as his office, Robert Zapata was on the phone, looking tired and annoyed. He motioned for Jackson to sit, but Jackson waited, not wanting to put pressure on his kidneys until he had to.

"Hey, Jackson. Take a load off." Zapata rubbed his eyes. "Who is this lovely woman with you?"

"This is Sophie Speranza from the *Willamette News.* She's writing a story and is here to observe." They both took seats, Jackson pulling a chair from a nearby empty desk. "I wanted to let you know what I'd done so far about Danette Blake."

"I'm listening."

About halfway through his summary, the front-desk officer stepped into the space and announced, "We've got another missing woman."

CHAPTER 8

"This is Elle Durham. She'd like to speak with you about her daughter." The desk officer backed out to make room, as a thin blonde woman in her late forties slipped into the crowded space. The woman had been attractive once, but now her skin seemed too loose for her face. Her gray cashmere pantsuit, on the other hand, fit well. Jackson couldn't name the designer, but he knew money when he saw it.

In a moment, he recognized her name. Her husband, Dean, now deceased, had invested first in timber, then real estate. The Durhams owned half of downtown Eugene and various other commercial properties.

Jackson looked over at Sophie, hoping she would leave without being asked. Her eyes begged him to let her stay. His expression said no.

"I'll be in touch about when we can finish this," she said, gathering her notepad and recorder. They all waited quietly while she put on her coat and left.

Zapata spoke first. "Hello, Ms. Durham. I'm Detective Robert Zapata. Please have a seat."

"I'm Detective Wade Jackson." He pulled the chair back for her.

"My daughter, Courtney, didn't come home last night and didn't call. I'm very worried."

"How old is she?" Zapata asked.

"She just turned twenty-one."

"She lives with you full-time?"

"Yes, of course." Mrs. Durham seemed surprised by the question.

"When did you see her last?" This was Zapata's area of expertise, so Jackson let him take the lead. Considering Danette's disappearance, he intended to hear this one out.

"She left for Diego's last night around eight thirty. Diego's is a nightclub."

"Has your daughter ever stayed out all night before?"

A long pause. "Yes, but she always calls."

"Did she drive to Diego's? Have you checked to see if her car is in the parking lot?"

"She always takes a cab if she plans to drink, so her car is still in the garage at home."

"Maybe she went home with someone and slept in." Zapata kept his voice soft.

"Courtney's not like that anymore. She has a steady boyfriend now." Elle Durham twisted her marble-sized diamond ring. "She would have called or come home by now if she was able to. It's four in the afternoon and no one has seen her. Not Brett, not Brooke. I've called everyone."

"Is Brett her boyfriend?" Zapata keyed something into his computer.

"Yes."

"What's his last name and when did he see her last?"

"Brett Fenton. He talked to Courtney on the phone yesterday afternoon."

"Ms. Durham." Zapata paused. "According to our records, you reported Courtney missing last March, and she turned up two days later in Seattle, having a good time."

"Courtney has changed." Elle's lower lip trembled and she bit down on it. "She wouldn't do this to me now. It's different this time, I can tell." Her voice rose at the end, pleading.

"I have five other cases," Zapata said. "Some of those missing people are young children. We can't afford to waste our time. I don't mean to sound uncaring, but I suspect your daughter will turn up soon, as she has in the past."

Elle stiffened. "Are you saying you won't look for Courtney?"

Zapata shook his head. "I'm saying I can't make this case a priority. Our resources are stretched thin."

"That's ridiculous." She took a sharp tone. "My late husband made significant donations to the Eugene Public Safety Department. My daughter is missing and I want a proper investigation."

Jackson was glad not to be sitting on the other side of the desk, and there was nothing he could say to be supportive.

"Of course." Zapata nodded at Ms. Durham. "What was Courtney wearing when she left the house?"

"I don't know. I was resting."

"Do you have a current picture of her with you?"

"Yes." She pulled a manila envelope from her shoulder bag and slid an eight-by-ten color print across the desk. Jackson stepped around to look over Zapata's shoulder. Blonde and beautiful, Courtney's only flaw was that her green eyes were set a little too close together. Still, she was hard to look away from.

Zapata read from his computer screen. "Her last report reads: 'Five-seven, a hundred and twenty pounds, with long blonde hair and green eyes. No scars, tattoos, or piercings.' Is all that still correct?"

"She has a tattoo on her lower back now. It's a pink-and-black floral design." Elle made a face. "It's hideous, but I couldn't have stopped her even if I had known in advance."

Jackson spoke up. "Have you noticed anything different about Courtney's behavior lately? Any new friends or hobbies or patterns?"

Elle spun around to him. "It's so hard to tell. Courtney always has something new going on. Lately it's been this crazy mountain bike–riding club. She comes home with scrapes and bruises, but she loves it." Elle let out a sigh. "I don't keep track of her friends anymore. I used to try, but it's impossible."

"Has she seemed moody or depressed?" Jackson asked.

Ms. Durham gave it some thought. "Courtney is always a little moody, but never depressed. I'm worried that someone drugged her drink or something. I don't trust that crowd at Diego's."

An awkward silence followed. Finally, Zapata said, "We'll do what we can to find her."

"That's it?"

"For now. I'll put out an alert, then go over to Diego's and talk to the staff. If you think of anything else that seems important, let us know."

Ms. Durham seemed reluctant to leave. She looked over at Jackson. "You think something has happened to her, don't you? What is it? Tell me." She sounded distraught for the first time.

"I'm sorry, I don't have any theories. Just questions."

Still, she didn't look as if she planned to leave.

"You should let us get to work," Zapata said.

"Fine." She slung her purse over her shoulder and walked out.

Zapata shook his head. "I feel sorry for that woman. If I had a daughter like Courtney, I'd lock her up."

"Does she have an arrest record?"

Zapata glanced at his monitor. "Shoplifting, public drunkenness, and indecent exposure. Nothing too serious, but still, looking for her is a waste of our time."

"Do you think there's any possibility Danette Blake's disappearance is connected to Courtney Durham's?"

"No." Zapata gave an emphatic head shake. "Courtney is off on a drunken adventure and forgot to call Mom, and Danette is probably a runaway. That's my best guess for now." Zapata stood. "Meanwhile, I've got to tell a different mother that her ex-husband quit his job two days ago and most likely left town with her kids."

"I'll keep looking into Danette Blake for a while if that helps."

"Thanks. It does."

* * *

The shabby duplex with the faded paint and empty driveway sank Kera's spirits. She had wanted Danette to move to Eugene so she could help her with Micah, but she had not envisioned her living here. Clearly, Danette was not around. She had hoped to find her daughter-in-law at home, hiding out, afraid to face her.

Kera parked her Saturn in the carport and climbed out. Instinctively, she looked around to see if anyone was watching. She wasn't too worried about a neighbor reporting a break-in, but Jackson's warning that thugs might be watching the house was still on her mind.

Kera marched boldly up to the front door and searched around for a spare key. Nothing above the doorframe and no fake-looking rocks. She moved around to the carport and headed for the side door. A small planter with an ugly cactus sat near the corner, catching the sun. Kera lifted the planter from the bottom to avoid the spikes, and there was a key. She started to be appalled, then remembered leaving her own apartment unlocked as a college student so her boyfriend could get in. Dumb.

The house smelled of baby and it seemed obvious nothing major was missing. A laptop sat on the dining table, a TV was tucked into a corner, baby clothes were piled on the couch, and the kitchen sink was full of dishes. Kera was anxious to access the computer, but first she checked Danette's bedroom. It was as Jackson described—closets and drawers full. Kera looked to the closet floor. Sport shoes, sandals, pumps. No woman would leave all her shoes.

Unless she wanted people to think she had not left of her own free will. Was Danette capable of that kind of manipulation? Kera's instinct said no. She headed back to the laptop and turned it on. Surprised it had been set to require a password, she typed in *Micah* and was allowed access. Her primary pursuit was the boyfriend, Chad. Kera hoped to find a picture, a last name, possibly a phone number or address. She glanced over her shoulder and out the front window. No one seemed to be aware of her presence here.

Kera opened Danette's last ten e-mails and quickly scanned them. Most were from a female named Lori who seemed to be a college student at Oregon State University and who chatted about her boyfriend and a professor she really hated. Two of the e-mails were from a guy who signed off as Tree. Kera assumed he was male from the juvenile content and abundance of typos. He also failed to include any contact information. Kera forwarded one of each of their e-mails to her own account rather than take notes.

She opened another group of ten and found nothing mentioning travel plans or Chad. The date on the last one was March 7, two days before Danette had moved to Eugene. It was tempting to respond to each of the mailers, asking if they had seen Danette, but Kera felt a little jumpy about being in the house. She would send the e-mails from her home.

Disappointed, she started to move on, then felt stupid for her oversight. She clicked open the Sent folder and found an e-mail that caught her attention. It was to a woman named Becca. In it Danette commented she'd enjoyed meeting Becca at the center and suggested they babysit for each other. Kera was curious about *the center*, so she forwarded the e-mail to her account as well. After ten more minutes, she moved on, feeling guilty about the invasion of privacy, especially since she had failed to discover anything that would help find Danette.

She found a folder labeled *Pics* and opened it. Photo after photo of Micah filled the top half of the file list, followed by pictures of friends—young people Danette's age—and a few of Margaret and Danette together. The mother and daughter looked unrelated. Kera wondered if Danette's father was tall and dark like Chad. She smiled, thinking about Jackson, who was also tall and dark haired with brown-black eyes.

No picture of Chad surfaced anywhere. Just as Kera opened a browser, she heard a car pull up outside. She jerked around and saw a patrol unit parked in front of the house. *Oh dear.* The officer at the wheel had a communicator to his mouth and she suspected he was calling in her license plate. She was going to be arrested. Kera's heart hammered as she envisioned herself being booked into the jail, stripped, and searched. She stood, took a deep breath, and willed herself to be calm. This was nothing compared to the events she'd already been through. Her life no longer had room for fear.

She picked up the key, went out the side door she'd come in, and walked straight up to the police car. The window was rolled up and the officer motioned her to step back. Kera complied. After a moment, he climbed out. "Put your purse on the ground and identify yourself." He seemed young, but he had the buzz cut and stiff-shouldered look of a cop who took everything seriously.

"Kera Kollmorgan." She set her purse on the asphalt. Did he think she had a gun? "My daughter-in-law, Danette Blake, lives here."

"Her neighbor reported a break-in. What are you doing here?"

Kera held out the key. "I have a key to her house. Danette's baby is at my home right now. Danette hasn't been seen since yesterday morning. I filed a missing-persons report at the department this morning with Detective Zapata."

"Answer my question. What are you doing here?"

"Detective Zapata asked me to find Danette's boyfriend's last name, so I came here to look for it."

"I doubt he meant for you to enter her house." Even his sarcasm was stiff. "If the woman is missing, this could be a crime scene." The officer hesitated, uncertain for the first time. "I need to see your ID."

"You want me to pick up the purse?"

"Yes."

Kera fished out her driver's license and handed it over.

"What is your name?"

"Officer Richard Anderson."

"I know Detective Wade Jackson. He can vouch for me."

Officer Anderson handed back her license. "Please leave the premises and do not come back. Let the police handle this situation."

The police aren't doing anything! Out loud, she said, "I'd like to go lock the house."

"All right."

She could feel him watching her. A voice came on his radio, and she heard her own name in an otherwise muffled report. It gave her stomach a jolt. Officer Anderson didn't try to stop her as she got in her car and drove away.

* * *

Sophie scooted across the parking lot of the *Willamette News* office with a little bounce in her step. She glanced over at the three-story printing building and wondered what would happen to that gigantic offset press when the newspaper folded. *Don't worry about it today*, she coached herself. Things were going too well.

First, she'd run into Kera Kollmorgan and heard the scoop on the missing-mother story, then she'd finally interviewed the reticent Detective Jackson. To top it all off, Elle Durham, who owned half of Eugene, had walked into the missing-persons office while she was there. Was one of the Durham heirs missing? Now that would be a story.

Was the missing Durham daughter somehow connected to Danette Blake, the missing young mother? Sophie rejected the idea. If someone had kidnapped Courtney or Brooke, it was about money.

Sophie trotted upstairs to her desk, refusing to feel guilty about her reaction to juicy stories. She had made peace with her role as an observer/chronicler of other people's misfortunes, and she compensated by writing stories about the "little guy who took a beating," whenever she could. She still had the "day in the life of a detective" feature in the bag too. It would just have to wait a little.

At her desk in her half-cubicle space, she logged in to her computer, slipped the disk with Danette Blake's photo into the machine, and printed a color copy.

On the way to pick up the print, a coworker stopped her. "Am I still on to shoot some photos at the police department this afternoon?"

"No, sorry. Maybe tomorrow. I'll keep you posted."

Sophie trotted with the print to her editor's office. The door was open, so she walked in just as Karl Hoogstad stood to adjust his pants. The news editor was midsize and round in the middle, with a strip of grayish hair clinging to the back of his head.

"You should knock," he said, not looking at her.

"Sorry. I've got a breaking story I'd like to get into tomorrow's edition."

"Yeah? What?"

"A missing young woman."

"As in vanished and no one has seen her?"

"Yep." Sophie slid the photo across the desk. "Her name is Danette Blake. She dropped off her baby with his grandmother yesterday morning and no one has seen her since."

A moment of silence while Hoogstad stared at Danette's picture. He pushed it back across the desk. "This is an abandoned-baby story, and we're not running it unless it's part of a trend."

"How can you know for sure something hideous hasn't happened to her?"

"Have you talked to the police department?" When Hoogstad scowled, the folds on his forehead wrinkled like those of a shar-pei.

"I thought I would run it by you first."

"Call the department. If they suspect foul play, I'll be so shocked I'll take you off the city-council beat and put you on crime full-time." He laughed in an unpleasant way.

* * *

Kera fixed sandwiches for herself and Maggie, who looked frazzled after only a few hours with the baby. Five minutes into the meal Maggie said, "What happens with Micah if Danette never comes back? I mean, what if she's dead?" Her voice collapsed on the last word.

Kera had not let herself think about the possibility Danette could be dead, but she had considered the idea Danette would not return voluntarily. "I'm willing to take care of Micah, but I understand if you think he should stay with your family."

"I can't do it." Maggie looked pained by the admission. "My health isn't good. I have fibromyalgia, and it's all I can do to work for a living."

"He can stay here as long as he needs to. I only work part-time now, so I wouldn't need a full-time sitter." Kera reached over and touched Maggie's hand. "Let's not think like that. It's only been a day and a half. She'll turn up." Kera sounded more sure than she felt. "I found an e-mail on Danette's computer that mentioned meeting someone at the center. Do you know what she meant by 'the center'?"

"No. Sorry."

"That's okay, I'll track it down. First, I'm going to send some e-mails, then I'll call the local TV stations."

"I should have thought of that." Maggie frowned. "I've never been good in emergencies."

After lunch Kera reread the forwarded e-mail from Becca. She sent Becca a message, asking for information about the center and encouraging Becca to call her. Next she checked her Facebook page. A few of Danette's friends had responded to her posts, but none had anything helpful to offer. Kera posted back and asked if they knew Chad's last name or anything about him.

She called KRSL and asked to speak to Trina Waterman.

"She's out on a story right now, can I take a message?" the receptionist said.

"I'd like to talk to someone about a missing-persons story."

"Just a moment."

A few minutes later, a fast-talking female voice came on the line. "This is Trina Waterman. I just walked in the door. Who are you and who is missing?"

"I'm Kera Kollmorgan. My daughter-in-law, Danette Blake, is missing."

"Your name sounds familiar. Have we met?"

"You interviewed me after the bombing at the Planned Parenthood clinic last fall."

"Oh yes. How are you doing?"

"Great. Except that Danette is missing."

"What are the details?"

Kera repeated her story.

There was a short pause. "That is peculiar. Have you been to the police?"

"I filed a missing-persons report this morning."

"Do they suspect she's the victim of a crime?"

"There's not much to go on. Her car hasn't been located, but everything she owns is still in her house."

"Do you have a digital image you can e-mail me?"

"Sure. I'd love to get her picture on the news. She could be in a hospital somewhere with no ID."

"No promises. I have to run everything by my producer." Trina gave Kera an e-mail address and got off the phone. Kera decided that on her next call she wouldn't mention Danette had dropped off her baby, just to see if she got a different reaction.

"I'd like to take a nap," Maggie said from the doorway. "Would you keep an eye on Micah?"

"Sure." Kera reached for the little boy, who grinned wildly at her.

CHAPTER 9

Danette thought she was awake, but couldn't be sure. With the blindfold over her eyes, her little world was dark, and the pills had knocked her out for what seemed like hours. She'd been half-awake and half-asleep for a while. Now her bladder felt as if it would burst. She forced herself to focus. Danette rolled to the edge of the bed and sat up. Her head felt light, her throat was parched, and her stomach growled. How long had she been in this room? Why were they keeping her?

She had a vague memory of being carried downstairs and dropped on this small, musty bed. The big guy had forced two tiny pills into her mouth and untied her feet. She'd been terrified, thinking, *Please don't rape me, please don't kill me*. He'd said something, then left her alone. She'd drifted off soon after.

Danette stood, waiting to see how her body would react. Her legs felt weird and her shoulders ached from having her arms pulled together in front for so long. The ache in her breasts made her think of Micah. She'd quit breast-feeding a few weeks ago and the baby had not been happy about it. A sob rose in her throat; she choked on it. Would she ever see Micah again? Danette fought for control. She couldn't break down. She had to stay alert and resilient if she wanted to survive this ordeal, whatever the hell it was.

The big guy had replaced the handcuffs on her wrists with thin nylon cord, so her hands had less mobility. Still, she was able to push the bandanna up and off her eyes. The room was just as dark without it. She was ready to yank it back into place if she heard footsteps coming. Her captor didn't want her to see his face, and it gave Danette hope she might eventually be released.

The gag in her mouth wouldn't budge without tearing off her lower lip. Danette shuffled forward, thinking there was a bathroom in the corner. *Had the big guy told her that?* Cautiously, she crossed the small space, found the switch inside the door, and flipped it on. The light was so dim she barely blinked after hours of darkness. Danette shuffled into the bathroom and used the toilet.

Having her wrists tightly bound made it difficult, but Danette searched the tiny room for something that might help. She found nothing. Not even a towel. She left the light on and shuffled back out into the main room. In the weak glow, she could see she was in a basement. Yet it wasn't a typical filled-with-crap basement. She was alone down here, with nothing but a bed, a couch, and toilet. She touched the cool stone wall, paralyzed with despair.

Another vague memory surfaced. She'd come awake once at the sound of footsteps on the stairs. The door to the room had opened and someone had come in. He'd offered her food if she promised not to say a word while the gag was off. She vaguely remembered chewing her way through most of a nutrition bar before she'd passed out again.

As her eyes adjusted to the weak light, she realized one long wall was stacked high with boxes. *What were they storing down* here? She thought about trying to open one. *Was it worth the risk of angering the big guy?*

She heard footsteps and yanked the cloth back over her eyes. A key clicked in the lock and a door swung open. Danette turned toward the sound, braced for assault. Two sets of footsteps moved toward her. A man's voice whispered, but she couldn't understand the words. Another man said softly, "The body's good but I need to see her face. Take the blindfold off."

"Trust me. She's pretty." Then louder, "Step over here to the light."

Danette was conflicted, as she had been since she'd landed on her face while getting out of the van. So far, as long as she cooperated with them, nothing bad had happened to her. Yet every fiber in her body wanted to refuse the command.

The big guy grabbed her arm, pulled her toward the bathroom, and stepped behind her.

"Keep your eyes tightly closed," he threatened. "If you want to live, don't look at him."

He untied the blindfold at the back of her head and lowered it to her collarbone, keeping his hands on the ends. His thick wrists rested on her shoulders. Danette kept her eyes closed, painfully aware the big guy could tighten the bandanna around her neck and strangle her in seconds.

"She's gorgeous," the other one said. His voice was not as deep or as loud as the big guy's. Danette wondered if she'd heard it before. "Good skin tone, but no strong ethnic features. The Dutchman will love her. We have a deal."

Danette shuddered. She'd just been sold like a side of beef.

As the blindfold came up, she relaxed her eyelids and got a nanosecond glance at the man who'd purchased her. All she could process was that he was not very big and his hair was light.

"Good girl." The big guy grabbed her arm. "It's time for another pill." He put two little white tablets under her tongue and they dissolved instantly. As Danette began to feel sleepy, the big guy put the bandanna back on her mouth, tied her feet, and carried her up the stairs.

* * *

Soon after Jackson and Katie arrived at Kera's, Mrs. Blake took off, saying she was going out to see an old friend for dinner.

"It's nice of her to give us some time alone," Jackson said, as he watched Kera change the baby. Katie was in the living room, texting a friend. For a moment, Jackson wondered what his life would have been like if he'd met Kera twenty years ago, instead of Renee, and they'd had a child together. What would their child be like? Would he have had more than one?

"I think she needed to get away from babysitting," Kera said with a laugh. "I don't blame her. She's not well."

They were silent for a few seconds as they both thought about Jackson's disease. People might say that about him now.

"How did your day go?" Jackson didn't want to talk about the whole RF thing yet. Kera picked up Micah and they sat beside each other on her bed.

"Good, I think. I filed a missing persons report and talked to Sophie Speranza."

"She told me she ran into you at the department."

"We had coffee together, and I told her about Danette. Sophie said she'd try to get her picture and story in the paper. We might as well enlist the public's help."

"Of course." Jackson hated the idea of Sophie getting to know Kera. She would try to use it to manipulate him.

"I went into Danette's house," Kera said softly.

Jackson felt a flash of concern mixed with irritation. "I advised you not to do that."

"I know, but Detective Zapata isn't taking this case seriously and I didn't expect him to get over there anytime soon."

She was right about that. "What did you find out?"

"I couldn't find the boyfriend's name anywhere, but I did see an e-mail that mentioned meeting another young mother at a center. So I'm looking into that."

"What center?"

"I don't know yet, but I'll find out." Kera paused, touched Jackson's leg. "A police officer came to Danette's house while I was there. He called in a report, then made me leave."

Jackson laughed out loud. Suddenly he had to pee. "Excuse me," he said, charging for the adjoining bathroom.

Kera made enchiladas, one of Katie's favorites, while Katie watched Micah in the living room. Jackson wandered back and forth between the two. At least his daughter was here, having dinner with them, so they were making progress. Katie still believed her parents would get back together now that Renee was sober, so she kept Kera at a distance, much to Jackson's anguish. He needed these two females to bond so he didn't have to spend his life like this, going back and forth.

At dinner, he delivered on his promise to Kera and Katie to discuss his medical situation. "I have an appointment with a urologist on Wednesday to talk about surgery. It's nothing to worry about," he said, looking at Katie. "I think they're just going to cut out some of the growth, which is a good thing."

Kera gave him a look. He took it to mean he was oversimplifying things. Jackson didn't feel the need to scare Katie with the whole truth yet. Hell, he didn't even know what the whole truth was.

Kera said, "I think they'll do a little more than that. They also need to protect your urinary system from having this happen again."

"Sounds like a good idea." Jackson faked a grin. As Kera was talking, it hit him for the first time that the surgery would leave him with quite a scar.

"Will you still pee normal?" Katie mumbled, her mouth full of corn.

"Of course." He felt like he had to go right now. He was learning to ignore the sensation until it became overwhelming.

"How long will you be in the hospital?" Katie wanted to know.

"For a few days." Jackson glanced at Kera. She rolled her eyes but didn't correct him.

"What if the fiber stuff comes back?" Katie asked.

"After the surgery, I'll take steroids to make sure it doesn't happen."

"Will they let me watch? You know, like on *Grey's Anatomy*, how they sit up there in the little room and watch surgeries?"

"I don't think so," Jackson said.

"Too bad."

While they cleaned up from dinner, they listened to the local news on the small television in the kitchen. Trina Waterman, a wispy blonde who looked just out of high school, led with "Last night, a young woman named Courtney Durham left Diego's nightclub on Pearl Street and has not been seen since."

As they flashed Courtney's picture on the screen, Jackson stopped wiping the counter and turned up the volume.

The anchorwoman continued: "Courtney is five-seven, a hundred and twenty pounds, with long blonde hair and green eyes. At the time of her disappearance she is believed to have been wearing black jeans, a black tank top, and a turquoise jean jacket."

Courtney's photo filled half the screen. Kera moved over and stood with Jackson in front of the small TV.

"If you have seen this woman, please call the police tip line." The phone number flashed on the screen in big white numerals.

Jackson was caught off guard by the story. He shouldn't have been. Elle Durham was worried about her daughter, and she had money to throw around.

The broadcast cut to Elle, seated in front of a gray wall, with perfect hair, clothes, and posture. Her voice quivered as she spoke: "My daughter Courtney is missing, and I'll do anything to get her back. If you have kidnapped Courtney, please don't harm her. I will pay for her return. Contact me directly at 606-2315."

"Oh crap." Jackson shuddered at the calls the poor woman would get.

"What about Danette?" Kera complained, her voice rising. "I talked to Trina Waterman this afternoon. I e-mailed her a digital file."

In the background, Waterman continued her broadcast: "Another young woman was reported missing today as well. Danette Blake, age twenty, has not been seen since a doctor's appointment this morning. The police are investigating, but so far they do not believe foul play is involved."

Danette's picture flashed briefly on the screen as Waterman spoke, then she switched to a traffic accident on Beltline Road.

Kera muted the sound. "Who is Courtney Durham? What is going on that two young women are missing? And why does Courtney's disappearance get more coverage than Danette's?"

Jackson had no good answers. "Courtney is a rich party girl who has willingly disappeared before. Mrs. Durham got airtime because the Durhams probably own the news building, maybe even the station."

Kera made the connection. "Oh, those Durhams." A second later. "That's bullshit."

"What's bullshit?" his daughter asked from the doorway, holding Micah on her hip.

"You don't get to say that word." Jackson tried to never swear in front of his daughter.

"Kera said it."

"She's earned the privilege."

"Sorry, I shouldn't have." Kera turned to Jackson. "Could these disappearances be connected?"

"It's possible, but I just don't see how. Zapata believes Courtney will turn up on her own. She has a history of bad behavior that includes running off without telling her mother." Jackson shook his head. "I wish Mrs. Durham hadn't announced her willingness to pay a ransom. She's going to get calls from thugs who will try to shake her down."

"What if Courtney was kidnapped? How much money can they demand?"

Kera was asking what he thought the Durhams were worth. Jackson could only speculate. "*If* she's been kidnapped, they know who she is and they'll probably ask for millions."

"I feel sorry for her," Katie said. "I guess being rich is not always a good thing."

Jackson looked at his daughter with pride. "It can be a problem. It's too bad making that kind of money can put your children at risk."

"In more ways than one," Kera added. After a moment, "What do we do next about Danette?"

"We keep talking to her friends. We try to find the boyfriend. We print posters with her picture and put them up all over town."

"Can I help?" Katie asked.

"Of course." Kera smiled at his daughter. "Once I get the post-ers printed, you can help me distribute them."

And I'll look for a connection between the two women, Jackson thought.

CHAPTER 10

Wednesday, April 8, 7:55 a.m.

Jackson hurried into the U-shaped building that housed city hall and police headquarters. Every time he noticed the nonstaggered masonry, he hoped the public-safety department would get a new building before the five-hundred-year earthquake hit. If the building collapsed, it would take all the patrol cars parked under it, leaving citizens to fend for themselves.

He had been at his desk only a few minutes when Sergeant Lammers called him back to her office. He stopped in the bathroom on the way, thinking his surgery couldn't come soon enough. The pain was easier to take than this constant pressure.

"Jackson, how are you feeling?" Lammers gestured for him to sit.

"Just fine."

"Good. I need you to investigate Courtney Durham's disappearance."

"Why? It's not my usual department, and Detective Zapata doesn't believe she's really missing."

"Elle Durham specifically asked for you to be assigned to her daughter's case. Since you don't have a homicide investigation right now, there's no reason not to make Ms. Durham happy."

"How did she come to ask for me?" Jackson was skeptical.

"She said you asked intelligent questions when she was filing the missing-persons report. I said you were our best investigator. She said she wanted you to find Courtney."

"Money talks."

"In this case, it does more than talk." Lammers let out a harsh laugh. "It may buy us a new building."

Jackson opened his mouth to speak, then changed his mind. He hated the politics of money. Even more, he hated being manipulated by it. Nothing he could say would change the reality. He was also pleased by the assignment. It would give him an excuse to keep investigating Danette's disappearance too. "I'll do my best to find her."

"Thank you." Lammers sounded sincere.

Jackson headed down the hall to Robert Zapata's desk. The officer was putting on his jacket. "Hey, Jackson. What's up?"

"Sergeant Lammers assigned me to Courtney Durham's case."

Zapata looked surprised. "Ms. Durham must be throwing her weight around."

"Did you see her on the news last night?"

"No. Did she make a public appeal?"

"She offered money to get her daughter back."

"Oh shit."

"Why do you think she's so desperate? I mean, since Courtney has a history of bad behavior that includes disappearing for days at a time?"

"Maybe it's a ploy to make her daughter feel guilty. You know, the 'look what you put me through' crap." Zapata picked up a black zippered notebook.

"Interesting. You're headed out?"

"I was going to stop by Diego's and talk to the staff and show Courtney's picture around." He put the notebook down, unzipped it, and handed Jackson a photo. "If you're taking the case, you might as well do the legwork."

"Taking this case wasn't my idea."

Zapata grinned. "Better you than me. I don't like wasting my time."

As Jackson pulled out of the underground parking lot, he thought about driving the few blocks to Diego's, then changed his mind. Courtney had been to the club late in the evening. If he wanted to catch the bartender or cocktail waitress who had served Courtney or the customers who might have seen her, it would be best to stop in after nine this evening. He headed for the south hills instead.

The Durham estate was off Fox Hollow on its own little street. From the bottom of the driveway, the building looked more like an elite luxury spa than a single-family home. Jackson guessed about five thousand square feet. As he drove up, he spotted a tennis court off to the left. He parked in front of the four-car garage and felt the cameras on him as he trotted over to the main entrance. He'd called ahead and Elle Durham was expecting him.

Still, the staff woman who answered the door said, "Ms. Durham is with her acupuncturist right now. She'll be out in ten minutes. Please have a seat." The woman started to walk away, but Jackson called out, "Excuse me. I need a moment of your time."

"Yes?" She looked surprised. She was in her fifties but looked well cared for and was comfortably dressed in black cotton slacks and pullover.

"What's your name?"

"Helen Joseph."

"What do you do here?"

"I'm the housekeeper."

"How long have you worked here?"

"Sixteen years."

"When was the last time you saw Courtney?"

"Late Monday afternoon. I saw her in the gym when I picked up the towels. I left here at five o'clock." Her answer sounded practiced, as if she'd been through it a few times. She didn't look worried.

"What gym?"

Helen pointed toward the back of the house.

Of course they had a gym. "Do you have any idea where Courtney is?"

"None." She kept her face deadpan. Jackson suspected she had some interesting stories to tell, but sixteen years on the job meant she was loyal and discreet.

"Thanks. I may have more questions later."

After she left, Jackson decided to look around. It was part of the job. The first two rooms he wandered into, a sitting room and a library, gave him little information except that the Durhams had more money than he'd realized. Hearing voices at the end of the second hallway, he headed in that direction. He needed to interview everyone in the household.

Halfway down, Elle came out of an intersecting hall. "Hello again, Detective Jackson. Thank you for coming." She grabbed his arm and steered him back the way she had come from. "Let's talk in my office."

The floor-to-ceiling windows let in the April sun, bathing the peach walls in a soft glow. Jackson could see why she wanted to spend time here. Elle Durham spoke into an intercom and asked someone to bring coffee.

Jackson decided not to let the meeting get too comfortable. "I saw your video on the news last night. Offering to pay a ransom before you get a demand is not a good idea."

Elle bristled. "I'm trying to protect my daughter."

"Has anyone called trying to collect?"

"Yes." Her eyes darted away. Elle plopped down, looking old and tired now instead of rich and well preserved. "I hired someone, a retired cop, to handle the calls for me. He says neither of the callers could produce any evidence they have Courtney."

"Who did you hire and where is he?"

"His name is Roger Ingram, and he's in the gym right now. So is Brooke, my other daughter."

Jackson didn't recognize the cop's name as he wrote it down. He'd been with the Eugene department nearly twenty years, so it was unlikely Ingram had been a local officer. "I'd like to talk to both of them before I leave."

"Of course. Is there anything else I can tell you?"

"I'd like to know about Courtney's social life. You mentioned a boyfriend yesterday. Tell me about him."

"Brett Fenton is an upstanding young man from a good family. He's the first boyfriend Courtney has ever had who I could say that about."

"I'd like to talk to him. What's his phone number?"

Elle pulled a cell phone out of her pocket, searched through her contacts, and gave him the number.

Jackson jotted it down. He thought about Danette's boyfriend, Chad, and wondered if he was somehow connected to Courtney.

"Does Courtney know a young man named Chad?"

"I don't think so, but I wouldn't know for sure."

Jackson let it go. It seemed unlikely that Courtney and Chad would travel in the same circles. "How long have Courtney and Brett been a couple?"

"About three months. They went to school together, so they knew each other casually before, but they met at a charity fund-raiser in January. I am very happy about the relationship." Elle gave him a look, as if warning him not to scare Brett off.

"What about ex-boyfriends? Who was Courtney dating before?"

Elle's stiffened and her thin face went a shade paler. "Oh dear. Her last boyfriend went a little crazy when she broke it off. He started out a little crazy too. I think he snorted cocaine like it was an asthma treatment."

"His name?"

"Courtney always called him Skeet, but I think his name was Steve."

"Do you know his last name or how to contact him?"

"No." She shook her head.

"I need you to call around and find out if you can." Jackson glanced at this notes. "I'd like to talk to Roger Ingram now."

The tall man in the blue tracksuit stepped off the elliptical machine and offered Jackson a sweaty hand. "Roger Ingram, retired Sacramento PD."

Jackson shook his hand, thinking that up close Roger looked sixty, but his hair looked thirty-five. "Wade Jackson, Eugene homicide detective." Jackson glanced over at the young woman on the stair stepper in the back of the room.

"That's Brooke Durham, Courtney's sister."

She looked up, gave Jackson a small smile, and went back to her workout.

"Did you know the Durham family before this situation?" Jackson asked.

"Elle and I met last year."

"Mind telling me how?"

Ingram pulled back. "Am I a suspect?"

"I like to know all the players and how they joined the game."

"I work part-time as a private detective, selective cases only. Elle hired me to investigate one of Courtney's boyfriends last June."

"Was his name Skeet or Steve?"

"No. It was Tristan Chalmers. He was clean, but liked to party."

"Tell me about the calls you got this morning." Jackson looked around the forty-by-forty gym for a bathroom.

"The first guy sounded older and fairly rational, but he couldn't produce any evidence he had Courtney."

"What did you ask for?"

"I said to put her on the phone or send me a digital picture. He said to give him a few minutes. He never called back." Ingram walked over to the small stainless-steel refrigerator in the corner and grabbed a bottled water. "The next call came from two young men. Very agitated. They threatened to hurt her if I didn't just shut up and get the money to them. At one point, they started arguing with each other, then eventually hung up."

"Have you handled situations like this before?"

"You mean a kidnapping?"

"A disappearance. If she'd been kidnapped for ransom, they would have called in the first twenty-four hours." Jackson took out his business card with his cell-phone number and handed it to Ingram. "Call me immediately if you hear anything."

Jackson headed toward the stair stepper, ignoring the pressure on his kidneys. Brooke saw him coming but kept up her workout. She looked a lot like Courtney, but with darker hair and not quite as pretty. Eventually Brooke looked up. "I only have a few minutes left, but we can start talking anyway."

"When was the last time you saw Courtney?"

"Monday evening before she went out."

"What was she wearing?"

"Black jeans, black ankle boots, black camisole, suede turquoise waist-length jacket, long silver-and-turquoise earrings." Brooke reported the list with labored breath, sweat dripping from her brow.

"What kind of mood was she in?"

"She seemed okay. A little irritated that Brett was having dinner with his parents instead of her. I think that's why she went down to Diego's on a Monday night." Brooke laughed. "That and the ladies' night specials."

"She and her boyfriend were fighting?"

"I think he's pulling away from her."

"You don't seem very worried about Courtney."

"That's because I know Courtney."

"You don't think she's been kidnapped?"

Brooke stopped climbing and shut off the machine. "Courtney is a wild child. She's been a little less crazy lately because of Brett's influence, but she's still Courtney. She'll turn up."

"Do you know her ex-boyfriend's name?"

"Skeeter? Aka Steve Smith? You think she's with him?"

"You tell me. Could she be?"

"Not voluntarily. In fact, I heard he went to jail."

Jackson jotted down Steve's last name and wondered how far he had to carry this charade. No one really believed Courtney had been taken against her will except possibly her mother. As Zapata had pointed out, Elle could be playing her part just to tweak her daughter's guilt. Jackson closed his notebook. "Anything else I should know?"

"You're leaking a little."

Jackson had just enough time to go home, change his pants, and consume a turkey sandwich before arriving five minutes late to his doctor's appointment. He hurried in, actually looking forward to the encounter. He was ready to do whatever was necessary to get these stents out of his body.

"How soon can I schedule surgery?" Jackson demanded as the doctor walked into the examining room.

"Slow down. We have a lot to talk about." Dr. Jewel looked too young to be a surgeon. Jackson wondered if he should find someone with more experience. The doctor continued, "The surgery you need is called a ureterolysis. It's a very rare procedure and I've only done one. No other doctor in Eugene has performed any. I know a retired colleague with some experience who will assist, so you'll be in good hands."

"Fine. I need to get this done. I feel like I have to pee all the time. This morning, I was leaking while I was questioning someone." There was no point in verbalizing how embarrassing that had been.

"I'll talk to my scheduler and we'll get you in as soon as possible." Jewel gave him a curious look. "Would you like to know what I'm going to do while I've got you open?"

Not really, Jackson thought. "Lay it out for me. My girlfriend and my daughter will want details."

"First, we'll cut your ureters free from the fibrous growth, then we'll open the peritoneal sac that holds your intestines." The doctor drew a little diagram as he spoke. "We'll tuck the ureters inside the peritoneum and sew it back up. The idea is to protect your ureters from the growth."

"You're rerouting my plumbing."

"Exactly."

"What about the stuff around my aorta?"

Dr. Jewel tried to hide his concern. "I've consulted with a vascular surgeon, and no one has ever seen anything like it. Most people with fibrosis around the aorta have had an aortic aneurysm that causes the growth. In those cases, a surgeon performs an aortic graft."

Jackson felt his chest tighten just thinking about it.

"You haven't had an aneurysm, so we believe swapping your aorta for a piece of Dacron is a risky surgery that may not help you."

"So what's the plan?"

"Two months after the surgery, we'll start you on prednisone. Hopefully, it will control the growth and you'll be fine." His tone was not reassuring.

"How long will I be off work?"

"Four to six weeks. It depends on how fast you recover and how much pain you have. We're going to cut you open from sternum to pubis and flop all your organs out of the way so we can get to the ureters. It's a bit of a shock to the system."

Jackson's bowels churned in protest. "Let's schedule it."

"I'll check with Mandy and have her give you a call."

As Jackson stood to leave, his phone rang. "It's Sergeant Lammers. A cyclist just reported finding a dead woman on the bike path behind Autzen Stadium. Her description sounds like it could be Courtney Durham. Get a team out there ASAP."

CHAPTER 11

Autzen Stadium, where the University of Oregon Ducks played football, appeared in the skyline as soon as Jackson turned off the Ferry Street Bridge. Skyboxes had been added a few years ago, and now it was one of the tallest structures in the southern Willamette Valley. Jackson drove past Alton Baker Park, lush with spring foliage, and headed out Centennial Boulevard. Technically, it was Martin Luther King Boulevard now, but after forty years of calling it Centennial, it was hard to make the change.

On a Wednesday afternoon in April, the massive parking lot was nearly empty. Jackson drove down the maintenance road that ran behind the property and connected to the river bike path. Near the water, the path disappeared into a thick grove of trees lining the Willamette River on both sides. The path ran for miles, connecting Eugene, Springfield, and Santa Clara. This area, though, was covered with wild grass, blackberry bushes, and a few stray oak and poplar trees.

He kept his speed down, watching for cyclists and who-ever else was out here today. The weather was warm for the first time in months, and two-wheeled riders had taken to the streets en masse. Walkers and joggers too, many of them in shorts, white winter legs flashing. He'd called out Lara Evans and Rob Schakowski as his initial team, but he expected to be the first of the detectives to arrive. His doctor's office was downtown, just across from the hospital and five minutes away.

Before the path reached the trees, it curved right and a patrol unit blocked the access. The officer was pulling crime-scene tape from the trunk of his car. Fifty feet away, a cyclist stood near a white bike leaned against a giant oak. Jackson parked behind the patrol unit on the asphalt path and got out of his car.

"Hey, Jackson, you got here fast." Mike Flaggert was a veteran cop Jackson had known since he was on patrol.

"I was only a few minutes away. What have we got so far?"

Flaggert nodded toward the guy near the tree. "The cyclist says he stopped to put air in his tire, saw the body, and called it in. I stayed away from the body because I know this will turn into a clusterfuck, and I didn't want to mess with the scene."

"Thanks."

Jackson headed toward the dark lump near a tall tangle of blackberry bush. As he approached, he slowed his pace and began to scan the ground for footprints and tire marks. The dead woman had not likely come here alone.

The thick wild grass didn't give any sign of being trampled. The early morning rain, which had cleared off hours ago, had likely washed away any tire marks. The evidence technicians would go over every inch of it anyway. Jackson walked toward the young man near the bike, who looked ready to bolt.

"Thanks for waiting. I need you stay for a while longer."

"How long? I've got to be at work by three?"

"Ten minutes. I need to check the body first, then ask you a few questions."

"As I told the other cop, she's dead for sure."

Jackson trotted over and squatted next to the body. Fully clothed in jeans and a jacket, the young blonde woman looked as if she might have simply gone to sleep. She was on her back with one arm down at her side and the other across her chest. Jackson studied her face. No one ever looked exactly like they did in photos, but Courtney Durham came close.

Jackson closed his eyes and asked God to watch over her soul.

He'd visited her home that morning and spoken to her family; Jackson felt like he knew this girl. He dreaded being the one to tell Elle. Mrs. Durham had asked him personally to find her daughter and he had failed. He hadn't had enough time. When Lammers had assigned him to the case this morning, this young woman was already dead.

Jackson pulled on gloves and felt for a pulse. The coolness of her skin seeped through the latex. Jackson gently turned her head, looking for a wound. Then he saw the marks, a faded, purplish-yellow band of overlapping bruises on each side of her neck. He leaned in to better see the discoloration. They were definitely ligature marks, but they were also partially masked by foundation makeup, suggesting Courtney had tried to hide them.

Otherwise, her pale skin, perfect nose, and full lips were still flawless. He scanned her body, taking in the intact clothing. There were no rips, no stains, no blood he could see. With gloved fingers, he examined Courtney's hands and found no defense wounds, but he noticed thin red lines around both wrists.

Had she been handcuffed or tied in some way? Jackson was reminded of a case he'd worked last fall. The thirteen-year-old girl who'd been left naked in a dumpster had abrasions on her wrists too. Based on what he knew about Courtney, these abrasions could have been caused by consensual bondage-type sex. The bruises on her neck could have been caused by sexual asphyxiation. For now, he pushed aside what he knew about Courtney. He had to stay open-minded. This young woman was dead long before her time, and he had to find out why.

Jackson pulled his camera from his black evidence bag and took a few photos to capture her position and distance from the bike path. He hated the inconvenience of using film, but the district attorney required it so defense lawyers couldn't claim they had digitally doctored photographic evidence. Jackson didn't know for sure this was even a crime scene, but it was always possible his actions would end up in court.

He heard a car coming up the path and turned to see the white medical examiner's van. After a moment, Rich Gunderson, dressed in his usual black, headed toward him with a large canvas bag slung over his shoulder. Jackson stood and stepped back from Courtney's body.

Gunderson called out, "What have we got?"

"Young female, no apparent signs of trauma. Bruises on her neck and mild abrasions on her wrists."

"Is she one of the missing girls I saw on the news last night?" Gunderson pulled his gray hair into a ponytail and slid on latex gloves.

"I think so. Where's Parker?"

"She's coming."

Jackson looked over at the path and saw Jasmine Parker climb out of the back of the van. Her tall, thin frame was stronger than it looked and she easily carried an oversized crime-scene bag. He'd seen Jasmine lug giant spotlights to a scene. Jackson was pleased to have bright sunlight to work under for a change.

As Gunderson knelt over the body, Jackson looked around for a purse or a wallet. He needed to see her identification. The small cloth bag was only a few feet away. Its color, the same as her jacket, made it hard to see in the green grass. As Jackson reached for it, Parker said, "Wait. Let me photograph it in location first."

Jackson let her take a few pictures, then reached for the purse. It was only about six inches square and held just the essentials: driver's license, a credit card, lipstick, and condom. *No cell phone?* He hoped to find a phone in her jacket pocket. It would make this investigation so much easier.

The name on the license was Courtney Durham.

Jackson stood, feeling the stents in his gut shift and squeeze. He reminded himself that it could be worse. Being alive automatically made him one of the lucky ones. Jackson put the purse into a paper evidence bag, filled out the label, and tucked it into the leather car-ryall where he kept his crime-scene tools, including two types of cameras, an assortment of brown paper evidence bags, extra film, a flashlight, crime-scene tape, paper booties, and a box of latex gloves. Eventually, he would take Courtney's purse to the lab for analysis, but he wanted to take a close look at everything first.

He turned to the cyclist, who was practically bouncing with impatience. "What's your name?"

"Kyle Larson."

"Let me see your ID."

Kyle handed him a well-worn state ID, the kind carried by people who didn't have driver's licenses. It matched the name he'd given.

"Tell me how you found the body."

"I was biking home from a friend's in Springfield, and I stopped here to put some air in my tire. It's got a slow leak." He pushed his hands through his thick, dirty-looking hair. Jackson guessed him to be about thirty. "I saw some legs on the ground by the blackberry bush. I walked over to see if the person was okay. She didn't look hurt, but she didn't look alive either."

"Did you touch her?"

"No." He shuddered. "I've never seen a dead person before, but I could tell. She was so pale and still, and there was a bug crawling on her face."

Jackson had no reason to think he was lying. "What's your phone number in case I have more questions?"

As he jotted down the number, he heard another vehicle pull up. "Thanks, you can go."

A young woman on a bike came up the path from the river. She saw the line of cars on the asphalt, slowed to a stop, and called out, "Hey, I need to get through."

Jackson moved toward her. "I'm sorry, but this is a police investigation. You'll have to find another route."

"That's crazy. I work at the gift shop in the stadium and I have to be there in ten minutes."

"Bike up to Alton Baker Park and come in that way."

"Oh fuck." She scowled dramatically before biking away.

Jackson tried not to let it bother him. During his two decades in the department, he'd noticed police officers commanded less respect than they used to. It disappointed him.

As Rob Schakowski walked up, his barrel-shaped body pushing the limits of his suit jacket, Jackson called over to Flaggert, "Will you get some crime-scene tape up over here too? We need to keep people from coming up on this side."

"That's gonna piss off the cyclists, joggers, and bird-watchers." Schak grinned at the thought. "What have we got?"

"Dead female named Courtney Durham. Age twenty-one. Mother reported her missing yesterday. Last seen Monday night. No signs of blunt-force trauma to the body, but bruises on the neck and mild abrasions on the wrists."

Schak looked surprised, an expression Jackson didn't see often on his partner's big, blunt face. "Any relation to Dean Durham, the rich real-estate tycoon?"

"His daughter. You didn't see Elle Durham on the news last night?"

"No. I had to drive to Roseburg yesterday to get a statement and didn't get back until late. Wow. Tough break for Mrs. Durham. First her husband, then her daughter."

"She'll blame the department." Jackson let out a breath. "Let's see if Gunderson has anything interesting to tell us."

They left the asphalt path and crossed the now-trampled grassy area. Gunderson was manipulating Courtney's arm. "Rigor mortis is completely set in, so she's been dead for at least eight hours." The ME lifted Courtney's hip and peeked down the back of her jeans, using a small flashlight. "Livor mortis on the posterior, so she most likely died right here and has been lying on her back since." He lowered her down. "I'm not going to get her temperature because I don't want to disturb her clothing. If she was out here all night when it cooled down, then she probably died around midnight, give or take a few hours."

Twenty-four hours after she disappeared, Jackson thought. *Where had she been during that time? What circumstances had stolen her life?*

"Could she have been killed elsewhere and dumped?"

"If the killer put her on her back right away and kept her face up during transport, I suppose it's possible." Gunderson took pictures as he talked. "You'll have to wait for the pathologist's report. Those bruises on her neck don't look like they could have killed her, but we won't know until we cut her open and see if her hyoid bones are broken. Even if she got drunk or high and passed out, it wasn't cold enough last night for her to freeze. Could be an overdose." The ME put the camera aside and stood. "Help me lift her into a body bag."

Jackson thought of the homeless man who'd frozen to death last winter a block from the Mission. He looked back at Courtney. It wasn't often bodies revealed so little about how they died. He squatted next to her feet and waited for Gunderson to get into place. As Jackson wrapped his hands around her leather-covered ankles, he noticed something on the sole of her boot. It looked like a little piece of tar. Had it come off the bike path? It seemed unlikely. Tar didn't stick to shoes unless it was warm and soft. April in Eugene wasn't warm enough to soften blacktop. Hell, August in Eugene was barely warm enough for that.

"Wait a sec," Jackson said to the ME. He called to Parker, who was on her knees, searching the area between the path and the body. "I need you to bag and tag something from her shoe." He didn't want the evidence to drop off during any of the transitions Courtney would go through in the next few hours.

Still squatting, Parker duckwalked the three-foot distance, her smooth face as expressionless as ever. "This little piece of black substance." Jackson pointed at the boot.

"It looks like tar."

"Get a sample of asphalt from the path and compare them. See if that's the source. I have a feeling it's not." Jackson thought about the parking lot at Diego's. Had it recently been repaved? He wished either he or Zapata had gone to Diego's last night to ask around. Guilt had been picking at his conscience since he'd received the call from Lammers. Jackson pushed it aside. It had not been his case until this morning, and Robert Zapata had prioritized the cases responsibly.

"You ready?" Gunderson asked.

"Wait. She's missing an earring." Jackson scooted two feet sideways and looked at the single earring. It was long and dangly with little pieces of real turquoise embedded in a silver mesh. Jackson took a couple of close-up shots of the earring, then scooted back while Parker shot images of Courtney's head, showing the missing jewelry.

When Parker finished, he and Gunderson lifted the corpse off the wet grass and onto a large black body bag. Jackson inwardly cringed, feeling what her mother would feel when she saw Courtney in the morgue. He could never look at a lifeless young woman without thinking about Katie and how devastating it would be to have someone knock on his door and tell him his daughter was dead.

As they set her down, air escaped in a half-moan, half-burp sound. Startled, Jackson jerked back. Gunderson chucked. "Sometimes the dead like to get in one last word."

Lara Evans walked up to the group. "Are you okay, Jackson?" She tried to sound casual. "You don't look so great."

"I'm fine, but I need to take off soon and let you and Schak finish up here."

"What's left?"

"Search the immediate area. We seem to have a missing cell phone. Talk to people at the stadium, see if we have any witnesses." Evans made notes, but she didn't need to. She would remember it all and think of things he hadn't.

"When do we meet up?"

"Probably around six. I'll call you."

Another car pulled up. The driver had the good sense to park off the path and not block everyone in. Jim Trang, an assistant DA, climbed out and headed toward them. Of course the DA's office had sent someone. With a high-profile case like the daughter of Dean and Elle Durham, the people in power would be watching everything. Jackson accepted that he wasn't leaving the area anytime soon. He hoped his kidneys could take it.

Suddenly Schak called out, "Look at this." Jackson jogged in his direction. Schak held up a disk-shaped purple object about the size of a hockey puck.

"What is it?"

"It looks like an asthma inhaler. It was under her body."

CHAPTER 12

Diego's was the closest thing Eugene had to a smutty nightclub, and even then, it was only occasionally risqué. Most evenings it was just another bar catering to the young and adventurous, but a couple of times a year it hosted a ball for people in black leather and dog collars who liked to be spanked in public. Oddly enough, the police were rarely called out to the club, unlike other drinking establishments where fights broke out every weekend.

Jackson pulled into the large shared parking lot behind the building, noticing how empty it seemed. Downtown Eugene had been in decline before the recession, but now it seemed abandoned in places. He strode up the alley and into the club, which was tucked in between a Greyhound station and a Thai restaurant. It took a moment for his eyes to adjust from the bright daylight to the dark interior. The club had a long mirror behind the bar, a disco ball over the dance floor, and red velvet-like cloth on the walls. Jackson headed straight for the narrow hall in the back. The retail space had housed many different businesses over the years and he hadn't been in the building since long before it was a nightclub, but the location of the bathrooms never changed.

"What can I get for you?" The bartender was a late thirty-something male trying to pass for twenty. His spandex pullover was so tight his nipples showed, and his platinum hair was not a color anyone had ever been born with.

"Just information." Jackson showed his badge, something he rarely did. "Detective Jackson, Eugene Police. I need to know if you've seen this young woman." He stopped himself from saying *girl*.

As Jackson reached in his carryall for Courtney's photo, the bartender glanced over at an older man seated at the end of the counter. Jackson looked over too, then made a mental note: medium build, salt-and-pepper hair, thin face, and black trench coat. "Who's that?" He nodded in the gentleman's direction.

The bartender shrugged. "Just a customer. I wanted to make sure he didn't need anything."

"What's your name?"

"Jason Speggel." He stared at the photo. "I've seen her. She comes in a couple times a month."

"When did you see her last?"

Jason worked his mouth around while he thought about it. "Couple nights ago?"

"Be specific. This is important."

"Is she okay?" He glanced at Courtney's photo again.

"What night was she here?"

"Monday." He snapped his fingers. "Of course. Monday is ladies' night. Drinks are half-price and the cocktail servers are guys."

"How late was she here?"

"I have no idea."

"Who would know?"

"I think Alec was working that section where she and her posse were sitting. He might know."

"First, I need Alec's phone number, then I want to know about the posse."

The bartender looked at the clock behind the bar. It was four forty-five. "Alec will be here in about ten minutes. Or so."

"Tell me about the posse."

"It's a bunch of rich-bitch party girls. One of them is named Madison, and I only know that because someone screamed her name Monday night when she came in. They were already half-drunk."

"How late does the group usually stay?"

He shrugged. "Alec would know."

Another patron sat down at the bar and Jason looked relieved. "Excuse me," he said, moving away. "I've got a customer."

Jackson perched on the nearest bar stool and filled in details on the sketchy notes he'd been taking. He was not optimistic he'd learn anything from Alec either. This may not have been Courtney's last stop for the evening. She could have gone to another club or to a private party. Jackson wrote *Find the cab-driver* at the top of his notepad.

Jackson ordered a cup of coffee, then called Katie and Kera and left them both messages. It would be a long night and he would likely work straight through it. He was relieved it was Renee and Katie's regular visitation day. For now, his daughter spent every other weekend at Renee's, plus every Wednesday night. Jackson was still skeptical his ex-wife's sobriety would last, but it was a relief to get a break. Being a full-time single parent and a homicide detective had overwhelmed him at times. Jackson had even considered resigning from the department and taking a DA investigator position with regular hours.

A guy who looked a lot like the bartender, only actually young, breezed into the club and called out, "Hey, Jason, note that I'm on time. You said it couldn't happen." He walked behind the bar and poured himself a soda from the fountain.

"Are you Alec?"

"Who wants to know?" The kid gave Jackson a playful grin. *Was Alec coming on to him?*

"Detective Jackson, violent crimes. I need to talk to you about one of your Monday night customers."

"Violent crimes, huh?"

"Let's go over to a table."

Once they were seated, Jackson showed him the photo.

Alec smiled. "That's Courtney." Then it hit him. "Oh no. What happened?"

"You tell me. Who was she with? When did she leave? Did anyone leave with her?"

Alec swallowed hard. "She was with her usual group. I only know Madison Atwell and Zoey Kingsley. The other two are kind of new. I think Courtney left around midnight, but I'm not sure. Most of the others had already left. I saw Courtney dancing, then about ten minutes later, I cleared their table."

"Who was she dancing with?"

"Some guy I'd never seen before."

"Describe him."

"About five-eleven and very lean. Blond hair, kind of long, but a nice face. He was wearing jeans and a black button-up shirt." Alec leaned forward. "Please tell me what happened to Courtney."

Jackson decided he had no reason to withhold the information. "She's dead. If she was a friend of yours, I'm sorry for your loss. But I need to keep asking questions. Do you know if any of her friends live over by Autzen Stadium?"

Alec blinked rapidly and seemed unable to speak.

"Are you okay?"

"Sort of." He blew out a breath. "I didn't know her personally, or any of them, except as customers. I only know last names because some of them pay with a credit card. I'm sorry."

"I'd like to look at credit-card receipts for Monday night."

"There's no names on them."

"I want to see the times."

Jason, the bartender, unlocked a small office off behind the bar and looked around for the receipts while the owner directed the search via a cell phone. Once they'd located the stack of paperwork, Alec, the cocktail server, thumbed through the pile.

"Did Courtney's dance partner pay with a credit card?"

"I don't know. I didn't take his drink orders."

After a quick search, Alec produced six small white slips of paper. "These have my server number on them. Should I put them in order according to the time they were paid?"

"Sure, thanks." Jackson started to wonder if he was wasting his time.

Alec said, "This one says eleven forty-five."

"Let me see the slip." Jackson looked for a credit-card number and found only the last four digits: 1075. He dug out Courtney's purse and checked her credit card. The numbers matched. Now what?

Alec stared at the turquoise bag. "How did she die? Was it alcohol related?"

Was he feeling guilty about serving her? "We don't know yet. Do you know what cab service she used?"

"Bailey's." His expression darkened. "I just remembered her cabdriver came in looking for her but Courtney was already gone. I didn't think too much of it at the time."

"She called a cab and left before it got here?"

Alec started blinking again. "I don't know. I was busy serving drinks, not hanging out with her."

"It's okay. Do you have a number for Bailey's cab service?"

"Jason has it behind the bar."

Jackson handed Alec his business card. "I need the name of the guy she was dancing with. Ask around tonight when the crowd is here. If you get it, please call me. I don't care if it's two o'clock this morning."

Jackson drank a second cup of coffee at the bar while he talked on the phone with the dispatcher at Bailey's Taxi & Limo Service. She reported that Courtney Durham had called for service at eleven forty. The driver, Stan Morris, had arrived at Diego's around midnight. He'd called in to say his fare had not materialized, so he was free to take other service calls. Jackson asked for the driver's contact information, then took a moment to put himself in Courtney's shoes.

I'm drunk and ready to go home, so I call a cab. Then something happens. Like the guy I was dancing with asks me if I want to go to a party. So we take off together in his car, and I'm too drunk to think about canceling my cab.

Was that even close?

Courtney had a steady boyfriend, or so her mother claimed, Jackson remembered. Maybe Courtney had gone outside for some fresh air while she waited for her cab, then something unexpected had happened. At midnight, on Monday, in Eugene? It seemed so unlikely.

Outside the building, Jackson scanned the businesses across the street, trying to determine if there was a potential witness out there somewhere. At midnight, none of the retail spaces on the block would have been open. If someone had assaulted or kidnapped Courtney while she waited out front for a cab, no one had seen it happen, unless they happened to be coming out of Diego's right behind her.

Jackson checked the sidewalk to see if Courtney had dropped anything—like an earring—but it was surprisingly clean. He searched the alley on the way to his car, stopping to examine a few pieces of trash, and did a quick search of the parking lot. No missing earring, no missing cell phone, nothing that looked like blood. He would come back tomorrow with his team and crawl on all fours if the investigation demanded it.

Right now, he had to inform the family.

Elle Durham surprised him by moving in close, laying her head on his chest, and weeping silently. Jackson grudgingly put one hand on her back to comfort her. It was his policy—and the department's preference—to not make physical contact with civilians while he was on the job. Especially women. Especially after two Eugene officers went to jail on multiple sexual-assault charges.

After a minute, Elle stepped back. "Excuse me for a moment." She headed to the office where they'd spoken yesterday. Instinct told Jackson to follow. Sometimes people were irrational in their grief.

Elle crossed the peach-colored room, dug into her purse for a prescription bottle, and downed a couple of pills. As Jackson started to ask what she was taking, she said, "It's just a tranquilizer."

"Can we sit and talk for a minute?"

She slumped into one of the padded chairs. Jackson took the other. Voice soft and trembling, Elle said, "I've worried about this for so long. Courtney is fearless and she took everything to an extreme. I suppose I should be relieved she died of an overdose instead of being murdered by some lunatic she picked up."

"Why do you assume she died of an overdose?"

"You said there were no obvious wounds. Knowing Courtney, it seems like a foregone conclusion." Elle cried as she talked.

"We don't know yet how she died. The autopsy will give us more information. The toxicology reports will come in soon and tell us more still." Jackson remembered the inhaler. "Did Courtney have asthma?"

"Yes. Why?"

"Her inhaler was under her body."

"She mostly used it when she was outdoors. Often only in the spring when the temperature changed rapidly." Elle rocked forward, grief consuming her. "Where is she now? I want to see her."

"She's in the basement of the hospital in an area called Surgery Ten. We would like you to officially identify her body as soon as you're able."

Elle sat up straighter and dabbed at the makeup around her eyes. "Brooke will be crushed. Will you tell her?" She looked even more gaunt than he remembered.

"Yes, but first I'd like to ask you a few questions."

"About what?"

"Courtney's last two days. She was missing for twenty-four hours and now she's inexplicably dead. I have to treat this as a possible homicide until the pathologist tells me differently."

"Did anybody even look for her?" A little flicker of anger surfaced.

"Detective Zapata put out an alert for her yesterday after you reported her missing. You went on television last night and notified the public. I was assigned her case this morning and spent the day investigating. We did everything we could in the little time we had."

Elle was quiet for a moment. "Dean and I used to go out looking for Courtney when she was still in high school. Sometimes she would go to a party and not come home. We worried ourselves sick over it." Elle's faced crumpled again and she fought for control. She seemed to be aging in front of his eyes.

Jackson grimaced as he remembered his own daughter's brief involvement with a group of promiscuous kids. "I'm sorry you had a hard time with Courtney. My daughter is fourteen and sometimes I'm terrified about her future."

"There's no point in worrying. Death gets everyone sooner or later."

Elle looked so sad, Jackson wanted to comfort her again, but he had to push past all the emotions and get to work. If Courtney had been murdered, or even accidentally harmed by someone, the window of opportunity for finding that person was closing fast.

"Courtney was at Diego's Monday night with a group of young women. Do you know who they were?"

"I told you this morning, I no longer try to keep track of her friends."

Jackson looked back at his notes. "Have you ever seen her with a guy described as five-ten, very lean, longish blond hair, and nice face?"

Elle looked puzzled. "It sounds like Brett, only Brett's hair is short. Who is this guy?"

"Someone Courtney was dancing with at Diego's. Maybe the last person to see her alive."

"You should ask Brooke about her friends. She would know more than I do." Elle's lower lip trembled. "Will you tell Brooke about Courtney? I don't think I can without losing it again."

"Is she here now?"

Just then a soft knock on the door interrupted them. A plump woman opened the door and said, "Dinner will be ready in about ten minutes."

"Thanks, Ursula. We won't be eating right now. Will you cover everything and save it for later?"

"Of course." The cook stayed in the doorway. "Is something wrong?"

"Courtney's dead, but I can't talk about it now. After you put everything away, you can go home."

Ursula's face crumpled. "I'm so sorry." She started to say something else, changed her mind, and left.

Elle pulled her cell phone out of her purse and pressed a single number. A pause, then, "Would you come to my office please? It's very important." Another pause. "Now please. We'll talk when you get here."

Jackson couldn't help but think about how cell phones had changed everyone's lives. This woman no longer had to walk around her very large house to speak to family members.

A minute later Brooke breezed into the office, took one look at Jackson, and said, "What has Courtney done now?"

"Sit down, Brooke. Detective Jackson has something important to tell you." Tears rolled down Elle's face.

Brooke looked concerned but she didn't sit. "What's going on?"

"Someone found Courtney's body today in the area behind Autzen Stadium. There's no obvious sign of trauma, so we don't know what happened to her yet. I'm sorry to be the one to tell you this."

"Dear god." Brooke looked stunned and grabbed for a chair. She plopped down and covered her face with her hands. Unlike Elle, Brooke cried noisily.

Jackson waited for her to get control. Finally, he said, "Brooke, I need to ask you some questions. I need to know about Courtney's friends, her habits, who she might have known who lived in that area."

Brooke looked over at her mother. "Can I have a Valium?" To Jackson, "How am I supposed to sit here and talk about her like nothing happened?"

"I know it's difficult, but if Courtney was assaulted by someone, we need to investigate. We need your help."

"You mean raped?"

"It's a possibility."

"Was she naked when you found her?"

"No." Jackson had to get control of the conversation. "Was there anything new in Courtney's life? A change in behavior? A change in mood?"

Brooke glanced at her mother. "She had a decent boyfriend for a change. And she was partying less, but nothing major."

"Do you know the names of the women she drank with at Diego's on Monday?"

"No. I'd stopped going there a while back. Too sleazy for me."

"Did Courtney have a friend who lived in the Autzen Stadium area?"

Tears rolled down her face as Brooke talked. "She used to party with some guy who lived farther down, closer to Springfield."

"What's his name and what does he look like?"

"I think his name is Zack. He's blond, skinny, and about thirty. I saw him once at Diego's." A pause. "Months ago."

Jackson felt a little tingle of possibility. Zack could be the guy Courtney was dancing with before she called the taxi. "Last name?"

"I don't know." Brooke reached to the desk for a tissue and blew her nose. "What do you think happened to her?"

"I really can't speculate. When she left the house Monday night, did she say anything to you about her plans?"

"Just that she was going to Diego's and would be home around midnight."

"Were you close to Courtney?" Jackson kept his voice soft.

"Of course." Brooke rushed to her mother, bursting into fresh tears as she knelt next to the chair and hugged her.

Jackson gave them a moment. He had more questions and normally he would have interviewed them individually, but he wasn't sure this was a murder investigation. Yet Danette's disappearance twelve hours before Courtney's nagged at him. It was very unusual for Eugene, a small city of about 157,000, and even unlikely for the larger metro area that included Springfield and other outlying towns. After a minute, he asked, "Do either of you know Danette Blake?"

Brooke kissed her mother's forehead and turned to Jackson. "I don't. Who is she?"

"A young woman who disappeared Monday morning."

"That's weird. Do you think there's some connection?"

"I'm just looking at all the possibilities. Where would Courtney go after leaving Diego's?"

"To a party, to a guy's house, maybe to the all-night pancake place on Franklin for something to eat." Brooke sighed. "Or to the coast, or maybe to Terwilliger Hot Springs. Courtney's impulsive."

Jackson jotted down the restaurant because it was the one place he could actually locate, walk into, and show her picture around. Anxious to talk to the boyfriend, Jackson decided to wrap up. "Is there anything either of you can tell me about Courtney that will help me determine where she was during the last twenty-four hours of her life?"

After a slight hesitation, Brooke said, "Courtney and Brett were fighting. If she was drunk, she might have called him to start an argument."

CHAPTER 13

"What do we do if Danette never turns up?" Maggie asked the unthinkable as Kera grabbed her purse and got ready to go out. Maggie held the baby and looked distraught.

"It's only been two days. We can't think like that yet."

"I know, but what if two days turns into two weeks, two months, two years? What do I do? Do I just go on with my life?"

Kera hugged Maggie around the shoulders, wishing there was more she could do. Not knowing the fate of your child would be the worst kind of torture. "Yes, you go on. Let's give this some time. I'm making headway."

Kera left the house feeling guilty about leaving Maggie with Micah again. Someone had to look for Danette though. She'd called Detective Zapata this morning and came away with the impression he thought there wasn't much he could do. Later she'd received a message on Facebook from one of Danette's friends who had said she thought Chad worked at the Red Apple Market on Sixth Avenue.

Kera's first stop was at the printer to pick up the posters she'd designed. Afterward, she would head to the market and see if she could determine Chad's last name. She planned to go back to Danette's house to finish looking around. Maybe if the police got called out to the duplex again they might realize how desperate she felt and start to help her.

The Red Apple was an old Safeway that had been converted to a neighborhood store catering to Latino shoppers. The interior was clean and bright and smelled like fajitas. Kera walked up to a young female cashier and asked to see the manager.

"She's not here right now. Can I help you with something?"

"I'm looking for a young man named Chad. He's tall and dark haired."

The cashier grinned. "He's good-looking too. He's in the cantina." She gestured with her thumb toward the back of the store.

Kera felt a thump of excitement in her chest. She hadn't expected to actually see or talk to Chad, but she couldn't think of any reason not to. She headed toward the wonderful smells in the back of the store. It wasn't noon yet so there was only one customer seated at the tables. A young man matching Chad's description had his back to her as he chopped tomatoes at the counter.

"Chad?"

He turned and looked her over thoroughly. "Why do you want to know?"

Kera refused to be intimidated by his dark-eyed stare. "I'm Kera Kollmorgan. Danette Blake is my daughter-in-law. Have you seen her?"

"Danette is married?" His suspicion turned to anger.

"No. Sorry. I just say that for convenience. I'm her baby's grandmother." Kera couldn't help but notice the knife in his hand.

He saw her looking but didn't put it down. "I haven't seen Danette in days, so I can't help you. I need to get back to work." Chad started chopping again.

"What's your last name?"

"None of your business," he said, keeping his back turned.

"I'm trying to find Danette and I'd like your help. Will you at least tell me if you saw her on Monday?"

He turned to face her again, his free hand clenched into a fist. "We were together last Saturday night, and I haven't seen her or talked to her since. I called once and she didn't answer. So I'm moving on. It's not like I planned to get serious about a woman with a baby."

"Did Danette ever talk about leaving her baby?"

He widened his stance and put his hands on his hips. "Not exactly, but she was freaking out about being a mother."

A customer took a seat at a nearby table.

"Now leave me alone. I can't help you." Chad walked over to greet his customer.

Kera left the store with mixed feelings. If Danette had run away from her baby, then she was probably safe and would call eventually. It also meant Kera might end up raising Micah, a prospect that both excited and scared her. *Would Micah be so much like Nathan it would hurt just to look at him? What would it mean for her future with Jackson? Was he prepared to start over as a parent?*

Before leaving, Kera picked up a package of sturdy tacks and double-stick tape for putting up posters, then headed for the young cashier's checkout stand. As she reached for her wallet, Kera said, "How do you spell Chad's last name? I need to send him an invitation."

"Whitehorse? It's spelled just like it sounds."

"Makes sense." Kera pulled Danette's picture out of her shoulder bag and showed it to the cashier. "Have you seen her?"

"No. Why?"

"She's missing. Can I put up a poster in your parking lot?"

"Sure."

After taping a poster to the light pole, Kera climbed in her Saturn and called Detective Zapata. Not surprised that he didn't pick up, she left him a message with Chad's last name and hoped he would at least run a background check.

* * *

Evans and Schakowski were already in the small conference room when Jackson arrived. They had both been at the department, waiting for his call. His stops at Diego's and the Durham house had taken longer than he'd expected. Jackson took a seat in one of the folding metal chairs. "I ordered a ton of Chinese food, so I hope you haven't eaten yet."

"Even if I had, I'd still eat my share," Schak said. "Is it just us three? I thought Mrs. Durham would have demanded the attention of everyone in the Violent Crimes Unit."

"I called McCray too." Jackson dug out his notepad. "We'll bring in more detectives if we have to. Right now, we don't even know if this is a homicide. If it weren't for the other missing woman, I'd bet money Courtney Durham overdosed."

"What missing woman?" McCray asked as he walked in. Ed McCray had been on the job long enough to earn his gray hair and weathered face. He was also tenacious and levelheaded, and Jackson always called him in on puzzling cases.

"Thanks for coming. Danette Blake, age twenty, disappeared Monday morning and has not been seen since. She dropped off her baby with her mother-in-law, went to an appointment with a psychiatrist, then vanished." Jackson looked at the other two detectives to see their reaction. It was not news to them. "While we investigate the death of Courtney Durham, we'll also keep Danette in mind. On the surface, these women have nothing in common, except they both disappeared on the same day."

"What do we know about Courtney Durham?" McCray took out a notepad and a stick of gum. He'd recently quit smoking and was trying not to outgrow his skinny brown corduroy pants.

"She went drinking at Diego's on Monday night. She was with a group of young women." Jackson flipped back through his notes. "I have the names Madison Atwell and Zoey Kingsley." He looked at Schak. "Your turn to take the board."

Evans jumped up. "I'll do it. Schak's handwriting would make a kindergarten teacher cry."

On the long dry-erase board, Evans wrote *Courtney* at the top on one side and *Danette* on the other, drawing a line down the middle. They waited while she filled in the details Jackson had just verbalized. Under Courtney's side, she wrote the friends' names, then turned to Jackson. "Want me to interview them?"

"Yes, and anyone else who was in the drinking group that night. Also, ask about a guy named Zack, who was seen dancing with Courtney." Jackson glanced at his notes, wishing he'd taken time to key them into a Word document before the meeting. "Courtney called Bailey's Taxi and Limo Service at eleven forty p.m. They sent driver Stan Morris to Diego's to pick her up. She had already left the nightclub when he arrived."

"Have you talked to him?" McCray asked.

"No. Put him on your list, along with the Pancake House, that all-night place on Franklin. Courtney's sister says she might have gone there after leaving the club. I have photo prints of Courtney being made now, so you can all pick some up when you leave."

"What have you got for me?" Schak wanted to know.

"Find out who Courtney had cell-phone service with and get a subpoena for her records for the last two weeks. We need to know who she called between Sunday and Tuesday night, and we need to look into the ex-boyfriends. Start with Steve Smith, who is also known as Skeet. And there's Tristan Chalmers from last June. There may be others in between. Courtney's sister, Brooke, might be able to give you more names."

Evans turned from the board. "What kind of young woman are we talking about here?"

Jackson tried to keep his voice in a just-the-facts mode. No matter what she had done, Courtney was still someone's daughter. "Her sister called her a wild child. Courtney had a habit of disappearing while partying. It apparently started in high school. She's also been arrested for shoplifting, public drunkenness, and indecent exposure."

"The Durhams are obscenely rich; why would she steal something?" Schak looked more puzzled than disgusted.

"Maybe just for kicks." Jackson had to flip back to his notes from that morning. Was it only this morning he'd first been out to the Durham house, not knowing Courtney was already dead? "Her mother said Courtney had recently joined a mountain bike-riding club. Maybe she's an adrenaline junkie."

The door opened and the desk officer came in with a cardboard box loaded with cartons of food. "Dinner is served," he said with a mock bow.

After he left, Jackson picked it back up. "I'll interview her current boyfriend, Brett Fenton, and hopefully have something to go on from there. Let's get back out there as quickly as we can."

Evans jotted the boyfriend's name on the board, looked at Jackson. "What about Danette? Is she anything like Courtney?"

"Not at all." Jackson reached for a carton. "Full disclosure here. Danette is Kera's daughter-in-law. I first learned about her disappearance from Kera. I've met Danette and spent a little time with her. What I know is she was a student at Oregon State until the baby was born, and she has no criminal history."

"You ran a check on her?" McCray made a little tsk-tsk sound.

"We all do it. It's one of the perks of the job."

No one argued.

"So what do these two young women have in common?" Schak voiced what everyone was wondering.

"Probably nothing. But if they have a connection, we have to find it."

Brett Fenton was playing basketball under the Washington Street Bridge with a group of other twenty-something young men. As soon as the weather warmed every spring, the outdoor court was in constant use, often by players who just dropped in for a pickup game. Not that you didn't see people out here in the winter, just not nearly as often. The uniform age of this group made Jackson think the game had been arranged in advance.

With the sun dropping in the sky, Jackson stood on the grass at the edge of the court and tried to see if he could pick out Brett, who apparently was blond, lean, and good-looking, similar to the man seen dancing with Courtney Monday night. Jackson pegged the guy in the white shorts and T-shirt, who seemed to be in better shape than the others.

When one of the players noticed him watching and called a time-out, Jackson moved toward the group. "Brett Fenton?" He'd called Fenton after leaving the Durhams and arranged to meet him here.

The blond guy in white jogged over. "I'm Brett."

"Let's go sit at the picnic table." Jackson wanted to watch Brett's face as they talked. He also wanted him to be sitting down and away from his friends when he heard the news of Courtney's death.

"What's going on with Courtney?" Brett wiped a drip of sweat from his temple. Jackson sensed Brett was trying to sound more casual than he felt.

"Someone found her body this morning behind Autzen Stadium."

"Oh no." Brett's hands flew to his face. "Oh shit."

"I'm sorry for your loss. I'm also sorry to pressure you at a time like this, but I need to ask a lot of questions."

Brett shook his head. "Give me a second." He got up and walked a few feet away. Jackson gave him a moment.

When Brett came back, his eyes watered and his breath came in short gasps. "What happened? I knew Elle hadn't heard from Courtney, but I wasn't too surprised."

"Why weren't you surprised?"

Brett's eyes flashed with guilt. "It's complicated. Courtney's complicated. I kind of broke up with her Monday morning."

"Why?"

"She's crazy."

"Party-till-you-drop crazy? Or alternate-view-of-reality crazy?"

"Spoiled-rich-girl crazy." Brett's shoulders shook and he let out a sob. "I can't believe she's dead."

"When did you see her last?"

A small pause while he thought. "Sunday night. I was over at her place."

"Has she called you in the last two days?"

Brett rubbed his forehead. "No."

Jackson was sure he had just been lied to. "I can get your cell-phone records in a couple of hours." *Maybe.*

Brett calculated the possible scenarios. Finally, he said, "Courtney called me from Diego's Monday night. She was drunk and I told her to leave me alone."

"What time?"

"Around eleven."

"Did you hear from her yesterday?"

"No."

"Were you worried?"

"Not until Mrs. Durham called and said Courtney hadn't come home. Even then, I wasn't really worried. If you knew Courtney, you'd understand."

Jackson was starting to feel like he did know Courtney. The table began to vibrate and Jackson realized Brett's legs were shaking. "You seem nervous. What are you holding back?"

"Nothing." Brett opened his eyes wider in an attempt to look sincere. "This is just freaky. I told her on Sunday I wanted a break from her. Now three days later, you tell me she's dead."

"Can you think of anyone who would want to harm her?"

"No."

Jackson stood. "Let's go down to the department and document an official statement. I want to know everywhere you've been since Monday night."

Brett choked back another sob. "Please don't arrest me. I think I know what happened."

CHAPTER 14

The interrogation room's pale-gray walls and cheap overhead lighting made everyone look a little ill, but Brett was devoid of color. The young man from an upper-class family had never been inside a police station before. Seated at the table in the windowless room he looked smaller and younger than he had on the basketball court. Jackson knew better than to let himself have any compassion. Brett was a viable suspect. Age no longer mattered when it came to murder. Two weeks before, an eight-year-old boy in another state had shot two men, one of whom was his father.

"This conversation is being recorded." Jackson didn't mention the camera. "The purpose is to simply get your statement on record. You are not under arrest, you are here willingly, and you have declined the presence of a lawyer."

Brett nodded.

"First, let's get your timetable nailed down. When was the last time you spoke to Courtney Durham?"

Brett cleared his throat. "Monday night around eleven o'clock. She called me from Diego's. She was drunk, so I told her I didn't want to talk to her."

"Where were you all day Tuesday?"

"I went to classes at the University of Oregon, then had dinner with some friends at Pegasus Pizza around six. Afterward I went home to study. I live with my parents, so they can confirm that."

"What are their names?"

"Sherry and George Fenton. They both teach at the UO."

This was mostly formality, which was why he hadn't called another detective in for the session. Jackson's instinct was to believe the kid, especially knowing what was coming next.

"What do you think happened to Courtney between late Monday night when she left Diego's and late Tuesday night when she died?"

"I think she was picked up by a company called ThrillSeekers. Courtney told me she had hired them to kidnap her."

"Why would she do that?" When he'd first heard Brett's story, Jackson had been stunned. Sometimes living in Eugene made him feel naive.

"She did it for the adventure. Courtney likes to live on the edge and she's tried everything else." Brett shifted, looking even more uncomfortable. "I also think she wanted her mother's attention."

"Did you know when the kidnap was supposed to happen?"

"No. Neither did she. That was part of the thrill."

"You went along with this activity?"

"No!" Brett pushed his hands through his hair. "Courtney told me about it after she had already hired them. I thought it was stupid and dangerous and begged her to call it off. But she wouldn't. So I told her I couldn't see her anymore."

"When did this conversation take place?"

"Sunday night at her house."

"When was your next conversation with Courtney?"

"Monday night when she called from Diego's."

"Did she mention the kidnapping?"

"No. She said she loved me and wanted to see me. She was drunk so I said no and got off the phone."

"When did you realize she might have been kidnapped?" Jackson was uncomfortable calling it a kidnapping if Courtney had arranged it, but there wasn't another term for this craziness.

"Her mother, Elle Durham, called me Tuesday afternoon and said Courtney hadn't been home. She wanted to know if I'd seen Courtney, which I hadn't. After I got off the phone with Elle, I wondered if Courtney had been picked up by the adventure company."

"Did you mention ThrillSeekers to her mother?"

"No."

Brett shifted again, like a kid with a guilty conscience. "I didn't know for sure that was what happened. Courtney could have been anywhere. I didn't want Elle to be mad at me for not telling her sooner."

"Tell me the details about the kidnapping. Where did they plan to hold her and for how long?" Jackson would ask these same questions tomorrow morning at ThrillSeekers. *How could such a business be legal?*

"I don't know any of that. I got so mad when she told me she'd already paid for it, I never asked. I just kept telling her to cancel it."

"Do you have any idea why Courtney is dead?"

"No." Brett hung his head.

Jackson debated whether to keep Brett on hold until he could confirm his story. He had already checked ThrillSeekers' website and called the company, which didn't answer. The owner, Zoran Mircovitch, had an unlisted number. Jackson would drive to Portland first thing in the morning with a search warrant.

"I'll let you go for now, but I want you to be available at a moment's notice. Don't even go see a long movie."

Back at his desk, Jackson checked his phone messages. Sophie Speranza had called, asking him to confirm the identity of the body found that afternoon. *Did he still owe her something?* He'd done the interview, so they should be square. Jackson pressed for a return call, regretting it instantly.

"You got back to me. Thanks."

"I can't give you any real information."

"Just tell me the identity of the dead woman."

"Courtney Durham."

"Was she murdered?"

"We're not sure yet how she died. We're waiting on toxicology reports."

"Off the record, what do you think?"

Jackson held back a chuckle. As if he would trust her with an off-the-record statement. "I really don't know yet. I have to get back to work."

"What about Danette Blake? Any word on her disappearance?"

"Not yet."

"Is Courtney's death related to Danette's disappearance?"

"It seems unlikely at this point."

"Can I quote you on that?"

"I'd rather you didn't. Gotta go." Jackson hung up before she could ask anything else. He decided he had evened the score and could go back to ignoring her calls, just as he did with all the other media people. The department had a spokesperson whose job it was to talk to the media so he didn't have to.

He checked his cell-phone messages. He'd missed a call from Katie. Earlier, he'd contacted his ex-wife and asked if she could keep Katie overnight. Renee had been happy to comply. His daughter had called just to say good night. It made him feel loved, and lucky, and guilty all at once.

* * *

Kera and Maggie sat down in the family room to watch the local evening news together, with Micah in Kera's lap. They shared an unspoken hope that someone out there had seen or heard something about Danette and reported it to the television station.

Keith Peterson, an aging redhead with a square jaw, led the broadcast with economic news, which seemed less depressing than usual. Trina Waterman, seated on his right, launched into the next report, her voice thick with suspense and conspiracy.

"In a breaking story, the body of a young woman was found in the wooded area behind Autzen Stadium today, about a half mile from the Willamette River. Police have not confirmed her identity. A passing cyclist found the body and called 911. He posted the event on Twitter, the online social-networking site, where it was picked up by our news organization. A call to the Eugene Police Department confirmed the cyclist's account, but no further details are available.

"In another story, there's been no update on the whereabouts of Courtney Durham, twenty-one, who disappeared Monday after visiting a downtown nightclub. Her mother, Mrs. Elle Durham, who publically pleaded for her daughter's return yesterday, was not available for comment."

Courtney's picture flashed on the screen with a number to call. "We'll have more on this breaking story as details emerge."

Maggie cried out, "Could the body they found be Danette's?"

Kera muted the TV. "No. The police have Danette's picture. They would have called us. The broadcaster made it sound like it could be Courtney."

"Poor girl."

"I notice they didn't mention Danette is still missing."

"She's not rich, blonde, and connected." Maggie's voice was thick with bitterness. "Danette was always a bit of an outsider in school with her brown skin and dark eyes. I didn't realize how deep the bias is."

"I'm not even sure the media realizes how biased it is."

* * *

While Jackson wrote up the paper for the search warrant, he called his team members to update them and to ask Schak to go with him to Portland in the morning. On the drive to Judge Cranston's home, he called Kera. It was after ten o'clock but he knew she would still be awake.

"It's Jackson. Are you okay?"

"More or less. I'm a little worried about Maggie. She seems to have lost hope and keeps talking about Stephanie Condon."

Stephanie was an Oregon teenager who'd vanished without a trace until her body had turned up eleven years later. Jackson hesitated to tell Kera about Courtney's fate. "Did you get some posters put up?"

"About twenty this afternoon. I focused on the area around Danette's duplex to start with."

"Did Katie help?"

"I called her, but she didn't get back to me. I found out a few things about Danette though."

"Tell me."

"Danette's boyfriend is Chad Whitehorse and he works at the Red Apple Market." Kera paused. "One of her friends who I'd e-mailed got back to me and said she met Danette at the Young Mothers Outreach Center on Seventeenth and Oak. The center offers drop-in babysitting, peer support, and networking with other resources, that kind of thing. Maybe you can check into it."

"I won't have time. I've been assigned a case with a suspicious death." Jackson drove up the ramp to the Ferry Street Bridge, grateful for the lack of traffic. "That's why you haven't heard from me until now."

"Is it Courtney Durham?"

"Was it on the news? We didn't release her name until moments ago."

"Trina Waterman didn't identify her directly, but she put the connection out there. Was Courtney murdered?"

"It's possible."

"That means Danette could be dead too." Kera's voice choked up.

"I don't think so." Jackson wanted to reassure Kera, but without giving her sensitive case information. "There are circumstances surrounding Courtney's disappearance and death that make me pretty sure Danette's situation is unrelated."

"That's good. I mean for Danette, but not for Courtney. Does her family know?"

"Yes. I told them this afternoon."

"Are you still working?"

"I'm about to wake up a judge to get a search warrant signed, then I'm leaving for Portland early in the morning. I'm not sure when I'll get to see you."

"Good luck with your case and call me if you can. I'll keep searching for Danette."

"Keep Detective Zapata in the loop, will you? He's a good man with too much work on his hands."

* * *

Danette woke to sheer blackness. The cloth was still over her eyes, but it was more than that. She was covered head to toe by a heavy blanket. Suffocating. She could barely pull in enough air. She was on her side, knees bent, and her head jammed against something hard and cold.

All at once she became aware of motion. The road hummed below her. She was on the floor in the backseat of a car. *Where were they taking her now?*

For a while, she tried to gauge the distance she was traveling, but there was too much slowing down, stopping, and rolling forward again. They had to be traveling in a well-populated area with stoplights. Danette prayed she was still in Eugene. If they kept her in town, she might find a way to escape and make her way back to Micah.

She wanted to stay awake, to be aware of her surroundings, but the drug and motion made it impossible.

Danette woke again when she was lifted from the car and carried across a small open space. The cold air, even with the blanket, made her think it must be the middle of the night. Still, Danette was hit with the call of freedom; it surrounded her, taunted her to scream and fight and run to safety. Her feet were tied, her hands were cuffed, and she had bindings around her mouth and eyes. She had learned the hard way all she could do was injure herself.

They entered a building where it was warmer, but still cool. The other, smaller man possessed her now and she heard him breathing heavily under the weight of her body. They crossed a room with a familiar smell she couldn't name, then jostled down a short flight of stairs. Another basement, Danette realized, as he dumped her on a mattress on the floor. Would this be the last place she ever knew? She vaguely remembered a reference to a Dutchman.

Who was he and what did he want with her?

CHAPTER 15

Thursday, April 9, 5:02 a.m.

Jackson met Schak at the department at five as planned. Each carrying a thermos of coffee, they headed down to the parking lot below the city-hall building. Typically, he would have made the trip alone, but Jackson didn't know anything about Zoran Mircovitch, and the presence of two detectives might deter the suspect from trying anything stupid.

"We're taking your car, right?" Schak said.

"Would you mind driving?" Jackson hated being a passenger, but the stents were driving him crazy.

"Are you in pain?"

"Sometimes. I just need to be able to shift around." Jackson hadn't told his coworkers about the stents and didn't plan to unless he peed his pants and had to explain.

They climbed into Schak's city-issued Impala, which looked much like his, and headed out of town as the sun rose on the horizon.

After a two-hour drive, listening to Led Zeppelin and Pink Floyd most of the way, they took the Burnside exit in Portland and started looking for 321 Oak Street. They found it off Third Avenue. The brown brick building had no signage that mentioned an adventure company. The entrance was locked, so they walked down the street to a Denny's and had breakfast.

Forty minutes later, they were back and waiting near the front door when a young Asian woman walked up to open it. She looked surprised and a little nervous to see them. "Who are you?" The woman fumbled with an oversized key collection.

"Detectives Jackson and Schakowski, Eugene Police. We need to speak with Zoran Mircovitch immediately."

She pushed open the heavy door. "He doesn't usually get here until nine."

They followed the woman into a small, austere lobby.

"Do you work for him?"

"Yes."

"Call him. Get him down here. We have a search warrant, so we'll get started anyway." Judge Cranston had limited the warrant to a search of the database for Courtney Durham's records, and if Mircovitch cooperated they wouldn't need to exercise it.

About twenty minutes later, Zoran Mircovitch rushed into his office. Jackson and Schak were still questioning his administrative assistant, who had already told them Courtney was a client but wouldn't give any details.

Mircovitch was in his forties and his sun-loving face was starting to wrinkle, but otherwise he was lean and muscular, a lifetime athlete. After introductions, they all took seats. Mircovitch pulled his hands together. "What's the problem?"

"One of your clients, Courtney Durham, is dead." Jackson took the lead. "We'd like to know why."

Mircovitch lost a little color. For a moment he was speechless, then finally blurted out, "I'm sorry to hear about her death, but I assure you, this company is not responsible. We operate under the tightest rules for safety and accountability."

"Tell us about ThrillSeekers and how you came to think kidnapping people was a good way to make money."

Mircovitch made a noise in his throat. "That is a very limited part of our business. Mostly we arrange outdoor adventures like skydiving, parasailing, and wilderness camping." He gestured at the walls, which were covered with blown-up photos of smiling people engaging in various outdoor activities.

"Did you arrange for Courtney Durham to be kidnapped?" Jackson kept up the pace.

"Yes. She asked for the service and signed a contract to that effect."

"How much did you charge her?"

A pause. "Twenty thousand."

Schak let out a whistle.

"Who did the actual kidnapping?"

Mircovitch turned to his computer and keyed something in. "I'm fairly certain who we contracted with, but I want to be sure."

"Someone you've used before?"

"Yes. Seth Valder."

Schak spoke up. "I've heard the name. I believe he owns a strip club in Eugene."

"Mr. Valder is a businessman," Mircovitch clarified, "and Lucky Numbers is one of his holdings."

"How did Valder know where to find Courtney?"

"She provided us with a list of places she would be over the next few weeks."

"Have you spoken to Valder in the last few days?"

"He called yesterday morning to report he had completed the contract."

Jackson was impatient with Mircovitch's spin. "I want to know every detail about Courtney's business with you. I want to see her contract. I want to see Seth Valder's contract. I want to know exactly what Valder said when he called yesterday."

"Of course. You have a warrant. You can see all of it." Mircovitch clicked a few keys, and the printer on a side table started spitting out paper. Mircovitch talked over the noise. "When Seth called, he reported he'd picked up Courtney, held her for twenty-four hours as stipulated, then released her in good health. According to my contract with him, he also made a brief video of Courtney near the end of her adventure to document her safety. He uploaded the file to our FTP site. Would you like to see it?"

"We would. How much did you pay Valder?"

"Ten thousand."

Jackson scrambled for what to ask next. Most of the deaths he investigated involved men who had killed each other over drugs, money, or ego, and often left some type of evidence. Occasionally, he was handed a stumper case, but this one was strange from every angle.

"How did Courtney die?" Mircovitch turned his thirty-inch monitor so Schak and Jackson could view the video.

"We're not certain yet."

Courtney's pretty face came on the screen, smiling strangely at the camera in a darkened room. "Hey, it's Courtney here. I just wanted to say I'm okay and this was all my idea." She made a kissing gesture with her lips, then laughed seductively. The video file went dark.

"I want to see the information for the file." Jackson stood and walked around to Mircovitch's side of the desk. "Move, please."

The business owner stood and pointed at a .mov file labeled DurhamSafetyProof. Jackson grabbed the mouse and clicked. An information box popped open and revealed the file had been created at 9:17 p.m., Tuesday, April 7. Courtney had been captive and alive at nine o'clock, then free and dead by midnight.

"Where were you Tuesday night between nine p.m. and two a.m.?" Jackson demanded.

"At home in bed with my wife."

"Where was this video recorded?"

"I don't know. I left that up to Valder. My contract with him only stipulates that the client be kept warm, dry, and safe."

"Where was Courtney released?"

"Again, I don't know. That's part of the thrill for the clients, not to know when they'll be picked up, where they will be held, or where they will be released. Once they sign the contract, which is also videotaped, the adventure is out of their control."

Schak spoke up again. "How many of these kidnappings have you done?"

"Only a few."

"Did any of them go badly?"

"No." Mircovitch reached for his water bottle.

He was concealing something. Jackson knew it instinctively. So did Schak, who suddenly leaned forward. "What are you not telling us? Remember, we have a warrant. We could spend all day here looking at files."

"No one was hurt, and it has nothing to do with Courtney."

"Tell us anyway." Jackson went back to his chair.

"We take every precaution to protect our clients and ourselves. Every nonconventional adventure has a safety word the client can use at any time and the whole thing stops immediately."

"And?"

Mircovitch drew in a long breath. "One client panicked during her adventure. She used the safety word, but the contractor didn't hear her right away. She wasn't happy with her experience, so we refunded her money. That's it."

"What's her name?"

"I don't have to tell you. I doubt if your warrant gives you permission to search for her in my files." Mircovitch crossed his arms and leaned back.

Jackson felt a flash of anger. This man's kidnapping sideline disgusted him. He wanted to shut it down, but this was not his jurisdiction and ThrillSeekers was not his primary focus. Courtney had been dead for more than thirty-six hours, and their window of opportunity was nearly gone. They had to get back to Eugene and talk to the contract kidnapper.

"I want Seth Valder's phone number and address." Jackson stood, relieved to stretch and take the pressure off his kidneys.

Mircovitch checked his cell phone, then jotted down a number. "I don't have his address."

"Let's go. You're coming with us."

"To Eugene? You can't take me to Eugene. I haven't done anything wrong and you have no reason to hold me."

Jackson pulled handcuffs from his inside jacket pocket. "You are coming with us, one way or another."

"Oh shit." Mircovitch glanced around as if he might not see his office again. "I have to make a few phone calls first. I have clients scheduled for this morning."

Jackson grabbed the cell phone out of his hands. "Not yet."

On the way out, Mircovitch stopped and spoke to his receptionist. "Cancel my appointments for the day, please. Then see if we have Seth Valder's address."

"That's not necessary. We'll find it," Jackson said, tugging on Mircovitch's arm.

They dropped Mircovitch at the downtown Portland police head-quarters. In a private conversation with the precinct captain, Jackson asked that Mircovitch be held and questioned about his seedy business for at least four hours. The captain wasn't happy about the unorthodoxy of the arrangement until Jackson mentioned the investigation involved the death of Courtney Durham, daughter of Dean and Elle Durham who contributed heavily to law-enforcement causes and state politicians who saw things their way. Jackson normally wouldn't allow someone's money to affect how he did his job, but he needed this favor. Valder was key to finding out what happened to Courtney, and he needed time to get to Valder. He wasn't about to let the sleazebag slip out of town after a warning phone call from Mircovitch.

As soon as they were in the car headed home, Jackson called Lara Evans and asked her to run a background check on Seth Valder. Next he called Ed McCray. "Schak and I just left Portland. I need you to find Seth Valder and bring him in for questioning. He's the owner of Lucky Numbers. Evans is running a background check so she should have his address in a moment."

"Is Valder considered dangerous?"

"He filled a contract to kidnap Courtney Durham, so he could be. Don't move on him alone. Take Evans with you. Schak and I will be there in an hour or so."

Schak, who was driving, gave him a look. Making that kind of time meant hitting eighty or more all the way.

In ten minutes, Evans called back. "Valder is forty-one and hasn't been arrested in the last twelve years. Before that he had a few drug charges and one fraud conviction. He currently owns Lucky Numbers and another business called Valder Enterprises, which we don't know much about. He resides at 27851 Fleck

Road, which is outside of Veneta, and owns a rental property at 2597 Royal Avenue."

"Go with McCray to Veneta to bring Valder in, then talk to Michael Quince and see what he knows about him." Detective Quince currently handled most of the sex-related crimes that came in to the unit.

"I'm on it."

An hour later, as they sped past the town of Coburg, ten minutes outside of Eugene, McCray called back. "We've got a situation here."

CHAPTER 16

Jackson pulled up in front of Valder's two-story house deep in the trees and parked next to a nearly identical city-issued car. McCray said he'd called for backup, but it obviously hadn't arrived yet. Jackson and Schak hustled to the front door. The tall windows on either side revealed two people standing in the room beyond the foyer. Jackson knocked loudly, then pushed right in.

McCray and Evans stood watch over a man seated on a low beige couch. Valder looked at least six-three, even sitting down. Jackson guessed his weight at 240, with most of it concentrated from the waist up. What Valder had lost in hair, he made up for with light-blue eyes and tight, tanned skin. The tan seemed unusual, considering the circumstances. Jackson wondered if there was a tanning bed in the house somewhere.

Valder looked up at Jackson. "You can take these cuffs off. I don't bite." He grinned and flashed perfectly capped teeth. "There are four of you here now. With guns. As I told the guy in corduroy, I'm agoraphobic, so I'm not going to run."

Evans spoke up. "He refused to come with us, and we didn't want to drag him out, so that's the situation here."

This was a first for Jackson. "How do we know you're not bullshitting us?"

"Call my manager at Lucky Numbers. Ask him when he saw me last."

"How long have you been agoraphobic?"

"I haven't left the house in a year. It came on gradually before that. I'm willing to talk here," Valder said, with slight edge of pleading. "I'm a legitimate businessman with nothing to hide."

Jackson motioned for McCray to remove the cuffs. Not that he trusted Valder, but if the big man relaxed, he would open up more. "Then you won't mind if we look around while we're here?"

"Go ahead."

Jackson turned to Schak. "Would you pull up those other chairs next to the couch? We'll interview him here." Jackson headed down the main hall in search of a bathroom.

When he returned, Schak and McCray were seated across from Valder, but Evans remained standing. They'd left Jackson the chair directly in front of the suspect. Jackson sat, thinking he'd never been in an interrogation situation like this one. It was unusual to have the whole team present, but at the moment he had no leads to send anyone out on. Brett Fenton was still a possibility, but so far they had no motive for him to kill Courtney.

Jackson pulled out his tape recorder and set it on the coffee table. "You don't mind if I record." It was not offered as a question.

Valder shrugged. "What do you want to know?"

"How much did ThrillSeekers pay you to kidnap Courtney Durham?"

"Technically, I contracted to help her act out her fantasy. For that, I was paid ten thousand dollars."

Valder was unfazed by the line of questioning, and Jackson felt a little less certain. "How do you know Zoran Mircovitch?"

"We've done some business together over the years. We met at a gym in Portland a long time ago."

"What kind of business do you do with Mircovitch?"

"It's mostly referrals. I send potential clients to him and he gives me a nice contract every once in a while. Why do you want to know?"

Jackson ignored the question. "Tell me about Courtney's contract. If you don't leave the house, how did you fulfill it?"

"I hired Eddie Lucas. He has little business called Dirty Jobs."

"At least he's honest in his advertising. Where can we find Eddie?"

"He's in the yellow pages."

"I'm doing you a favor by not dragging your ass in to the department for questioning," Jackson snapped. "Just tell me how you contacted him."

Valder looked offended. "I'd heard his name before, so I looked him up in the phone book. Really."

Jackson turned to McCray. "Let's find Eddie Lucas and bring him in. Evans, go with him, please."

The two detectives trotted out of the house.

Jackson turned back to Valder. "When and where did Eddie pick up Courtney?"

"Monday night as she came out of Diego's. He waited in front, then grabbed her and stuck her in the van." Valder shrugged, seeming unconcerned.

"Did she struggle? Did Lucas use force or restraint? I want details." Jackson's voice got loud again.

"I wasn't there. All I know is she was cuffed, gagged, and blindfolded. She wanted it to be real, and she was fine when she got here."

"When did Courtney arrive?"

"Little after midnight."

"How long was she here?"

"About twenty-four hours. That's what the contract said."

"Who videotaped her when she was here?"

"I did." Valder jerked forward. "What happened? Did the little rich girl change her mind and sign a complaint? Or is her mother making a stink about it?"

Did Valder really not know Courtney was dead? "You didn't see the news this morning?" Jackson assumed Sophie's story had been in the newspaper, but he'd left the house before his arrived.

"I spend my mornings on E-Trade. What happened? What's this all about?"

"I'll tell you in a minute. Right now I need a few more answers. Where did you keep Courtney for the duration of her confinement?"

"Here. In a room in the basement." Valder kept his face impassive.

"What happened when her confinement was over?"

"Eddie picked her up."

"Did you arrange a time in advance?"

A slight hesitation. "Yes."

Jackson noticed the pause. Out of the corner of his eye, he saw Schak react too. "What happened to the arranged time?"

"Nothing. Eddie came back a little early, that's all."

"Where did he take her to be released?"

"To Autzen Stadium, out near the back by the bike path. You must know all this. What's going on?"

"Who decided where to drop her off?"

"I did. Eddie was just the leg man."

"Why that spot?"

Valder shrugged. "It's a secluded area, yet right in the middle of town. Creepy, but easy for someone to get to."

"What kind of shape was Courtney in when she left your house?"

"She was fine. I have a video to prove it."

"She's dead now. Any idea why?"

Valder blinked his eyes and let his mouth fall open. "Courtney's dead? Oh shit. That's terrible."

Jackson wasn't buying it. "I think you knew already. Did Eddie call after the drop and tell you what happened?"

"Eddie called to say the job was done and everything was fine." Valder clenched his teeth. "What happened to Courtney? How did she die?"

Jackson stood. "Let's go take a look at where Courtney stayed while she was here."

Valder sat for a long moment. "I don't have to show you."

"We can have a search warrant within an hour. I've got at least another hour's worth of questions."

"Fine, I'll show you." Valder stood and was taller than Jackson had guessed. "As I said, I have nothing to hide. I helped a young woman act out her fantasy. That's it." Valder moved toward the center of the house, his arms at his sides, not swinging like most people's did when they walked.

As they headed down the wide hall, Schak turned to Valder. "Who else lives here?"

"Just me."

"Who brings in supplies for you?"

"An employee."

"His name?" Schak kept up the questions.

"He goes by G, but his legal name is Gary Gwartney." Valder paused and looked over his shoulder. "G had nothing to do with this."

At the end of the hall, they reached a stairwell heading down. At the bottom, the steps opened into a small alcove with a door on either side. "The basement was originally built as a bomb shelter," Valder explained. "So there's a bathroom and a refrigeration unit down here. I also keep a generator and supplies."

Valder opened the door on the left and the three of them entered a room that was about fourteen feet square. A narrow bed occupied one corner, a couch was in another, and one wall was lined with boxes. Most displayed food labels, and they looked sloppily stacked. There was a narrow door in the corner opposite the bed.

Jackson took in the gray brick walls and cold cement floor and wondered why in the hell a spoiled rich girl would want to be held captive here. *She must have been mentally ill,* Jackson thought. What had her boyfriend Brett said? That he thought Courtney had done it for her mother's attention.

"Jesus," Schak muttered. "This is so fucked up." He looked at Valder with such contempt Jackson stepped in.

"Did you give her food and water while she was down here?"

"Of course. She also had a communication unit she could contact me with if she wanted it to be over."

"What kind of communication unit?"

"You know, a walkie-talkie."

"Did she use it?"

"Nope. She toughed it out." Valder's expression said he admired Courtney's fortitude.

"Have you held anyone else down here?"

Valder shook his head. "I'm not a kidnapper. I'm a businessman who caters to the diversity of human desires."

"The strip-club business?" Jackson retorted. "What else?"

"There's only so much I can do from my house." Valder tried to look rueful, but he was being evasive.

"Mind if I look around?"

"That's why we're here."

Jackson headed toward the bed, not even sure what he was looking for. Bloodstains? Courtney had made a video here, showing herself to be unharmed.

While Jackson pulled up the blanket and looked for trace evidence on the bed, Schak examined the couch. After a moment, he said, "This is a hide-a-bed."

"Yep."

"Why two sleeping spaces?"

"I told you. This room was originally built as a shelter for the family. Back in the late seventies, when nuclear war was the big threat."

Jackson checked the bathroom, which held only a toilet, a sink, a roll of toilet paper, a small hand towel, and the faint smell of Windex. The space had been recently cleaned. He stepped back out into the main room.

"I'd like to get some evidence technicians down here."

Valder visibly stiffened. "You'll need a warrant for that."

"I'll get one." The windowless room suddenly started closing in around him. What else could they accomplish here right now? Valder acted like a man with nothing to hide. Meanwhile Eddie Lucas, the last person to see Courtney alive, was still out there.

"What was it like for her down here?" Jackson tried to imagine the twisted scenario. "Was she free to roam around? Or read?"

Valder sounded impatient. "Her hands were cuffed together and she was blindfolded. No entertainment. She wanted the real experience."

Jackson had to get out. "What do you say, Schak? Seen enough?"

"For now."

They headed back upstairs with Jackson feeling guilty about needing to escape the room. His next call would be to the pathologist. He needed to know how and why Courtney had died. What if Courtney's death was some inexplicable freak thing? He wanted to charge Valder with something, but Jackson suspected it would be a waste of time. Victor Slonecker, the district attorney, would ultimately decide if Seth Valder went to trial.

When they came back into the living area, with daylight streaming in through its tall front windows, Jackson felt his chest loosen. Being underground had never affected him that badly before. Was he becoming claustrophobic?

"How long have you been agoraphobic?" he asked Valder again, as the suspect walked into the kitchen. It was huge, spotless, all stainless steel and black marble.

"That's hard to pinpoint." Valder opened the refrigerator. "Would you like something to drink?"

"Bottled water if you have it." Jackson never purchased bottled water; it was a waste of money, but he was thirsty and he never drank anything from an open container given to him by a stranger. "When was the last time you left the house?"

"About a year ago. I went in to the club for St. Patrick's Day, but no amount of alcohol could get me to stay. The disease had been coming on for a while."

Valder handed Jackson and Schak each a bottle of water. "What now?"

"A few more questions."

Valder sighed and slumped into a kitchen chair. "I should have never taken this job."

"Why did you?"

"The money was good and it was a favor to Mircovitch."

"Did you owe him for some reason?"

"No. I figured it couldn't hurt to have him owe me."

Schak asked, "How many jobs have you done for ThrillSeekers?"

"Just two. This was the second."

"What was the first job?"

"We took a couple out into the Deschutes wilderness and dropped them off with just the clothes on their backs and a GPS locator. They were outdoor-fitness freaks. They wanted to test themselves."

"Who's we?"

"Eddie did that job too. I don't venture into the wilderness." Valder gave him an odd smile.

"I'd like you to call Eddie right now. Ask him to come out here."

"I don't have to do that."

"It would certainly be cooperative and go a long way toward keeping me from hauling you down to the county jail." Jackson grinned back at him. "It's not a pleasant experience even for people who aren't agoraphobic."

"But you already know that," Schak added. "You've done a little time."

"I wondered when you would get around to that."

Jackson heard a car pull up outside. He hoped it was the patrol-unit backup McCray had called for. He planned to keep a twenty-four-hour watch on Valder.

CHAPTER 17

The Young Mothers Outreach Center on Seventeenth and Oak had once been a small bank but now looked like a combo day-care/computer center. It smelled like babies, with hints of formula, applesauce, and dirty diapers. Cribs lined the left wall in the front half, and the area rug near them was littered with colorful plastic toys. With Micah snuggled into a harness against her chest, Kera looked around for someone in charge. The two young women who were taking care of the babies didn't seem like management types. Eventually, she would talk to everyone here if she had to. Beyond this, she didn't know what else she could do to find Danette. Maggie had gone back to Corvallis, and Kera had to make some decisions about how to care for Micah and what to do about her own job.

In the back half of the partially divided room she saw young women at computer stations. Kera headed past the cribs and cupboards and walked up to someone sitting at a desk filling out paperwork. She looked nineteen or so and had two eyebrow piercings.

"Hi. I'm Kera Kollmorgan."

"Your baby is so cute." Micah smiled at the girl, doing his baby best to attract attention.

"Oh yes." Kera kissed his sweaty little forehead. "He's my grandson, and his mother's name is Danette Blake. Do you know her? She comes here sometimes."

"No, but this is only my second visit. Ask Gwen," she said, pointing at a young woman standing next to a computer station. "She's a volunteer and knows everybody."

Gwen looked up as Kera approached. Gwen was dark haired, goth pretty, and about twenty-five. The client she'd been assisting muttered under her breath about the "damn online applications."

"Hi, I'm Kera. This is my grandson, Micah, and we're trying to find his mother, Danette Blake. Do you know her?"

"Sure, but she hasn't been here this week."

"She's missing." Saying the words made Kera choke up, and she struggled for control. She had hoped she was past this phase.

Gwen scowled. "What do you mean missing?"

"She left Micah with me Monday morning and never came back. I found out she came in to this center sometimes, so I'm looking for any information you might have."

"Wow." Gwen reached over and squeezed Kera's arm. "I'm so sorry. Let's sit down and talk." She touched the girl at the computer on the shoulder. "Keep going with the application. I'll be back."

They sat at a scarred wooden table that had likely been donated. "Danette hadn't been coming here that long," Gwen said, "so I don't know her well, but I'll help if I can. What can I tell you?"

"I'm trying to determine if she purposely abandoned her baby." Kera left out the other option.

"It's possible," Gwen said without hesitation. "I know Danette had a conversation with our director about adoption."

"She was thinking of giving up her baby?"

"I'm not sure. A lot of the women who come here don't have any family in the area. Some of them end up placing their baby in state custody; we never see them again, of course." She smiled at Kera. "But Danette had family support."

"Does the center encourage women to give up their babies?"

"Of course not." Gwen paused, reconsidering her answer. "Unless they're drug addicts or abusive to the child, then we call social services."

"Did Danette talk to you about Micah? Did you get a sense she was giving up on being a mother?"

"Danette was frustrated and depressed. She said she didn't feel bonded to her baby. Yet she was here, getting help with day-care and participating in group sessions, so she was trying to make it work." Gwen abruptly stood. "I think you should talk to our director. He's actually here this morning."

Kera followed her down a short hallway that led to two offices. Gwen knocked on one door, then gently pushed it open. "Elias? Do you have a minute? There's someone here you should talk to."

"Of course. Come in." The voice was friendly. Kera stepped in behind Gwen.

"This is Kera Kollmorgan. She's looking for Danette Blake. I know Danette talked to you about some things, so here we are."

The man stood and reached across his messy desk to shake her hand. "I'm Elias Goodbe. How can I help?" He was gray haired and lean, with well-balanced features and a contagious smile.

As Kera sat, Gwen excused herself and left.

"My daughter-in-law, Danette Blake, left her baby with me Monday morning while she went to an appointment, but never returned. She hasn't contacted me or her mother either. I'm trying to figure out if she abandoned her baby purposely or if something horrible has happened to her."

Goodbe made a sympathetic sound. "You must be very worried. I'm not sure I can help, but I'll try. What appointment did she go to?"

"It was with a psychiatrist named Stella Callahan."

"We referred Danette to Dr. Callahan. Stella does some pro bono work for the center, and Danette seemed to be in need of counseling beyond what our volunteers could offer."

"Do you think Danette was having some kind of breakdown?"

"I'm not qualified to say. I'm really just an import businessman who happened into social work though circumstances and need." He smiled, and Kera felt drawn to his charm. Goodbe continued, "We were worried Danette was severely depressed and might need medication to get through her postpartum experience. So we sent her to Stella."

"Did Danette talk about giving up her baby?"

Goodbe hesitated. "I'm not sure it's ethical to share that information with you. You say she disappeared on Monday?"

"Monday morning."

"I understand your concern. Danette did ask me about adoption, but only in a hypothetical way. She mentioned there was someone she trusted to raise Micah." Goodbe nodded at the baby. "I assume that's you."

"Most likely. Danette's mother isn't well." Kera still felt she hadn't learned anything new. "Do you have any idea where Danette might be? Where she would have gone if she did decide to walk away from this little boy?"

He shook his head. "I'm sorry. I really don't. Feel free to ask any of the volunteers."

"Do you operate entirely on volunteers?"

"Almost. I have a paid manager, but Gwen and the others are giving their time. Gwen originally came here looking for help and now is a volunteer, and our computer expert, Tasha, is filling a community-service order from the court. A few of our volunteers come here as part of their own therapy. So we have a variety of motivations, but it works."

"It's wonderful what you're doing here. I didn't even know the center existed until I started searching for Danette." Kera got an idea. "I think you could use some publicity, and I know a reporter for the *Willamette News* who would probably give you a great little write-up."

Goodbe seemed to pull back physically from the idea. "I don't know about that. I'm afraid we'd be overwhelmed with requests for services and have to turn people away. I think we're doing fine with word-of-mouth referrals. Maybe when we have more space and more money coming in."

Kera picked up her purse. She didn't really follow his thinking, but it wasn't her business. She stood to leave. "I'm a nurse at Planned Parenthood. Is it okay to refer young pregnant women here?"

"Of course." Goodbe stood too. "I'm sorry about Danette. Let me know if you find her."

"Thanks for your time."

On the way out, Kera chatted briefly with both of the young women in the day-care area. One had met Danette but had nothing new to offer. Kera remembered the posters in her car and made a quick trip out to get one. With permission, she taped one of the posters on the front window facing out. Anyone coming near the front door would see it. The effort failed to make her feel optimistic.

* * *

Jackson met with the task force at three. The little room was charged with energy. They all had information to share and a sense that they were about to make a breakthrough.

"McCray, will you take the board? We have a lot to document." Jackson glanced at his notes, which he hadn't had a chance to process yet. *Where to start?* "We now have three suspects: Zoran Mircovitch, Seth Valder, and Eddie Lucas, with Lucas being our most viable."

"What about the boyfriend, Brett Fenton?" Evans seemed to vibrate with eagerness. "Did you rule him out?"

"Make that four suspects," Jackson corrected. "Mircovitch is spelled *M-i-r*," he said to McCray. "In fact, let's start with the boyfriend. He claims he broke up with Courtney on Sunday. She supposedly called him from the club Monday night. He says she was drunk, so he hung up on her. My instinct says he's telling the truth." He turned to Schak. "Did we get her phone records?"

"Not yet. Verizon was supposed to fax them to me this morning."

"Call the company again as soon as we're done here. We have to know if Courtney made any phone calls Tuesday night after she recorded that video in Valder's basement."

"Will do," Schak said, sounding a little defensive. "The ex-boyfriends were a dead end. Steve Smith is in jail in Salem, and Tristan Chalmers has a new girlfriend and a solid alibi."

"Great news. What's your gut feeling about Seth Valder? Is he really agoraphobic? Or is it all bullshit?"

"I think it would be hard to fake that, but I'm happy to hang out at Lucky Numbers and see if he ever shows up in the club." Schak flashed a grin, then turned serious. "I think he's hiding something. The more he tried to be all open and honest about Courtney's little adventure in his house, the more suspicious it made me."

"I know what you mean. Like hiding in plain sight." Jackson turned to Evans. "Did you get anything on Valder from Detective Quince?"

"Quince says he's running prostitutes, but they can't get any of the women to testify against him."

"Let's get a warrant for Valder's phone records. I'd like to know who he's been talking to lately. I don't like the bastard, and even if he's not directly responsible for Courtney's death, I'd like to rattle his world a little."

The district attorney rushed into the room, late as usual. Despite his hurry, Victor Slonecker looked immaculate in an expensive gray suit. His thick black hair and angular face gave him public appeal, and Jackson believed Slonecker's controlled ambition would take him all the way to state attorney general.

"Thanks for coming," Jackson said, rising to shake his hand. "This is an unusual case, and we could use your guidance." He and Slonecker worked together well, but Jackson always felt a little unsure of how to address him.

"What do we know about how Courtney died?" Slonecker sat and put his briefcase on the floor.

"Not much yet," Jackson answered. "I called Gunderson last night to see what he found under her clothes. He reported that Courtney's body has no signs of trauma except the bruises on her neck and the minor abrasions on her wrists. No obvious evidence of sexual assault either. The autopsy is scheduled for early tomorrow, and we'll know more then."

Slonecker was still looking at Jackson. "What do you know about ThrillSeekers? Mrs. Durham called me this morning and she wants someone held accountable for Courtney's death."

Jackson was caught off guard. "When did Elle Durham find out about ThrillSeekers? Did she know about Courtney's contract *before* the kidnapping?"

"I don't know," Slonecker said, sounding impatient. "I just know she's angry and wants me to press charges against everyone involved. What did you find out about the company?"

"It's located in Portland and run by Zoran Mircovitch. Courtney hired them to abduct her for thrills. She signed a contract and made a video verbalizing her agreement to be held in confinement for twenty-four hours. She had a safety word she could have used at any time to end it. At the end of her ordeal, her caretaker—if you can stomach that term—made another video in which Courtney again verbalized her consent and appeared completely unharmed."

"Good god." Slonecker looked stunned.

"Whether any of that is illegal, I don't know," Jackson added. "The Portland police are aware of our investigation and are keeping an eye on Mircovitch. Meanwhile, Mircovitch contracted with Seth Valder, owner of Lucky Numbers, to fulfill the contract. Valder, in turn, hired Eddie Lucas, owner of a business called Dirty Jobs, to do the actual kidnapping."

"Where did they hold her?"

"At Valder's. He showed us the room."

"Do we have any of these men in custody?"

"Not yet." Jackson had a flash of doubt about his decisions. "Seth Valder is agoraphobic and says he hasn't left his house in more than a year. A uniformed officer is parked in his driveway to ensure Valder doesn't have a miraculous recovery and disappear overnight. We're looking for Eddie Lucas now. We were just getting to that when you walked in."

Jackson glanced at McCray, hoping he would have something solid to report.

McCray cleared this throat. "We put out an attempt-to-locate for Lucas and a uniformed officer is parked in front of his house."

"What about his business?" Jackson tapped his notepad.

"He runs it out of his house," Evans reported. "It's a one-man operation. His ad in the phone book says he will…" She looked down at her notes. "Crawl under your house looking for the leak or remove the dead squirrel from your attic."

There was a moment of quiet while they thought about what it would be like to have that job.

"Mr. Dirty Jobs kidnapped Courtney and took her to Valder's home, then picked her up again twenty-four hours later and dropped her behind Autzen Stadium. Is that the scenario?" Slonecker made it sound too stupid to believe.

"That is the story Seth Valder tells. We don't have Lucas' side of it yet."

"I know you already know this, but finding Eddie Lucas is critical." Slonecker grabbed his briefcase and stood to leave. "Meanwhile, I want a twenty-four-seven watch on Seth Valder. I may place him under house arrest for criminal negligence."

No one said anything. As much as they all wanted Valder to go down for his part in the charade, Courtney's video, made at 9:17 Tuesday night, would make it hard to convict him of kidnapping.

After the DA left, Jackson looked back through his notes from their last meeting. Their focus had been so different yesterday morning. Still, they had to review what they'd learned. He looked up at Evans. "Did you track down the guy named Zack?"

"Zack Underwood is a musician. He says he and Courtney are friends. They danced together that night, but then she left. Other people at the club say they saw Zack there until closing."

"Thanks, Evans. We now know Courtney was kidnapped, by arrangement, from Diego's that night. According to Seth Valder, she was also dropped off in good health behind Autzen Stadium around ten o'clock the next night. The big question is: What happened then?"

A rap at the door, then the desk clerk stepped in. "I have a fax for Detective Schakowski."

"About damn time." Schak bolted to the door and grabbed the thick stack of papers.

While Schak scanned Courtney's phone records looking for the narrow time frame between Courtney's drop-off and death, Jackson turned to Evans. "Did you run a background check on Lucas?"

"He was arrested for stealing a car when he was nineteen. It was his aunt's car and she dropped the charges. He was charged with possession of marijuana a year later. That's it. Other than a few traffic violations, he's been a good boy—that we know of—for a decade."

"Let's get out there and find out everything we can about Lucas. We need to know if he has any family or friends he would stay with if he knew we were watching his house. Let's get word out to our neighboring states to look for his van. If he heard Courtney died, he might panic and run."

McCray nodded. "I already did that."

"Let's check Valder's rental unit too."

"I've got a phone number," Schak said, his voice charged with excitement. "On Tuesday April seventh at 10:13 p.m., Courtney called 606-1330 and spoke for three minutes and forty-two seconds."

"I'll have the owner of that number in a second," Evans said, pulling a small white laptop from her bag.

"That's handy," McCray commented.

"I just bought it. I think I love it."

Anticipation hung thick in the air as they waited. After two minutes Evans announced, "Brett Fenton."

CHAPTER 18

"He lied to me," Jackson said, feeling neither surprised nor disappointed. "He told me the last time he spoke to Courtney was Monday night when she called from Diego's."

"He must be hiding something," Schak said.

"What if he went down to the stadium after Courtney called?" Evans voiced what Jackson was thinking.

"He said he was home with his parents. Did we check his alibi?"

An uncomfortable silence.

Jackson stuffed his notes into his evidence bag. "McCray and Evans, stay on Eddie Lucas. I want him in custody. Schak, call Brett Fenton's parents and see if we can pinpoint exactly where he is. We'll bring him in for another round of questioning."

Jackson spent the next twenty minutes typing all his handwritten notes into a Word document and organizing them by subject. He'd taught himself to type, and over the years, he'd slowly gotten better despite his oversized fingers. This was an important process because it not only helped him stay organized, it reminded him of the little pieces of information that might otherwise get lost in the constant shuffle of new leads. Such as whether anyone had bothered to verify the main suspect's whereabouts at the time of the victim's death. *Damn.* That was sloppy. Brett had told them about ThrillSeekers and sent them off in another direction. No point in dwelling on it. Self-directed anger was too distracting and he couldn't afford another mistake.

Now that he knew Courtney had been alive at 10:13 p.m. and called her boyfriend, the idea that Eddie Lucas had dropped her off unharmed seemed plausible. In fact, Jackson now felt certain Courtney had died right there in the grass where the cyclist found her. She had probably called Brett to ask for a ride. Why would he lie about that? Unless he'd gone down there to pick her up, then for reasons still unknown, killed her. *How?* The bruises on Courtney's neck didn't appear as though they would be lethal. He'd seen hickeys that looked worse. Hopefully tomorrow's autopsy would tell for sure.

Jackson stared at the file on his monitor. Under *Physical Evidence*, he had listed: bruises on neck, abrasions on wrists, asthma inhaler under body, tar on shoe, missing earring. He had nothing.

He called the crime lab on Garfield and asked for Parker.

"Hey, Jackson. I was just going to call you before I left."

"What have you got for me?"

"Not much. The search of the area around the body didn't produce anything significant. Some trash, a couple of needles with heroin residue, a running shoe, a red bandanna, and a very weathered paperback novel. Sorry, no blood and no cell phone."

"You were going to call me, so you have something."

"The asthma inhaler found at the scene was empty."

Jackson's brain scurried to process the possibilities. "How do you know that?"

"I opened it up. It felt light, so I checked."

"Do we know for sure it was Courtney's?"

"Not yet. I extracted some saliva from inside the mouth mechanism and sent it to the state lab for DNA analysis, but I won't get the results for a couple of days."

"Assuming the inhaler was Courtney's, it seems likely she had it in her hand sometime before she died." Jackson was mostly thinking out loud.

"Seems likely."

"Can a healthy twenty-one-year-old die from an asthma attack?"

"Children sometimes do, but with adults it's rare. The pathologist should be able to tell you though."

"How far was the red bandanna from the body?"

"Let me check." After a pause, Parker said, "About twenty feet."

"So it could have been around her mouth or her eyes at one point."

"I'll send it to the lab as well."

"Thanks. Send the needles too. The victim was known to use recreational drugs." Jackson tried to remember what else he had planned to ask. "What about the black substance from her shoe?"

"It's roofing tar, so it didn't come from the asphalt path itself. Unless you have another sample for me to compare it to, there's not much else I can tell you about it."

Jackson let it go. They knew where Courtney had been now. Where she picked up the tar hardly mattered. "Thanks, Parker." He hung up and keyed the new information into his notes. He suddenly remembered what Elle Durham had said about Courtney's asthma. That she mostly used her inhaler when she was outside and especially when temperature changes triggered the need for it.

Jackson played out a scenario based on the information he had. Eddie Lucas had dropped Courtney off in the grassy area behind the stadium. Courtney called her boyfriend to pick her up. While she waited, she got cold and had an asthma attack. She took out her inhaler, used it up, and dropped it like trash. Then Brett showed up and they argued about the kidnapping adventure. He lost control and killed her.

Or?

Courtney tried to medicate herself but the inhaler was empty or nearly empty. When Brett showed up, Courtney was already dead of an asthma attack. He panicked and left and later lied about getting the call. Had Courtney died there in the grass because she couldn't get enough oxygen? How long would it take? Why hadn't she called 911? Jackson didn't buy this scenario.

Either way, it seemed as if her arranged kidnapping was only indirectly to blame for her death. Unless Eddie Lucas had hung around until after Courtney called Brett, then came back and killed her. Weird, but possible.

Jackson's stomach growled, reminding him it was getting late in the day. A good father, he thought, would put this case aside, pick up his daughter from her after-school drill-team practice, then go home and have dinner with her. Most of the time, he was that kind of father. Last night, he'd asked Renee to keep Katie for another day or so. This was not a case he could walk away from, even for a few hours. There was something inexplicable going on and it pulled at him with a force he couldn't resist.

Jackson heard footsteps and looked up as Schak approached his desk. "Fenton's parents say he's in class but should be home by five. You want me to handle this?"

"I'll go with you." Jackson grabbed his jacket, gun, and evidence bag. "The more I think about this case, the less sense it makes. I keep thinking we're missing something big."

Later, as they headed downstairs to the parking lot, Schak said, "Now that we know Courtney Durham arranged her own kidnapping, do we assume the other woman's disappearance is unrelated? What's her name again?"

"Danette Blake." Jackson hadn't thought about Danette all day, or called Kera to see how she was doing. More guilt. "It seems very unlikely the cases are in any way related, but we'll ask Brett Fenton if he knows Danette."

"Eddie Lucas too? If we get him into custody?"

"Why not?"

They took separate cars, thinking if Fenton didn't come home, they could split up for whatever came next. Jackson took the lead, heading up City View, then turned onto Panorama near the peak. The Fentons' huge home was constructed of white stucco, a rarity in Oregon where timber was plentiful. Jackson went past the driveway, turned around, and parked on the other side of the street. Schak parked near the driveway.

Twenty minutes later, Brett's black Nissan 370Z came up the hill. As he approached the driveway, Jackson saw the young man glance first at Schak's blue Impala, then at Jackson's similar car across the street. All at once, the Nissan accelerated, speeding past both of them.

Schak took off, squealing his tires and hitting his siren as a warning. Faced the wrong direction, Jackson had to crank his car around while he radioed in the pursuit. He pressed the accelerator and shot up the hill. What was Fenton thinking? Unless the kid abandoned his car and took off on foot through someone's backyard, there was no way he would escape. Even then, they would pick him up eventually.

At the top of City View, the road looped around and turned into Shields Avenue. The street was lined with houses, and Fenton was moving too fast for a neighborhood. Heart pounding,

Jackson prayed everyone would stay inside, having dinner. As he crested the hill, he saw Schak's cruiser make an abrupt right turn on Suncrest. Fenton was heading farther up the forested hillside into the Hawkins subdivision of new homes. *Damn.* Jackson radioed in the new direction.

He made the turn, feeling slightly out of control. This street was narrower, so he eased off the accelerator. Abruptly, Schak screeched to a stop a hundred feet in front of him. Jackson slammed his brakes and skidded in behind Schak's cruiser. As Schak bolted from his car, Jackson saw the little black sports car stopped in the street ahead of his partner's car. A little farther up, he saw a mother and child step safely onto the sidewalk.

Their suspect had stopped for a pedestrian. So Fenton wasn't a psychopath. *Would he take off again? Was he that guilty? Or just scared?*

The young man had apparently had enough of the chase. He pulled over to the curb, got out of his car, and raised in hands in the air, looking around the upscale neighborhood to see who might be watching.

Brett Fenton burst into silent tears moments after Jackson sat down at the interrogation table. Jackson waited for him to get control. Tears were not all that unusual from suspects. Confrontation, guilt, frustration—it could all come together to make a grown man cry.

"This is a second interview with Brett Fenton. It is Thursday, April ninth, and the time is 6:15 p.m. Are you ready to begin, Brett?" Jackson glanced around at the closet-size room. *Let him confess, quickly, please.*

"I should wait for my lawyer. I know my parents called him." Brett wiped his eyes with his sleeve and tried to look brave.

"You can if you want to. We'll be back when he gets here." Jackson clicked off the recorder and stood. Schak followed his cue. Before they reached the door, Brett called out, "Don't leave me here. Please."

Jackson was reminded that Brett was still a twenty-one-year-old kid who lived with his upper-middle-class parents and had never been in trouble. He turned and sat back down. "Do you want to talk now?"

"Yes."

Jackson put the recorder on the table and pressed the red button. The concealed camera was also videotaping. "Why did you kill Courtney?" He'd changed his mind about starting gently.

"I didn't!" Brett choked back a sob. "I didn't even see her that night. She called me and wanted me to pick her up, but I refused. I wanted no part of the whole stupid kidnapping thing."

"Why did you lie about the last time you talked to her?"

"I don't know."

"Bullshit."

"I was scared. You had just told me she was dead. It freaked me out."

"What did Courtney say when she called?"

"She bragged a little and said something like 'I did it. I survived a day of captivity. They couldn't break me.' "

Jackson was surprised but kept his face immobile. "What did her kidnappers do to try to break her?"

"Probably nothing. Courtney was a drama queen. She was just proud of herself for not quitting and getting dropped off early."

"What did she say next?"

"She asked me to pick her up. I said no." Brett covered his face. "Of course I feel horrible about it now."

"Did she tell you where she was?"

"Yes. She used it to make me feel guilty about leaving her there in the dark by herself."

"Did she specifically say where she was?"

"Behind the parking lot at Autzen Stadium, near the bike path."

"Where were you when you got the call?"

"I was driving home from a friend's."

"Were you alone?"

"Yes."

"Where did you go after Courtney called?"

"I went home."

"Did anyone see you come in?"

"My parents were in bed, but my mother probably heard me. She's a light sleeper."

"How did Courtney sound to you?"

"She was bragging and kind of excited at first, then she was pissed at me for saying no. Courtney had mood swings like that all the time."

"She sounds pretty hard to get along with," Schak said, sounding empathetic.

"She was. She was also great fun, and great—" Brett cut himself off.

"What were you going to say? Great in bed? Was Courtney sexually exciting?" Schak followed up.

"Yes. She was sexually exciting." Brett looked down.

Schak continued with a soft tone. "She also made you angry sometimes?"

"Of course."

Jackson picked up. "What about that night after the kidnapping when you went to get her? Did you fight about her abduction adventure?"

"I didn't go down there!"

Jackson was determined to find a crack and worm his way in. Fenton had lied to him before. He wouldn't let him get away with it again. "Did she ever cheat on you?"

Brett hesitated. "I don't know."

"But she might have?"

"With Courtney, anything is possible."

"Did you ever hit her?"

"No." He looked offended.

"Did you ever squeeze her neck too hard?" Jackson was thinking of the bruises.

Something flashed in Fenton's eyes. "No."

"What about during sex? Some people like to have their airflow restricted for orgasm. Did you ever choke Courtney during sex?"

A long silence.

"Just tell me, Brett. Help me understand what happened. Help yourself by telling the truth."

"She wanted it. She had trouble—"

The door swung open. A desk officer stepped in and said, "I have two lawyers here to represent Brett Fenton. Mr. Adam Traynor and Mr. Roger Barnsworth."

Damn!

Most of the people he interrogated in this room had no one to represent them. The Fentons had money, so they'd sent their personal lawyer and the best defense attorney in town. "He only gets one lawyer," Jackson said. "The other can wait in the lobby."

The clerk turned back to the hallway and relayed Jackson's message. After a murmured discussion, a large black man with a shaved head strode into the room.

Jackson stood to shake his hand. "Mr. Barnsworth, good to see you again." The criminal defense attorney had represented Eugene's ex-mayor during a murder investigation last fall.

Barnsworth nodded, grabbed the extra chair by the wall, and sat down next to his client. After cursory introductions were made, Barnsworth said, "Have you charged my client with a crime?"

"Not yet."

"What are the circumstances?"

"His girlfriend is dead, he was the last person to talk to her, and he lied to us about it."

Barnsworth's brow creased into a tiny scowl. "I'd like to confer with my client alone."

"I'd like to finish this conversation. Mr. Fenton has been very forthcoming, and I believe he would like to continue."

Brett looked back and forth between the two men.

Jackson prodded. "You were just going to tell us about how you choked Courtney during sex."

"No you're not." Barnsworth grabbed his client's arm. "Brett, I want you to stop answering questions."

"I didn't do anything wrong. I don't want to look guilty. The asphyxiation thing was a week ago."

Were the bruises that old? "Whose idea was it?"

"It was Courtney's. She was—" Brett stopped, then slumped forward.

Jackson waited. His suspect wanted to talk about this.

"She was sexually frustrated," Brett finally said. "Despite her enthusiasm for sex, Courtney didn't have orgasms easily." Brett looked away at the wall. "She tried. We tried." He glanced back at Jackson. "I worried that's what the whole kidnapping thing was about. That she wanted to punish herself. Or maybe get raped. Or have sex with some lowlife stranger just to see if it would make her come."

Jackson sat back and gave himself a moment. This was not what he'd expected to hear.

"What kidnapping?" The defense attorney looked dumbfounded.

Jackson looked at Barnsworth. "Courtney arranged for her own kidnapping as a thrill. An adventure. When it was over, she

called Brett to pick her up and died soon after that. We're trying to find out why, and Brett is helping us understand Courtney.
Please let him continue."

"I won't let him incriminate himself."

Jackson met Brett's eyes. "What do you think was going on
with Courtney? What was her main problem?"

"I don't know." Brett rubbed his face again. "Too much money,
a dead father, and not enough attention from her mother. Elle
Durham is great in some ways, but I think she competed with her
daughters and messed with their heads."

"Do you think Courtney was mentally ill?"

"She had problems for sure. She'd been seeing a shrink for
months."

A tingle ran up Jackson's neck. "Do you know her doctor's
name?"

"I think it's Callahan."

Now Jackson's whole body thrummed with adrenaline. "Dr.
Stella Callahan?"

"Yeah. Why? Do you know her?"

Jackson looked over at Schak, who nodded, then back at
Brett. "Do you know Danette Blake?"

"No. Should I?"

"Have you ever heard her name before?"

"No."

Jackson saw no indication Fenton was lying. "Will you excuse
us?"

He stepped out of the room and Schak followed, leaving the
door open. Jackson kept an eye on Barnsworth, who was warning
his client about offering too much information.

"We need to talk to Callahan right away," Jackson said, keeping his voice low. "Two young women disappeared on the same
day and they were both seeing the same shrink. Now one is dead

and other hasn't been seen since her last appointment. Why didn't I make this connection sooner?"

"None of us did." Schak shrugged. "Because the adventure kidnapping was the big lead, and no one told us Courtney was seeing a shrink."

"We'll need a warrant. Callahan won't tell us anything without one. Will you get started on the paper?"

"I'm already writing it in my head."

Jackson went back into the interrogation room and sat. "When did Courtney start seeing Dr. Callahan?"

"She was already going to appointments when we got together. She quit for a while, then started up again."

"How does Courtney know Dr. Callahan?"

"I don't know. Her mother might be able to tell you." Brett seemed more relaxed, as if he sensed the pressure was off him.

Jackson decided to relieve him of that notion. "The pathologist can lift fingerprints off neck skin. If you choked Courtney to death, we'll know tomorrow after the autopsy. By then, you'll have lost your chance to confess and plea-bargain."

"Don't say anything," his lawyer warned. Barnsworth turned to Jackson. "If you're not prepared to charge my client, I'd like him to be released now."

"That's not going to happen. He's our primary suspect, and so far he has no alibi for the time frame of Courtney's death."

"Talk to my parents. I'm sure my mother heard me come in."

"I plan to do that." Jackson clicked off the recorder and stood to leave. "An officer will escort you to a holding cell. Mr. Barnsworth, your time here is up."

The attorney gave Jackson a scornful look, then clapped Brett on the shoulder. "I'll go see a judge and have you out of here before nightfall."

Jackson planned to see a judge too—and a psychiatrist.

CHAPTER 19

Jackson hung up his desk phone and swore out loud. He'd called Judge Cranston twice and couldn't get hold of him. Walter Cranston was a sixty-year-old Republican who had worked as a prosecutor. Jackson always went to him first with any warrant that might be iffy. He'd also called Dr. Callahan and left two messages, emphasizing the urgency of his request to talk. He debated with himself about whether to call Judge Marlee Volcansek, a lifelong Democrat and member of the ACLU, who might be less inclined to force a psychiatrist to talk about her patients.

Jackson dialed Volcansek anyway. A new sense of urgency pulsed through his veins. What the hell had happened to Danette? Could her disappearance somehow be related to Courtney Durham's? On the surface, it made no sense, yet the connection existed and he had to pursue it. What if Callahan knew about the kidnappings? What if the psychiatrist was a predator?

Judge Volcansek answered on the fifth ring. "I assume this is important or you wouldn't be calling me at home during the dinner hour."

"You assume correctly. I need a warrant signed."

"I'm in the middle of making homemade pasta and need to put the phone down. Why don't you stop by and talk to me about it while I cook?"

"Thanks. Are you still on Crescent?"

"I am."

On the drive over, Jackson called his daughter and was relieved when Katie picked up.

"Hi, Dad. It's about time you called."

"Sorry, sweetie. I'm on a difficult homicide case right now."

"I know, but it doesn't seem fair. You've got those stents and that weird disease. Why didn't they give the case to someone else?"

Her concern was like a gentle kiss on the forehead. "A young woman is dead and her mother asked me personally to take the case."

"Because you're the best, right?"

"Some days. What have you got going on?" He pulled to the left and took the Ferry Street Bridge.

"Same old stuff. Drill-team practice, a hideous math test on Friday that I don't want to study for, and—"

In the not-too-distant background, Renee yelled, "Why haven't you unloaded the dishwasher yet?"

"I'm talking to Dad."

"Honey, don't yell back. It hurts my ears and pisses her off." Jackson kept his voice gentle, but Renee's outburst concerned him. He associated the yelling with drinking. In theory, Renee had been sober for about six months. He hoped for Katie's sake it wasn't over.

"Make it fast, I need some help in here," Renee said, her voice fading as she moved away from Katie's phone.

"Finish what you were telling me, hon."

"I don't remember."

"Is everything okay over there?"

Katie lowered her voice to a whisper. "She gets all stressed out after work, then mellows out later. I think she's hooked on those antianxiety pills."

Jackson's hands tightened on the wheel. He was glad he'd finally bought a wireless earpiece for talking and driving. "How stressed? Is she verbally abusive?"

"Oh no. Nothing like that. Don't worry, Dad. It's not like when she was drinking."

If Jackson hadn't been driving, he would have closed his eyes as he prayed for strength. "Do you want me to come and get you?" Jackson had full custody. Renee's time with Katie was at his discretion.

"No. You have a case to clear." In a less certain voice, Katie asked, "What about this weekend? I'd like to come home and work on the trike." The three-wheeled motorcycle they were building together from an old Volkswagen was nearly complete, and they were both excited to take it on the road.

"We'll do that. I promise."

"Okay. Call me tomorrow after school. Love you, Dad."

"I love you too."

Jackson flipped his phone shut and swallowed hard. As a younger man, he would have never believed he could love someone as much as he loved his daughter. Sometimes, like now, it made him feel dysfunctional and powerless.

He rolled down his window, sucked in some oxygen, and realized he'd missed his turn.

He could smell warm pesto as he approached the judge's front door. Jackson's stomach growled. He'd sent Schak out to question Brett Fenton's parents and told him to take a dinner break afterward. Jackson hadn't eaten since their breakfast in Portland this morning, which was why he often lost five or six pounds during an intensive murder investigation.

He almost didn't recognize the judge when she opened the door. She was wearing a jade velour tracksuit and her long hair swung freely. Jackson had never seen Marlee Volcansek in anything but her black robe and pulled-back hair. Her face was as tight as ever though, thanks to Botox and fillers.

"Come in," she said, gesturing and walking away.

Jackson followed her into a massive kitchen with shiny stainless-steel appliances and a sunset-pink granite countertop. Even if he got around to remodeling his modest older home, his kitchen would never have this much space.

"Thanks for taking time for this."

"It's my job." She turned and he saw her smile broadly for the first time. "What's the warrant about?"

"I need to question a psychiatrist about two of her patients. One disappeared Monday morning after her appointment with Dr. Callahan, and the other died Tuesday under very suspicious circumstances." Jackson didn't want to bring up the adventure kidnapping if he didn't have to. It would only muddy the issue. "I need to know what the connection is, and I suspect Callahan is the only one who knows."

"I saw the news about the disappearances the other night, and I read about Courtney's death in the paper this morning. The other young woman is still missing?"

"Yes. Until today, I thought she probably ran off because she couldn't handle her baby. Then I learned Courtney was also seeing Dr. Callahan. I have to get the psychiatrist to open up about these women. I also want to look at both their files and see if they have anything in common."

Volcansek turned a burner down and wiped her hands on her apron. "The dead woman no longer has any doctor-client confidentiality to protect. The missing woman, what's her name?"

"Danette Blake."

"Danette still has a legal privilege to protect. I'm not sure you have compelling evidence for violating that privilege."

"Dr. Callahan was the last person to see Danette."

"Do you suspect the psychiatrist of harming her, or conspiring to harm her?"

"It's starting to look like a possibility."

Volcansek carried the cooked pasta to the sink and dumped it in a colander to drain. "Do you suspect the doctor of harming or conspiring to harm Courtney Durham?"

Jackson fought to control his impatience. "At this point, no. Something weird is going on here, and I need to find out what it is. What if Dr. Callahan has other young female patients who are at risk?"

"Did you write the warrant for a limited search?"

Jackson hadn't written it, or read it. "Of course."

"Okay. I'll skim through it." She dried her hands. "Have you eaten?"

"No, but I'm fine."

"Nonsense. Eat some pasta while I read." She went to the sink and scooped some short curly noodles into a bowl, then ladled some pesto sauce over the top. "Italian sausage?"

"Sure." His stomach growled in response.

As she reached into a drawer for a utensil, Jackson set the subpoena on the breakfast table near the window.

He was scraping the bottom of his bowl before the judge finished reading. She made two strikethroughs, then signed the paperwork. "Now get going. My husband will be home soon and I still need to make artichoke salad."

Jackson drove to headquarters and sat at his desk to read through his notes. *What was he missing?* As an intelligent, twenty-year cop, he didn't believe in coincidence. Two young women with the same shrink disappear on the same day. There had to be a connection. Only Courtney was never really missing. What had Brett Fenton said? That Courtney might have done it to get her mother's attention? Was Danette pulling some kind of stunt for the attention too? Had Dr. Callahan somehow given both of them the same idea?

His cell phone rang, jolting him out of his thoughts.

It was Schak. "Hey, Jackson. Mrs. Fenton didn't actually hear Brett come home Tuesday night, but she says she got up around midnight to get a drink of water and his jacket was on the couch and his car was in the driveway."

"Midnight gives him plenty of time to drive to Autzen Stadium, choke the life out of Courtney, and drive back home."

"Courtney called him at 10:13, so yep, it's doable. Have you heard from the shrink?"

"Not yet, but I have a signed warrant. I'll park in front of her house if I have to."

"Any word on Eddie Lucas?"

"Nothing there either. Go home and get some rest. It's been a long day."

Jackson called Mrs. Durham and left her a message asking her to get back to him. While he waited for his return calls, he opened his carryall and removed the evidence bag holding Courtney's purse. He'd intended to look at the purse before now, but first the ThrillSeekers lead had consumed the investigation, then Brett Fenton's lie.

He pulled on gloves, clicked on his desk lamp, and held the small greenish-blue bag under the light. He scanned every inch of the cloth, looking for blood or semen or anything unusual. A tiny stain in the corner looked like blue ink, but nothing else popped for him. Jackson removed its sparse contents one at time and held them under the lamp.

The driver's license was standard issue, except Courtney's head shot in front of the blue curtain actually looked quite good, even though she wasn't smiling. The credit card was issued by Bank of America and wasn't set to expire for ten years. Jackson had never been issued a card that was good for more than two years at a time. The tube of lipstick was surprisingly smudged, and the color a dark watermelon pink. The condom was made by Trojan and revealed nothing new about the victim's sexual preferences.

Jackson stuck his hand inside the little bag, feeling around for a zippered compartment. He found a little flap instead. His slid two fingers into the opening in the cloth and bumped up against a small vial. He couldn't manipulate his big fingers inside the small opening, so he used his other gloved hand to push against the vial through the cloth from the outside. In a moment, the vial lay in his palm. His guess was amyl nitrate, a street drug used to enhance sex. It fit with Brett's account of Courtney's struggle to have an orgasm. The one-inch vial was half-full of clear liquid. Maybe Courtney had seduced Brett into having sex with her there in the open area behind the stadium. Another effort to find the right mix of variables that would sexually satisfy her.

Brett was due for another round of questioning, but not until tomorrow. Jackson intended to let him sit in a cell overnight.

What about Danette? He felt a headache coming on. Too little sleep, too much caffeine, and too much forced analysis. As he dug some aspirin out of his desk drawer, Lara Evans walked up. Her eyes were still bright with energy, despite having been on the job for twelve hours that day. It was the Provigil she took when working round-the-clock cases. Her energy made him feel even more beat-up after a long day of stents rolling around in his gut and only four hours of sleep. Jackson wished he had her prescription, developed to keep military pilots awake.

"Any news on Eddie Lucas?"

Evans shook her head. "It's not good. I finally talked to one of his neighbors who said she saw him throw a duffel bag in his van this morning and take off like a bat out of hell."

"Great. He's probably in Canada by now."

"Could be. McCray and I called every hotel and motel in the Eugene/Springfield area. He didn't check in using his own name or license-plate number, and no one recognized him by description."

"Good work."

"What's next?"

Jackson tapped the paper on his desk. "I have a warrant to search some files at Dr. Stella Callahan's office. She's the psychiatrist Danette Blake saw before she disappeared, and we learned from the boyfriend that Courtney Durham was seeing Callahan as well."

"That can't be coincidence." Evans pulled up a chair. "What's your theory?"

"Either Callahan is a predator or associated with predators, or somehow inspired both girls to stage a disappearance for attention."

Evans made a face. "What do we know about Callahan?"

"Nothing."

"I'll go run a background check, then I'd like to go with you to search her office."

"Thanks."

While he waited for the psychiatrist to call, Jackson tried Elle Durham again. This time she picked up and in a sleepy, slurred voice said, "What do you want?"

"It's Detective Jackson. I need to ask you a few more questions."

"I don't have any answers. Why does God hate my family? Do you know?"

She was high on something, but Jackson didn't think it was alcohol. "I'm sorry for your pain, Elle. I don't know why these things happen. My parents were murdered, so I know a bit about how you feel."

"Was Courtney murdered?"

"We don't know yet. Her autopsy is tomorrow morning, and I'll call if I learn anything new. Do you know Stella Callahan?"

"Yes." A pause. "She's an acquaintance."

"Did you know Courtney was seeing her professionally?"

"Of course. I recommended Stella. She's very good. Courtney was getting better."

That was an arguable point. "How long have you known Dr. Callahan?"

"A few years. Hang on a sec." During the break, he heard fumbling and swearing. "Sorry about that. I met Stella at a chamber of commerce luncheon. We were on a committee together and became friends. She really helped me after Dean died."

"I'm glad she was there for you." Jackson cringed, remembering her husband had gotten drunk and electrocuted himself in their hot tub. "I hope you'll start seeing Dr. Callahan again. You know, to help you with Courtney's death."

"There's not much point."

He wasn't sure what else to say, so he asked, "Do you know Danette Blake?"

"No. Should I?"

"Probably not. Thanks for your time."

Around nine o'clock, Evans waltzed up to his desk with a funny smirk on her face.

"What is it?"

"Stella Callahan has no criminal record, no unpaid parking tickets, no pending lawsuits."

"But?"

"She used to be Stan Callahan."

"No shit?" Jackson was too surprised to process what it might mean to his investigation.

"Five years ago, Stan Callahan legally changed his name to Stella. They have the same social-security number. Stan Callahan has no criminal record either."

"Did he have a sex-change operation?"

Evans handed him a printed file. "I don't know. He was living and practicing in Medford. After he changed his name, he moved to Eugene and opened a practice here as Stella."

"Any ideas for how this affects our cases?"

Evans laughed a little. "As far as I know, there's no documented reports or research showing that transsexuals are prone to any type of crime."

"As a woman, she wouldn't likely have sexual feelings for her female clients, would she?"

"It depends. Sometimes, a partner in a heterosexual marriage will have a sex-change operation, and if the other partner is accepting of it, they stay together. They often continue to have a sexual relationship. I think." Evans looked as confused as Jackson felt.

"I'll have to ask her about it."

"I want to be there."

"She may not call back. We might have to track down the owner of the building and search her files without her." Jackson continued to think of Dr. Callahan as a woman because that had been his first perception.

"I'll see what I can come up with."

"You don't have to do it now. Go home and get some rest."

"Will you call me if you question the doctor tonight?"

"We'll see how late it is."

Evans touched his shoulder. "Okay, but I'm available."

"I appreciate that."

After Evans left, Jackson stretched out on the soft couch in the room they used to question minors. He hoped to sleep for a few minutes, but he couldn't stop thinking about Stella Callahan and whether she still had a penis. If she did, had that penis been interested in Danette? Interested enough to seduce or kidnap her? He'd left Stella three messages, all telling her to call him immediately, no matter what time it was.

Just as he was drifting off, the front-desk officer came into the room. "I knew you were still here."

Jackson sat up, wondering what time it was.

"I've got the Redding California Police Department on the phone. They have Eddie Lucas in custody."

Thank god. Maybe he would finally get a break in this case.

Jackson hurried out to the front desk and picked up the outside line. "Jackson here. I issued the attempt-to-locate and arrest warrant for Eddie Lucas."

"Captain Sam Pogue. We've got Mr. Lucas in a holding cell at our department. A uniformed officer tried to pull him over for making an illegal turn and he took off. It wasn't much of a chase. Lucas turned down a dead-end street moments later and it was over. The officer brought him in and our desk clerk recognized his name from the interstate watch list."

"Great news. How soon can your department transport him here? I'm investigating a suspicious disappearance and a suspicious death."

"First thing tomorrow when the day shift comes on. We'll have Lucas there by early afternoon."

"Thanks. If there's going to be a delay, call me."

Jackson gave the captain his personal cell-phone number and got off the phone. Now that he had the Callahan connection and Brett had moved into prime-suspect position, Lucas didn't seem as important to the investigation. Still, Jackson felt better knowing that everyone who had been involved in Courtney's kidnapping adventure was being watched by police officers.

He went back to his desk and gave Evans a call to update her. She would sleep better knowing some of her hard work this day had paid off. He took a Vivarin tablet to keep him awake for the session with Callahan. As soon as he swallowed it, Jackson wondered what effect it would have on his heart and his kidneys. He would have to ask his new doctor. The thought pissed him off.

Stella Callahan finally called at ten fifteen, as Jackson was getting into his car to drive to her house. "I'm sorry for the delay in returning your call. I was at the Hult Center watching a performance by Ballet Fantastique. Afterward I went for a drink with a friend. I just now turned on my phone."

"I'd like to meet at your office in twenty minutes."

"Is this about Danette Blake? Why can't it wait until morning?"

"It's also about Courtney Durham, and I have to attend her autopsy in the morning. The first three days of a homicide investigation are critical."

Callahan drew in a sharp breath. "Homicide? Are you saying Courtney was murdered?"

"Her death is suspicious, and I need to talk to you."

For a moment, all Jackson heard was the noisy bar in the background.

"I didn't even know she was dead." Callahan's voice shook with emotion. "I still won't violate patient confidentiality."

"I have a search warrant for your files. I could have tracked down the owner of the building and started going through them without you, but my preference is to ask questions. I'll see you in twenty minutes."

Jackson hung up before she could argue. He was too tired for bullshit.

The building was dark, and no cars were in the parking lot. Jackson hoped the shrink wouldn't blow him off. If she did, he'd find her, cuff her, and bring her in to the department. He was through treating Callahan with kid gloves. Either she was involved in both kidnappings or there was something in her files that linked Courtney and Danette. He wanted that information right now. Jackson wondered if he should have called Evans. Was there any chance the doctor would get violent if backed into a corner?

He had his phone in hand to make the call when a small SUV pulled into the lot. *Finally!*

Dr. Callahan opened the door to the downstairs lobby. Jackson touched his weapon out of habit as he climbed out of the car. He trotted toward the door, feeling the stents shift and pinch in his gut. He'd never thought he would look forward to a major surgery with such enthusiasm.

Inside the building with the lights on, Jackson could see Callahan was still dressed for the theater in a gray pantsuit and lavender shirt. Choking on the psychiatrist's perfume, he followed her up the stairs.

Once they were in her office, Callahan turned to him. "I fully intend to read the subpoena and not let you see anything that isn't specified."

"I'd like to get most of what I need from asking questions." Jackson handed her the paperwork. "I still need you to photocopy everything in Danette Blake's and Courtney Durham's files and deliver it to police headquarters first thing in the morning. Your cooperation is vital."

"I'd like to help you. I just don't see how I can." Callahan sat and skimmed the subpoena.

Jackson decided to deal with the gender issue first. "I know you used to be Stan Callahan when you practiced in Medford. Why did you become a woman?"

Callahan pressed her lips together, stared at him for a long minute. "The subject is irrelevant, but let's get it out of the way." She squared her wide shoulders and took a breath. "I was born a hermaphrodite, someone with mixed genitalia. My parents saw a penis and decided I should be a boy. They were wrong. After a lifetime of living in the wrong skin, I decided to get comfortable with myself. I started taking estrogen. I grew my hair out, moved to Eugene, and began dressing and living as a woman."

"Which gender are you sexually attracted to?" Jackson hated this conversation, but he had to know who the doctor really was.

"I'm mostly asexual. I've never had much of a sex drive, and my genitalia are too confusing for most men to deal with. So I simply abstain."

"Are you now, or have you ever been, sexually attracted to young women?"

"No." The doctor looked amused by the question.

"Do your clients know anything about your gender issue?"

"No."

Jackson didn't know where else to go with the subject. Worse yet, he didn't know how to verify anything the doctor had just told him. "Tell me how Courtney came to be your patient."

"I assume her mother referred her to me."

"How do you know Elle Durham?"

"I met her and Dean through the chamber of commerce. Elle and I were on a committee together and we became good friends."

"You were friends with both Dean and Elle or just Elle?"

"I knew them both, but Elle and I spent more time together."

"Do they know you used to be a man?"

"No." The doctor's neck muscles twitched.

Was she lying or withholding? "Does Elle know?"

"She knows I'm asexual." Callahan frowned. "Why are we talking about me and my relationships? Do you suspect me of something?"

"I suspect everyone. It's my job. When did Courtney first come to see you?"

"I think it was in December, but let me check." Callahan rolled the desk chair over to a file cabinet behind her and flipped through folders in the top drawer. She pulled two files and rolled back to her desk. "Might as well get these out if I have to copy them for you."

"Thanks." Jackson waited while Callahan looked for Courtney's intake record.

"Yes. December thirteenth was her first appointment. I believe she called a week before that."

Jackson jotted down the date. "What was her basic problem? Why was she here?"

Callahan calculated how much she could withhold.

Jackson tapped the subpoena on the desk between them.

"Specifically, she had a sexual dysfunction. Generally, self-destructive impulses. Yes, I think those conditions are related."

Jackson would get back to all that if he needed to, but first he was looking for a connection. "When did Danette come to see you?"

Callahan pushed Courtney's file aside and flipped through the second one. "March twentieth. She'd only had three regular appointments."

"Why was she here?"

"She was depressed and overwhelmed by the responsibility of caring for her baby. She also had issues with her mother's unwillingness to help her with the child."

"Did she ever talk about giving up Micah?"

A small pause. "Yes."

"Don't make me read the whole file. I'm trying to find out what happened to these young women."

"Right at the end of our session, Danette said she was thinking of giving her baby to his grandmother to raise."

"Do you believe Danette is capable of simply taking off? Of leaving the baby and going somewhere else to start over?"

Callahan mulled it over. "Yes. It's certainly possible."

"Did you prescribe her medication?"

"An antidepressant. She had postpartum depression."

"Do the two women know each other?"

"I don't think so. They live in very different worlds."

"Did you prescribe Courtney medication?"

"I considered it, but she was already self-medicating with alcohol and illegal drugs and had no desire to stop. I didn't want to add to the mix. I worried she would overdose." Callahan twisted a strand of hair. "How did Courtney die? You indicated she was murdered."

"We're not sure yet. Her body had no obvious signs of blunt-force trauma." Jackson didn't want to say too much. If Callahan were involved, she might accidentally provide details she shouldn't know and incriminate herself.

"Have you done toxicology tests?" she asked. "Did Courtney overdose?"

"They're being processed." Jackson shifted uncomfortably from the pressure he now felt. "How did Danette end up here?"

"Young Mothers Outreach referred her. I do a certain amount of pro bono work, and they call me when they have someone who needs immediate treatment and can't afford it."

Jackson recalled Kera mentioning Danette's association with the center. "Why did Danette need immediate treatment?"

"The assistant director, Lisa Harkin, thought Danette suffered from postpartum depression, which can be very serious and lead to psychosis. After the initial consultation, I put Danette on Paxil. During her last visit, I changed her prescription to Lexapro."

"Tell me what you know about Young Mothers Outreach." Jackson made a note of the name.

Callahan stood. "It's late and I'm tired. Can we do this tomorrow?"

"We're almost done."

"Would you like some water?" She moved toward a mini refrigerator under a workspace behind her desk.

"If it's bottled."

Callahan handed him a container of water, then paced as she talked. "The center was started by Elias Goodbe, who's also a member of the chamber of commerce. I think he was looking for a tax shelter and decided to do something good for the community at the same time. The charity offers a few basic services to young women with babies who have limited resources. Services such as daycare, help with finding jobs, some counseling, and help with accessing other resources, like me."

It was another long shot, but Jackson asked it anyway. "Is Courtney in any way associated with the outreach center?"

A short pause. "Not that I know of."

"What aren't you telling me?"

"This conversation is straying outside the scope of your subpoena." Callahan sounded sure of herself, but her sudden rapid eye movement indicated discomfort.

"I'm prepared to handcuff you and take you into the interrogation room at the department if I don't believe I'm getting the truth here."

"Elle Durham, Courtney's mother, contributed money to Young Mothers Outreach." Callahan's voice rose in pitch. "That's all I can tell you about a possible connection."

"But not all that you know?"

"As far as I know, Courtney and Danette were not acquainted and have nothing in common except they both were my patients. Danette probably abandoned her baby, and Courtney probably overdosed, I'm sorry to say. I think you're making too much of this."

"Did you know about Courtney's kidnapping?"

Callahan was taken aback. "I saw Elle's public statement on the news Tuesday night, but I didn't take it seriously."

"Why not?"

"I know Courtney. I know Elle. I understand the game."

Jackson unconsciously leaned forward. "What game is that?"

"Their relationship is complicated, and I'm not going to discuss Elle."

"Did you know Courtney arranged for her own kidnapping through a company called ThrillSeekers?"

She pulled back, eyes widened. "I did not know that." Callahan was either a good actress or was genuinely surprised.

"She never discussed it with you?"

"No. I would have discouraged her."

"Is it possible you gave her the idea that disappearing would be a good way to get attention?"

"Of course not." Now she looked offended.

"What about Danette? Could you have inadvertently given her the idea that she should walk away from her troubles?"

"Absolutely not." Callahan folded her arms across her chest. "What are you getting at here?"

"I'm just trying to figure out why two of your patients went missing, voluntarily or not, on the same day."

"I'm sorry, but I don't know. I will think about it though. At the moment, I'm very tired and I'd like to wrap this up."

Jackson too was bone weary. "Just a few more questions. Was there anything unusual about Danette's last appointment with you?"

"Not really." Callahan looked down at the folder in front of her. "Except that it wasn't her regular day. Danette normally came on Thursday, but she called Sunday night and asked if I could squeeze her in the next day."

"So you made room for her?"

"Yes, I think I had a cancellation." Callahan reached for her desk calendar. "Oh, that's weird." She looked up at Jackson. "Courtney is the one who canceled. Danette took Courtney's usual appointment time on Monday."

CHAPTER 20

The full impact of what the switched appointment could mean didn't hit Jackson until he was in the cruiser, turning the key, and staring at the parking lot. He shut off the car. Danette could have walked out of the building at ten that morning and found someone waiting for her, someone who was expecting Courtney Durham. Someone not very bright, like Eddie Lucas.

Holy crap. Had Danette been kidnapped by mistake?

If so, where the hell was she? Where was her car? Jackson's head pounded with the craziness of it. Danette and Courtney were the same height and age, but that was about it. Courtney was blonde and fair skinned, and Danette was a brunette with light-brown skin. Had the Dirty Jobs guy really made that mistake? Jackson recalled Danette had been wearing a hooded sweatshirt. If she'd had the hood up covering her hair, it was certainly possible. Lucas might have simply seen a pretty young woman of the right size leaving the office where his target was supposed to be and assumed it was Courtney.

Then what had happened? Dread invaded his weary bones. Jackson started the car and turned on the heater. The warm, sunny days of April quickly chilled into winter-cold evenings. When did Lucas realize his mistake? After he showed up at Valder's? Or had Lucas recognized his error sometime before? If he'd made it out to Valder's, why hadn't they simply let Danette go when they'd realized she wasn't Courtney? Would they kill Danette to protect themselves?

Who were *they*? Eddie Lucas and Seth Valder?

Lucas was in jail in Redding, California, about five and a half hours away, and would be transported to Eugene in the morning. Seth Valder was, in theory, trapped in his own home by agoraphobia and a police officer in the driveway. Jackson checked the time on his cell phone: 11:33. He wanted to drive out to Valder's and slap him around, but he had to play this right. The first to squeal got the deal. He suspected Lucas was just a grunt guy who'd made a horrible mistake and Valder had made Danette disappear. He needed Eddie Lucas to turn on Seth Valder.

Jackson put the cruiser in gear and finally left the parking lot. He'd planned to head over to Kera's and curl up in her arms for a few hours of sleep, but that would have to wait. He tried to map out all the scenarios in his mind. First, they had to bring Valder in and let him sit in a holding cell until after they questioned Eddie Lucas. How serious was Valder's agoraphobia? Would he become violent or hysterical when they forced him out of the house?

Jackson drove the ten blocks to city hall and barreled into the department's headquarters. He used his card to get through the security door, then doubled back to the front-desk officer who sat behind the plexiglass.

"Jackson, you're working late."

"I think I caught a break in this case. I need you to send a second patrol unit to Seth Valder's place at 35829 Territorial

Highway. Contact the officer watching the house. Instruct him to knock on the door and ensure Valder is still there. I want the front and back doors watched closely. Give both officers my cell-phone number and tell them I'll be out soon."

Jackson needed another detective to brainstorm with and back him up on this arrest. He figured Schak had gone to bed early and already had a few hours sleep. Evans had wanted to be in on Callahan's questioning. He called them both, and even without hearing the details, they readily agreed to get dressed and go back to work at midnight. Law-enforcement personnel, including judges and district attorneys, weren't clock-watchers. They acted when they needed to.

He also called McCray, who took a while to answer. "Hey, Jackson. What have you got?"

"I think Eddie Lucas kidnapped Danette Blake by mistake, then Seth Valder made her disappear. So I'm bringing Valder in."

"No kidding? That's wild. Should I meet you out there?"

"I've got Schak and Evans on the way. I need you to write up a search warrant for Valder's house and computer first thing in the morning and get it signed ASAP. Be very inclusive. I want samples from everything. If Danette's DNA is anywhere on the premises, I want to find it. I'll be at the autopsy at eight, then we'll meet up and go search Valder's house from top to bottom."

"You've got it." McCray paused. "How did you come up with that theory?"

"Danette and Courtney were seeing the same shrink. Danette took Courtney's canceled appointment."

"Oh man. Talk about wrong place at the wrong time."

"I think so. I'll call you in the morning."

Jackson called Dr. Callahan, hoping she would still be awake. Stella answered on the third ring. "Yes? What now?"

"I need your expertise on something. I have to bring in for questioning someone who is agoraphobic. How can I keep the drama to a minimum?"

"Oh dear. It's likely this person has a prescription for anxiety attacks. Make sure he or she takes a healthy dose of medicine before you attempt to move them outside. If the agoraphobic doesn't have a benzodiazepine handy, you can always use a blindfold. If you're going now—and I assume that's why you called at this late hour—then the fact that it's dark outside should help."

"Thank you."

"Do I still need to photocopy and submit those patient files?"

"Yes, please."

Thirty minutes later, Jackson was cruising down Valder's private driveway in the dark, his stomach gurgling from hunger and stress and his heart hammering with adrenaline and caffeine. What if he was wrong about this and the whole thing was a coincidence? Would Valder sue the department for harassment? Jackson wondered if Valder owned a gun.

The second patrol unit was in the driveway and so was Evans' car. Lara Evans lived in West Eugene, so she'd had a ten-minute head start. She was waiting in her cruiser for him. Jackson felt for his Sig Sauer, a reflexive habit, then climbed out. He coached himself to move slowly and carefully. Valder wasn't going anywhere.

As he neared the patrol unit, the officer stepped out. "Officer Hutchison. Are we taking him in?"

"Yes, but I'd like you to stay out here for now and watch the front door in case Valder makes a break for it. Be ready to pursue. Detective Schakowski should be arriving soon. After he gets here, block the driveway with your car until I signal."

"Got it."

Jackson and Evans strode up the walkway, weapons drawn. Jackson rang the doorbell, waited five seconds, then rang it again. He continued the pattern until Valder shouted from the other side of the door. "What the fuck?"

"Eugene police! If you have a weapon, put it down. Open the door slowly. We have the house surrounded."

After three long seconds, the door opened and Seth Valder hung back out of reach. He stood there in sweatpants only, puffy eyed and irritated. "What do you want now?"

"You're coming to the department for questioning. I'd like to be sympathetic to your condition, but this is the way it has to be." Now that Jackson could see Valder had no visible weapon, he holstered his Sig Sauer and readied his taser. Evans kept her firearm drawn.

"Oh Jesus." Valder took another step back and vigorously rubbed the top of his hairless head. "Oh Jesus." Shirtless, he looked even bigger than he had yesterday.

Next to him, Jackson felt Evans shift her weight, readying for a confrontation. "I'd like this to go as smoothly as possible." Jackson used his calm-father voice. "Do you have antianxiety medication you can take?"

"Oh Jesus."

Had Valder even heard him?

"Do you have antianxiety medication?" *Where the hell was Schak?*

"I'm not sure. I haven't taken any in a while." Valder's eyes jumped around, and the head rubbing continued.

Jackson had never been in a situation quite like this. He wanted to avoid a physical confrontation if possible, but he also had a deep distrust of this sleazebag.

"Turn around and put your hands behind your back. I'm going to cuff you."

"What is this about? I told you everything."

"Turn around and put your hands behind your back."

"I want to call my lawyer."

Jackson held out the taser. "If this is easier for you…"

"Oh Jesus." Valder finally started to turn. Jackson heard Schak coming up the walk and felt his body let go of some tension.

"Schak? Step into the house and watch this guy from the front while I cuff him." Evans might be offended but she would understand. Schak was seventy pounds heavier than Evans, and Valder would respect that.

When Schak was in position, Jackson stepped forward and grabbed Valder's right wrist, then quickly cuffed it to the suspect's left. "Let's go find your meds."

The four of them moved down the hall with Valder in the lead. By the time they reached the master bedroom, Valder had begun to hyperventilate. He plopped on the edge of the bed. "Check the cabinet above the sink," he said, gesturing with his head toward the master bathroom.

Jackson glanced over at Evans, and she moved in to make the search. He kept the taser ready. He'd discovered its usefulness soon after being issued one. Too bad it had taken the department so damn long to adopt them.

In a moment, Evans came back with three small pill bottles. She read from the labels. "We've got hydrocodone, Keflex, and diazepam."

"Open the diazepam."

"There's one left."

"Oh Jesus." Valder started to shake. "It's not enough."

"You might as well take it."

Evans went back for a glass of water, put the pill in her open palm, and held her hand up to his mouth. She understood Valder had to be the one to actively reach for and ingest the medicine, which he eagerly did. Evans offered him water. It ran off both sides of his mouth as he gulped it.

"How long will it take to kick in?" Jackson wanted to know.

"My stomach is empty, so twenty or thirty minutes." Valder shook his head. "It's not enough to make me walk out the front door."

"We'll see. Let's go stand next to the door so you can get used to the idea."

They stood around for twenty minutes, watching Valder as he sat in a chair near the front door with it partially open. Jackson took a moment to update the two officers outside. He decided to keep them at the house until he had a warrant and they could come back and thoroughly search it.

When he went back in the house, Jackson noticed Valder's eyes were less jumpy and his pupils had dilated a little. It was time. He remembered what Callahan had said about a blindfold. "I'll be right back."

Jackson retrieved a T-shirt from a drawer in the bedroom.

"What's that for?" Valder wanted to know.

"A blindfold. A psychiatrist said it would help."

"I doubt it."

Valder let Jackson tie it around his eyes and reluctantly stood when Jackson prodded him. As Valder shuffled forward, hand-cuffed and blindfolded, with a detective at each elbow, Jackson visualized Courtney coming into this house with the same bind-ings. Danette too. Danette, of course, had been terrified.

Valder stopped in the doorframe and swore. "I can't do this."

Jackson and Schak propelled him forward. "I've experienced five thousand volts of electricity," Jackson said. "Whatever you're feeling now is nothing in comparison."

"No!" Valder struggled to free himself from their grip.

"Evans, get ready to stun him if we jump back."

"With pleasure."

Valder buckled and he was suddenly two hundred–plus pounds of dead weight. Jackson let go, so Schak did too. Valder dropped to his knees, then pitched face-first onto the sidewalk, panting like a dog on a hot August day.

Schak looked over at Jackson, his expression barely visible in the darkness. "What now?"

"We drag him. Maybe once he's in the backseat, he'll be calmer."

As they hauled the large, panting, moaning man toward Jackson's car, Jackson was aware that in some police departments, they would have simply beat the suspect into unconsciousness. Especially knowing what they did about him. But it was not in his nature, and it was not the culture of the department either. Eugene's citizen watchdog group reacted rather strongly to violent police behavior.

As they tried to lift and drag Valder into the backseat, which was partitioned from the front with plexiglass, he started thrashing violently, twisting his torso and slamming his head against their thighs and groins. Feeling his kidney pain flare like a hot knife in the gut, Jackson gave up.

"Let him go and step back."

Schak moved quickly for a barrel-shaped man. Jackson nodded at Evans and she pulled the taser's trigger as Valder lurched to his feet. The prongs hit the suspect in the bare chest, and for a split second he was still. Valder collapsed on the ground again, writhing and moaning. Jackson had experienced the sensation during training and wanted to feel sympathy for Valder, but he was too tired.

"Let's get him downtown before he comes out of it."

As they hauled the limp but heavy man into the backseat and secured him with ankle chains, Jackson said, "I did everything possible to prevent this outcome."

"You sure as hell did," Evans said.

Jackson paced the room, struggling to stay awake as Valder was processed into the jail—strip-searched, questioned about his medical condition, and given a dose of Valium. Valder had come in wearing only sweatpants, slippers, and a T-shirt around his face, so there wasn't much to put into the plastic bag for his possessions. From the intake area on the ground floor, a deputy escorted Valder upstairs to the main jail and interrogation room.

"Should I leave him cuffed?" the deputy asked.

"Yes."

Valder's body seemed to fill the tiny room, and the pale-green walls were especially sickly to Jackson. His head pounded from exhaustion as he took a seat. He'd been awake and working for nearly twenty hours. Valder didn't look much better. His eyes were glassy and his shoulders slumped. Jackson hoped to catch him off guard.

"Where is Danette Blake?"

"Who?"

"The first girl Eddie Lucas kidnapped. The mistake." Jackson paused, giving Valder a moment to process the line of questioning. "Lying to me will work against you in the long run. Danette was in your house, and we'll find proof. All we need is a single piece of hair. You might as well tell me what happened."

"I don't know what you're talking about. I told you all about Courtney. If Eddie has something else going on, you need to talk to him."

"I have Eddie Lucas in custody, and I expect him to turn on you to save his own skin. This is your one chance."

Valder blinked and his shoulders tightened. After a long moment he shrugged. "I don't have anything else to say." His speech sounded a little slurred.

"Maybe Danette was never in your house, so you think you're safe. Or maybe Eddie realized his mistake, killed her and dumped her, and never told you about it. If you don't talk to me, he'll blame you for it. It will be his word against yours."

Valder didn't respond. Jackson tried again, but Valder shut down. After a few minutes, the suspect put his head on the table and closed his eyes.

Crap! How much Valium had they given him?

Jackson stepped out and called for a deputy. He was done for this day.

CHAPTER 21

Friday, April 10, 9:06 a.m.

Sophie couldn't stop thinking about Courtney Durham and Danette Blake. She was supposed to be writing a roundup story about three recent deadly accidents involving drunk drivers. The news angle was: Why the sudden increase? It was no mystery to her. The economy was bad; people were unemployed, depressed, and drinking more. The bigger question was what to do about it.

Meanwhile, nobody seemed to be investigating the disappearance of Danette Blake. Sophie had called the police department and been referred to Detective Zapata, who said foul play did not seem to be involved. He based the assumption on the fact that Danette's car was also missing; therefore, she had driven away in it. If Courtney Durham hadn't also disappeared Monday, Danette's case would be easier to dismiss. Having Courtney's body turn up had piqued Sophie's interest to the point of near obsession.

"Hey, Sophie, how's your drunk-driving story coming?" Her boss, Karl Hoogstad, had wandered up behind her.

"I got some great quotes from the Alcohol Abuse Prevention Network. I'm digging up some statistics from the early eighties to see if there's a pattern between unemployment and alcohol-related crimes."

"Great. I like it." Hoogstad clapped her shoulder and headed downstairs. Probably going to the cafeteria, Sophie thought. The statistic idea was impromptu, but it made sense, so she started accessing online Lane County files.

Her cell phone rang in her bag under her desk. Sophie dug it out and glanced at the caller ID: Elle Durham. *Finally!* She'd been trying to talk to Elle ever since Jackson had confirmed the dead body was Courtney. Sophie answered the call, grabbed a pen and tablet, and turned her back to her cube neighbor.

"Ms. Durham, thank you so much for getting back to me."

"This is a very difficult time, and I don't usually welcome attention from reporters, but you seemed so concerned." Elle Durham's speech was a little sloppy. "I want someone to expose ThrillSeekers for what they are, the greedy bastards!"

Sophie had no idea what she talking about, but her adrenaline was pumping. "What was Courtney's involvement with ThrillSeekers?"

"According to Brett, that's Courtney's boyfriend, she hired the company to kidnap her just for thrills. Now my baby's dead, and the police won't tell me how she died. I think those bastards at ThrillSeekers drugged her or something."

Sophie put on her headphone so she could type as she talked. She keyed *ThrillSeekers* into Google. "Have you spoken to anyone at the company?"

"I tried, but the receptionist won't tell me anything and she won't put the owner on the phone." Elle was both high and distraught. It made her a little hard to understand.

"Do you have any idea how much she paid them?"

"Brett wouldn't tell me."

"Will you give me Brett's phone number?"

"Just a minute." Ms. Durham came back with the number. "I don't think Brett knows much. Will you call ThrillSeekers? I thought maybe a reporter could get somewhere with them."

Bloody unlikely, Sophie thought. *Unless she pretended to be a potential client.* "I'll find out what I can. Now I have a question for you. Did Courtney know Danette Blake?"

"You're the second person to ask me, but I don't know who she is."

"Who else asked you? Was it the police?"

"It was Detective Jackson."

So Jackson thought the women's disappearances could be related. Now Sophie felt sure the connection was worth pursuing. "Why would Courtney want to be kidnapped, Elle? Do you have any idea?" Sophie wished she were recording the conversation on her desk phone.

Ms. Durham started to cry. "It makes her sound so crazy. Courtney wasn't mentally ill. She was just unhappy. That's why I sent her to a psychiatrist."

"Which psychiatrist?" Sophie remembered Kera telling her Danette had disappeared after a doctor's appointment.

"Why does it matter?"

"I think it might be important. Another woman Courtney's age is missing."

"That person you just asked about, what's her name? Danette?"

"Yes. She's been missing since Monday morning."

"That's so sad." Elle let out a sob. Sophie wondered how much she'd drank. After a moment, Elle said, "Courtney's doctor is Stella Callahan."

Sophie jotted down the name. "Thanks. Is there anything else you can tell me about Courtney's abduction?"

"The bastards dropped her off in a field. She had asthma!"

"That sounds irresponsible. I'll see what I can find out. Let's stay in touch."

Sophie knew she would soon think of other questions, but right now she wanted to call Kera Kollmorgan and find out which doctor Danette had seen Monday. Then she would call ThrillSeekers and try to set up an adventure.

This was a story.

Jackson got up late after a short night of waking up every hour to pee. He glanced at the clock and realized he had to be at an autopsy in forty minutes. He bolted for the shower, feeling like he had lead in his legs. He'd almost driven over to Kera's at three in the morning, but had decided it was too selfish. He was glad now he hadn't. Between him and the baby, the poor woman wouldn't have gotten any sleep. He wished Kera were here right now, brewing a pot of coffee, smelling delicious, and telling him he'd done the right thing and it would all turn out fine.

He let the hot shower pour over his still-tired body. *Would they ever be able to live together?* His daughter vehemently opposed the idea, and Jackson wasn't sure how he felt about raising a baby that wasn't his responsibility. He tried to tell himself it was too early to assume Danette was dead and never coming back, but he wasn't convincing.

After the shower, Jackson glanced at himself in the mirror and groaned. He splashed cold water on his eyes, hoping to shrink the bags that were dark and swollen like a waterway about to burst. Wearing only a towel, he trotted up the hall and into the kitchen to start a pot of coffee. Damn, the place was a mess. What the heck day was it anyway? Oh yeah, Friday; autopsy at eight.

He dressed, gulped a cup of coffee, and poured a second cup into an insulated travel mug. On the way to his car, he realized he didn't have his carryall. Cursing under his breath, he went back into the house. This was not a good sign. He needed to be alert and sharp. He had two important suspects to interrogate. Valder was in isolation at the county jail. It was less convenient having him there instead of in a holding cell at the department, but Jackson had decided to cover his own ass by booking Valder into a facility where he would get the appropriate medical attention for his phobia.

It was Eddie Lucas he was counting on today. If Lucas didn't confess, they would probably never find Danette's body or be able to prove Lucas had kidnapped her and Valder had killed her. Or maybe Eddie killed her when he realized his mistake. Jackson worried he might not ever know. Not knowing was tough to accept. It would be even harder for Kera and Mrs. Blake. Jackson needed to give them closure.

Back in his cruiser, he drove too fast and made calls on the way. He checked in with McCray, who was writing up the paperwork for a complete search of Valder's property, including his computer, phone records, and bank accounts. It was asking a lot from a judge, especially based only on his theory of mistaken-identity kidnapping. Evans and Schak would soon be on their way to Valder's home to wait for the go-ahead on the search. Jackson would join them after the autopsy.

When he called Kera, she didn't answer. Had she gone back to work at the clinic? Jackson left her a message: "Sorry I couldn't come by last night. I was on the job until about three this morning. I think we've caught a big break in this case and it involves Danette. I wish I could tell you more. Hang in there. Call and leave a message so I can hear your sexy voice."

In the basement of North McKenzie in an area known as Surgery Ten, a small crowd had already assembled near the bank of stainless-steel refrigeration units.

Normally, only the pathologist, the medical examiner, and the lead detective would be present for an autopsy. Today the district attorney and one assistant DA, Victor Slonecker and Jim Trang, were also standing around the table where Courtney's lifeless naked body was exposed to the group.

"I'll get started now," Rudolf Konrad said drily, giving Jackson a look. Konrad was forty-something, but his round face and thick blond hair made him look younger. Jackson had been late to his first autopsy with the new pathologist, and apparently he hadn't gotten over it.

"Sorry to be late." Jackson resisted the urge to explain that he had worked from five yesterday morning until three this morning.

"We drew blood and sent the samples to the state lab with orders to prioritize them, and we hope to have toxicology reports by late this afternoon or tomorrow," Konrad said, glancing at the medical examiner, who had most likely performed the tasks.

Gunderson spoke up. "I sent her clothes to the city's crime lab after I examined them. I found almost nothing noteworthy on her clothing. Except in the pocket of her jeans, there was a tiny plastic bag containing a white powder, which may turn out to be cocaine."

The assistant DA said something under his breath to Slonecker, his boss. The pathologist ignored him and began meticulously searching Courtney's skin, starting with her feet. Jackson grew uncomfortable. Five men were looming over and staring at the naked and perfectly sculpted body of a young woman. It felt voyeuristic and wrong. Yet they were all just doing their jobs. Slonecker and his assistant were present because Courtney Durham was high profile, and Jackson guessed the DA was under some pressure from Elle Durham to prosecute her daughter's killer. Jackson wasn't sure yet a crime had been committed against Courtney. If it had, he would do his part to bring her justice.

Still, he couldn't help but think the rich girl's selfish and out-rageous behavior may have led to Danette Blake's abduction and death. It was hard not to be angry about that.

"I'll start by examining her posterior," Konrad said, for the sake of the recording. Gunderson stepped up and the two men expertly rolled the corpse.

Reddish-purple bruising covered Courtney's back, buttocks, thighs, and calves. "Significant livor mortis on entire back of body," the pathologist reported, his voice deep and full, yet dead-pan. Although disturbing to look at, the discoloration was simply blood pooling in the lowest parts of a lifeless body. Still visible in the curve of her lower back was a massive tattoo, a complex design of flowers, vines, butterflies, and a sunrise. It took Jackson by surprise. He knew tattoos were more mainstream now, espe-cially for young women, but he still thought of them as working-class body art. Apparently he was wrong.

What could he do to keep his daughter from ever doing this to herself?

Konrad searched Courtney's posterior, starting at her feet. "Slight discoloration in the heel of her left foot. Could be due to lividity. There are no needle marks under the toes and no trace evidence. The tattoo around her ankle is several years old and healed well with no scarring."

Jackson struggled to pay attention. The travel mug of coffee was in his car getting cold.

Konrad continued his inch-by-inch examination of Courtney's skin until he reached her shoulders. "I'll now examine the anterior surface."

He and Gunderson rolled Courtney over and the process started again.

"Her hands show no signs of defense wounds, but there are abrasions around both wrists consistent with being bound."

"Bound by what?" Slonecker asked.

Jackson answered, "Seth Valder, our main suspect, admits Courtney was handcuffed while she was in his house during her kidnapping adventure."

"Hmm." The district attorney kept his face neutral.

Konrad worked his way up to Courtney's head and neck, stopping suddenly to reach for a special magnifying glass. He examined her neck for an endless five minutes while they all waited silently.

"There are layers of bruises on both sides of her neck," Konrad reported. "Some occurred weeks ago and others are newer. Because the bruises accumulated over time, it seems unlikely that any one event connected to the markings caused her death. I won't know until I have the body open and can examine the hyoid bone."

Konrad made a soft noise in his throat. "There appears to be a layer of makeup over some of the bruises. In that makeup, I believe, is a partial fingerprint."

"I'll be damned," Jim Trang said, breaking the stunned silence. "Can you lift it?"

"I think so. I'd like to come back to this area and spend more time after I complete the rest of the autopsy."

"This is too critical to wait," Slonecker argued. "If there's a print, we need it now. A fingerprint means she was strangled."

"Not necessarily." Konrad finally looked up from his close scrutiny. "These bruises are consistent with sexual asphyxiation. If they contributed to her death, it could have been accidental suffocation. Also, the fingerprint may belong to the deceased."

No one in the room wanted to believe it. Jackson remembered threatening Brett with the possibility of finding his fingerprints on Courtney's neck. He'd thought at the time it was just a bluff.

"Let's cut her open and look at her hyoid bone." Slonecker was clearly impatient with the process.

"I'll get there," Konrad said, "but first, I'll examine her genital area."

Jackson looked away as the pathologist probed between Courtney's legs. Even in death, she deserved some privacy.

Konrad took swabs from every orifice and placed them in tiny glass containers. After a moment, he said, "No sign of swelling or tearing. No semen present. It seems reasonable to conclude she was not raped in connection with her death."

Slonecker spoke up. "Any sign of consensual sex?"

"There are no signs, but it's still a possibility if a condom was used and discarded." Konrad glanced at Jackson. "Was a condom found at the scene of her death?"

"No."

Slonecker folded his arms across his chest. "Doesn't that contradict your theory about the neck bruises being related to sex?"

"Not at all." The pathologist's voice was still deadpan. "The neck bruises could have been caused by consensual sex engaged in over a period of weeks before her death. Or even hours before her death. The pressure on her neck during climax may have even killed her. If they used a condom, or he failed to ejaculate, that sex may have occurred moments before she died. I have drawn no conclusions except that she was not forcibly raped in a way that caused visible damage."

The room was quiet while Konrad pushed two gloved fingers into Courtney's rectum. Jackson was watching the pathologist's face and saw him make a small frown.

"What is it?"

"She has anal scar tissue."

"What does that mean?"

"I can't know for sure, but my best guess is she was repeatedly assaulted at an earlier time."

Jackson drew in his breath. Jim Trang mumbled, "Oh god."

"How sure are you about this?" Slonecker asked. "Is there any reason to tell her mother? Elle Durham is very anxious and calls me twice a day."

Konrad responded, but Jackson wasn't listening. He was thinking about Courtney and her irrational behavior and how it could all be a byproduct of childhood sexual abuse. Even the sexual dysfunction that Dr. Callahan had been treating her for made more sense now. Poor girl. Who had done this terrible thing to her? How much did it matter to his investigation?

The sudden whine of the Stryker saw caused Jackson to jump. He never got used to this part of the process, no matter how many times he'd been through it. Konrad made a Y-shaped cut into the chest cavity, then grabbed the loose flap of skin and flipped it up on her face. It made a loud sucking sound, and the smell of decaying organs filled the air. Jim Trang bolted from the room. *It must have been his first autopsy*, Jackson thought.

After taking a section of her lung and examining it up close, Konrad said, "Her lungs were deprived of oxygen, which is consistent with suffocation."

"Are you calling it a homicide or not?" Slonecker demanded.

"Not yet. We're going to look at her hyoid bone too."

"We found an asthma inhaler under the body," Jackson added. "Her mother confirmed that Courtney had asthma attacks sometimes when she was outside."

Konrad glanced over at Gunderson, the medical examiner, who had failed to report the information. "It's not often a person dies of an asthma attack," Konrad announced, "but during an episode, the chest muscles tighten, making the bronchial tubes constrict. The lining becomes swollen and sticky with mucus. Less air flows into the lungs, and less oxygen enters the bloodstream."

Jackson remembered his conversation with Parker at the lab. "A crime technician says her inhaler was empty."

"She could have had an asthma attack and not been able to treat herself," Gunderson noted.

"Let's look at her hyoid bone right now," Slonecker demanded again. "I need a ruling and I need to get back to work."

A flicker of irritation flashed on Konrad's face. "Certainly."

A few minutes later the pathologist announced, "The hyoid is intact, making it unlikely this woman was strangled with significant force, yet the surrounding blood vessels are occluded."

"What are you saying? Was it a homicide or not?"

"My report will say her cause of death is undetermined."

CHAPTER 22

Jackson checked his cell phone as he left the parking garage. His only call was from Sergeant Lammers, requesting a meeting with him in Chief Warner's office ASAP. Oh boy. The chief only took a direct interest in cases if they were high profile, like the situation with the mayor last fall. And now again with the daughter of a rich, prominent family who used their money to make good things happen in Eugene.

The drive from the hospital to city hall took four minutes. Jackson bounded up the stairs from the parking garage and headed straight for the bathroom. The pink in his stream startled him. His urologist had not mentioned blood.

From the privacy of the bathroom, he called Dr. Jewel. The chief could wait five minutes. The receptionist tried to tell him the doctor couldn't come to the phone, but Jackson said, "I'll hold for him, even if it's twenty minutes."

"That's really not necessary. The doctor will call you back."

"I'll wait. Please tell him it's important."

As he waited, Jackson rehearsed what he would say to Warner and Lammers. Finally, Dr. Jewel came on the line. "Wade, what's going on? Is there a problem with the stents?"

"There's blood in my piss."

"A little bit of blood is fairly common. What color is your urine?"

"Ugly pink."

"When is your surgery scheduled?"

"I don't know. Your office was supposed to call me."

"Just a moment."

The handle rattled on the bathroom door. Jackson ignored it.

Dr. Jewel came back on. "I'd like to do this operation Monday morning at six. I assume that works for you?"

His body screamed yes, but his head wondered if he could wrap up the bulk of the Courtney/Danette investigation by then. If not, could he let himself turn it over to his team?

"The bleeding is a concern," Jewel prodded.

"Okay. I can't stand these stents anyway."

"My assistant will give you all the presurgery instructions. In the meantime, take it easy. Sit around and read or watch TV for a couple of days."

Jackson jotted down the information on the back page of his notebook. He wondered when he could make time to preregister at the hospital. He would also need to eat at least one decent meal before Sunday afternoon when he had to start his presurgery fast.

He left the bathroom and headed for Warner's office. Two and half more days with the damned stents, then major surgery, during which he could die for any number of reasons, and now an ASAP meeting with the chief. Life was good.

Sergeant Lammers caught Jackson in the hall just outside Warner's office. She grabbed his arm. "Just a heads-up that Elle Durham is Warner's cousin, so Courtney is like a niece to him. Be careful what you say about her." Lammers reached for the door. "I hope you have some good news."

Jackson felt his kidneys bleed a little.

Warner was on the phone when they walked in, and it reminded Jackson to shut his cell phone off. Sergeant Lammers had a reputation for smashing and/or throwing other people's cell phones if they interrupted her conversation.

Jackson stood while they waited, because he was more comfortable that way. Lammers gestured for him to sit. Chief Warner was a little short and didn't like people towering over him. The chief finally hung up and looked directly at Jackson. "What the hell is going on with this case? Elle Durham has called three times, and I don't have any information to give her. She says you don't return her calls."

"Her daughter's only been dead two days, and I have worked round the clock to find out why. I didn't return Elle's calls yesterday because I was interrogating suspects all day." Jackson had tried not to sound defensive, yet there it was.

"What did you learn?"

Jackson suspected the chief knew nothing about his investigation, so he started at the beginning. "Courtney hired someone to kidnap her just for the thrill."

Warner's fleshy face scrunched into a scowl. "What the hell are you saying?"

"She arranged and paid for her own kidnapping by a company that specializes in extreme adventures. Her boyfriend, Brett, thinks Courtney did it to get her mother's attention."

"You know, Elle is—" Warner stopped, paused, then started again. "I knew Courtney needed some professional help, but I didn't know it was that bad."

Jackson wondered if the chief knew about Courtney's childhood sexual abuse. For a split second, he wondered if Warner was the pedophile predator who'd committed the crimes. It was always a family member or close friend of the family. Just as quickly, he let the ugly thought go. Warner was a good man.

Lammers jumped in. "What happened? The kidnapping went bad?"

"According to all testimony and videotape evidence, the kidnapping went as planned and Courtney was released unharmed around ten p.m. Tuesday night. Sometime before midnight, she died for unknown reasons. There was an empty asthma inhaler under her body, and her lungs showed signs of oxygen deprivation. It's possible she simply died of an asthma attack."

"Oh, that is tragic," Warner said, looking relieved.

"Her cause of death is undetermined. Courtney also has bruises on her neck consistent with choking. Her boyfriend, Brett Fenton, admits to engaging in choking during sex at Courtney's request." Warner started to interrupt, but Jackson kept going. "Courtney also called Brett to pick her up. He says he didn't go down there, but he also lied to us at first and said he hadn't heard from her. He's still a suspect."

"Is he in custody?"

"He was last night. His lawyer may have secured his release by now."

"Bring him back in. If that young man hurt Courtney, I want him prosecuted."

"There's another wrinkle in this case," Jackson said, wishing he didn't have to mention it.

"I'm listening." The chief leaned forward and Lammers gave him a look he couldn't read.

"Another young woman, Danette Blake, disappeared Monday morning. She left her baby with a sitter, kept an appointment with her psychiatrist, then simply vanished. Here's the connection. She and Courtney were both seeing the same psychiatrist.

In fact, Danette took Courtney's Monday morning appointment after Courtney canceled." Jackson wished he had a glass of water to wash down the lump in this throat. "My working theory is that ThrillSeekers' local contract man kidnapped Danette by mistake, thinking she was Courtney leaving the shrink's office."

After a full two seconds of silence, Lammers said, "Most criminals are idiots, so it's certainly possible. What's your theory about where Danette is now?"

"I think they may have killed her to simply clean up the mistake. The man who contracted for Courtney's kidnapping is a local named Eddie Lucas. He was picked up last night in Redding, California and is being transported here now. I'll be able to question him this afternoon."

"What a mess." Warner made a point to catch Jackson's eye. "Don't misunderstand me, I want Danette's case solved too, but remember Courtney is your priority. If you think the boyfriend killed her, then sweat him until you get a confession. Let one of your team members interrogate this other guy, Eddie what's-his-name."

Jackson nodded and stood to leave. "I have a lot to accomplish today."

"Keep me updated," Warner said as Jackson walked out, hands clenched tightly inside his jacket pockets. He hated being told how to run his cases. The idea that Courtney was somehow more important than Danette because of her family's money was such bullshit. Jackson was pissed at himself for not speaking up and saying so.

"Jackson," Lammers called out, catching up to him as he strode toward his work space. "Are you okay? I mean, physically. You look a little gray."

"I've had about seven hours of sleep since Tuesday, but I'm fine."

"When is your surgery?"

He stopped and turned to face her. "Monday morning. I just found out. I'll be out for the next couple of weeks. I hope that's okay."

"It's fine. I'm confident you and your team will resolve both cases."

"Thanks. I am too."

They stood at the edge of the area housing the desks of the violent-crime detectives. The desk officer rushed up from the wide hallway leading to the front of the building. "Jackson, an officer has located the car."

"What car?"

"The blue Toyota on the attempt-to-locate. Officer Lopez spotted it near the university. A young male was sleeping in the vehicle, so she woke him and asked to see his ID and registration. The car is registered to Danette Blake. The man's name is Josh Wilson and he has a record of heroin possession and petty theft. He says he found the vehicle with the keys in the door and borrowed it for a few days."

"Where did he find it?"

"In a parking lot on Lincoln Street."

"Where is the car now?"

"Near Fifteenth and Agate. The officer is still in the area, waiting for instructions."

"Tell her to watch the car until I get there. Where is the heroin addict?"

"Another officer picked him up and he's being booked into the jail now."

"Call the sheriff and ask him to designate Josh Wilson as a no-release." Without the request, even a car thief would be matrixed out of the system in less than twenty-four hours because of overcrowding.

"Yes, sir."

"Thank you."

"What does this mean for you?" Lammers asked.

"It means Danette didn't drive away from her appointment and abandon her child. It supports my theory that she was abducted from the parking lot of her psychiatrist's office by the same person who kidnapped Courtney."

"Let me know if you need more detectives."

On his way to the university area, Jackson made a call to Evans, who was waiting with Schak in front of Seth Valder's house. He told her about Danette's car. "You may have to search Valder's place without me, depending on what I find and when Eddie Lucas arrives."

"No problem. Keep us posted."

Danette's car fit right into the college neighborhood, with its big vintage houses and environmentally friendly vehicles. Jackson was surprised an officer had spotted the ten-year-old Toyota. Maybe the cop had noticed the junkie sleeping in the backseat and gotten lucky the vehicle was on an attempt-to-locate list. It didn't matter.

The patrol unit was parked across the street, and the officer climbed out of her car when she saw Jackson approaching. Jackson pulled on latex gloves. If Eddie Lucas had touched the car and left a print…

Officer Lopez, a middle-aged female, limped across the tree-lined street and introduced herself.

"Anything interesting I should know up front?" Jackson reached for the passenger-side door, which was near the sidewalk.

"It smells like vomit. Brace yourself."

"What about the junkie? Did he say anything to indicate he knew the woman who owned the vehicle?"

"No. He was practically incoherent, but he told me where he found the car."

"Have you searched it?"

"No. As soon as I saw the name on the registration, I knew it belonged to the missing woman. So I called for another officer to take in my arrestee and didn't touch anything in the car."

"Good work."

Jackson put in a call to the crime lab, asking to have the vehicle towed back to the evidence bay. A spring shower came out of nowhere, so Lopez took refuge under a nearby tree and Jackson climbed in the Toyota to conduct a quick search. The stench almost drove him straight back out. The sour vomit smell made his eyes water, so he rolled down a window. Three days worth of junkie garbage littered the front seats and floor: a half-eaten burger, food wrappers, two stolen wallets, now empty, and used needles. The backseat was covered with a dirty blanket and a gray sweatshirt, and the worst of the smell seemed to come from the floor back there. Jackson didn't expect to find anything that would actually help him locate Danette, but he had to look anyway.

He started with the glove box, which produced all the usual registration and insurance papers, as well as a flashlight and a sci-fi paperback. He poked around in the garbage on the floor, grateful he was wearing gloves. He reached under the front seat and came out with a handful of papers. Sifting through them, he found a catalog for summer classes at the University of Oregon, a handout with a list of social services, and a bright yellow flyer with information about the Young Mothers Outreach Center.

Dr. Callahan had said someone at the center had referred Danette to her for treatment. He wasn't sure it mattered now. It seemed obvious Danette had disappeared from the parking lot of her shrink's office. Assuming he could take the junkie's word for where he'd found the car. If the druggie was willing to admit he stole the Toyota, why lie about where he found it? Jackson might eventually question Josh Wilson about Danette, but it seemed like a waste of time right now. Unlike meth addicts, who might kill someone for the ten dollars in their pocket, heroin addicts were rarely violent and not organized enough to make someone disappear.

Jackson glanced at the address on the flyer, pocketed the paper, and got the hell out of the car. Gulping deep breaths of wet fresh air, he glanced over at Officer Lopez, who was trying to keep a straight face.

"Told you it was bad."

"You did. Offering me a mask would have been more helpful." He grinned. "Will you stay with the vehicle until the crime lab gets here to impound it?"

"Of course."

Back in his car, Jackson called McCray. "How are we doing on the subpoena?"

"Judge Cranston is reading it now. He's a little skeptical about your mistaken identity kidnapping theory."

"Tell him we've located Danette's car. A junkie found it in the psychiatrist's parking lot with the keys in the door, so he stole it. It's sitting here on Fifteenth and Agate right now."

"No shit? Your theory is sounding more and more viable."

Had McCray doubted it? Jackson almost laughed. He didn't blame him. "Call me and Evans when you have the subpoena, then head straight for the phone company. I want Valder's phone records immediately."

Jackson called headquarters. "Have we heard from the Redding police this morning?"

"Not yet."

"Get on the phone with the captain who contacted us last night. I want to know when Eddie Lucas will be here. I need to talk to him ASAP."

"Yes, sir."

Jackson was anxious to interrogate Seth Valder as well. The strip-club owner had been in no condition to answer questions the night before, and letting the agoraphobic sit in jail for a while would help break him down. Meanwhile, his strategy was to lean on Lucas first and offer him a deal for giving up Valder.

Jackson headed for the outreach center on Seventeenth and Oak. He might as well stop in and check it out while he was in the neighborhood. Until he had Eddie Lucas in custody or a search warrant for Valder's house, he was on standby.

The Young Mothers Outreach Center shared a parking lot with Goodbe Imports. The center was in a small concrete building with windows on the street side only. Jackson vaguely recalled it might have once been a bank. Inside, it smelled of baby powder and the walls had been painted creamy yellow. The back half was filled with computers and tables, and it reminded him of the space at the employment office.

A dark-haired woman in her twenties approached him immediately, and another young woman with a baby in her lap eyed him warily. Jackson realized he was not a typical visitor here and might be causing some alarm.

"Hi. I'm Gwen. How can I help you?"

He introduced himself. "I'd like to ask some questions about Danette Blake. Are you the person in charge?"

She smiled. "I like to think so, but not really. Our director is Elias Goodbe, but he's not here right now. His assistant, Lisa Harkin, is in her office though. Follow me."

As they walked into a short hallway, Gwen turned and said, "You're the second person to come in here asking about Danette. She must really be in some kind of trouble."

"Who was the other person?"

"A woman named Kera. She had Danette's baby with her."

Kera had checked out the center? Once he processed the information, Jackson was not surprised. Kera didn't sit around waiting for things to happen. She would look for Danette until she had exhausted all reasonable leads. For Kera's sanity, Jackson needed Eddie Lucas to tell him where the body was buried. He dreaded telling Kera about finding Danette's car, but he knew hearing bad news was better than a lifetime of wondering. He didn't know how parents of missing children went on with their lives.

Gwen led him into a small, windowless office and introduced him to a woman in her midfifties with a gray-white ponytail.

"Lisa Harkin." She shook his outstretched hand and gave him a warm smile. "Have a seat."

"Do you know Danette Blake?" Jackson eased onto the wooden chair.

"I did her intake here at the center, so I spent a few hours with her. I can't say I know her well. I understand she's missing."

"She was last seen at an appointment with her psychiatrist. Did you refer Danette to Dr. Callahan?"

"I did. I was very concerned about Danette's depression and thought she needed professional help. I ran it by the director and he agreed to the referral."

"You mean Elias Goodbe?"

"Yes."

"What's the connection between Goodbe and Callahan?"

"My understanding is they're friends, but I don't know how they met."

"Do you know Elle Durham?"

"Yes. She's one of our benefactors."

"What about Courtney Durham?"

Lisa shifted in her chair. "I've met her and Brooke. Why? Do you think Courtney's death is related to Danette Blake's disappearance?"

"It could be. Does Elias Goodbe know Elle Durham?"

Lisa looked up at the doorway just as Jackson sensed movement behind him. A man's voice said, "I'm Elias Goodbe and I should probably be the one answering these questions."

Jackson stood and turned to face him, noticing Goodbe looked much like his assistant—gray, but fit and attractive. Jackson introduced himself. "I would like to talk to you."

"I don't have much time, but my office is right next door."

They entered a slightly larger office with a small vertical window. Jackson had to move a stack of papers from the guest chair before he could sit. Goodbe motioned him to put the papers on the already overflowing bookcase. Jackson thought he smelled stale smoke on Goodbe's clothes.

"To answer your question, yes, I know Elle Durham. We're both members of the chamber of commerce and we've served on committees together. Elle is a wonderful woman who has suffered more than her share of tragedy. I'm sure Courtney's death is hitting her very hard."

"Did you know Courtney?"

"She was a volunteer at the center briefly, but I didn't know her well."

Jackson thought he detected a flicker of distaste in Goodbe's expression. "What did you think of Courtney?"

"She was a troubled young woman." Goodbe paused and looked thoughtful. "Yet she was a good person at heart."

"What do you know about Danette Blake?"

Goodbe shook his head. "Not much. Lisa thought she was suffering from postpartum depression, so we referred her to Stella Callahan, who does some pro bono work for us." The director clasped his hands together. "I understand Danette is missing."

"Since Monday. After seeing Stella Callahan."

Jackson waited, hoping Goodbe would volunteer something. He sensed the director was uncomfortable.

Goodbe finally said, "I wish I could help you. These last few days have been distressful for me personally, hearing the news about these young women. I don't know what else I can tell you."

"Do you know Seth Valder?" Jackson tossed it out on a whim.

"No." Goodbe squinted a little. "Should I? Who is he?"

"He owns Lucky Numbers, a strip club out on Highway 99." Jackson watched for a reaction but didn't get one. His phone rang and he flipped it open. It was the department. "Excuse me. I have to get this."

"A Redding police officer just walked in the door with Eddie Lucas," the front-desk officer reported.

"I'm on my way."

CHAPTER 23

Lucas had the thin face, nervous eyes, and sparse hair of a man who'd spent most of his life worrying about something. Today was no exception. Even with his hands cuffed in front, he was chewing his fingernails as Jackson walked into the interrogation room.

"Eddie. I've been looking forward to seeing you."

"I go by DJ now."

Jackson sat on the other side of the scarred wooden table. He set out his recorder. "Eddie, if you tell me the truth, I'll use this tape to convince the district attorney to cut you a deal. If you lie to me, I'll convince a jury you're as guilty as you look." Jackson gave him a shitty smile. "Ready?"

"You're wrong about me," Eddie said, sounding high-pitched and eager, his black Kid Rock T-shirt making him seem younger than his thirty-two years. "I've been on the right side of the law for a long time now. They picked me up on some stupid left-turn thing."

"Why did you run?"

Eddie shrugged. "I don't know. Sometimes I see cops and I panic. I keep hoping I'll get over that."

"You're looking at a murder charge in the death of Courtney Durham. I guess that's reason to panic."

His suspect swallowed hard. "That's crazy."

Jackson wanted to get to the heart of this conversation, but he had to put Lucas on edge first. "We know Seth Valder hired you to kidnap Courtney. We know it was her idea, and that she was fine when she left Seth Valder's house in your van. What happened after that? Did you panic and kill her because you were afraid of getting busted for your part in the whole thing?"

"Hell no." Eddie shook his head vigorously. "I let her off over there on that bike path behind the football stadium, just like Seth told me to. Then I drove away. Courtney was fine. She said, 'Thanks for the ride,' and blew me a kiss when she hopped out."

"When did you learn she was dead?"

Eddie's eyes darted around as he tried to find the best answer. "I didn't know she was dead until you mentioned it just now."

Jackson laughed a little. "Why did you suddenly leave town yesterday?"

"My mother is sick. I was on my way to Fresno to see her."

Jackson leaned forward. "Look, Eddie. You need to cut the bullshit. I have Seth Valder in custody too. I'm prepared to charge both of you with two counts of kidnapping and murder." Jackson put extra volume on the word *two* and watched Eddie's reaction.

* * *

Two counts of murder? Eddie felt queasy. His tongue slid back and forth across his bottom lip and he was powerless to stop it. "Who else is dead?" He had to ask, but he already knew.

"Danette Blake. The first woman you kidnapped." The detective stared at him with the coldest eyes. "If you cooperate, the DA will offer some kind of deal with minimal jail time. He's on his way over here now. I want the whole story before he gets here. He's not a patient man."

Eddie remembered that day. It had seemed like such easy money at the time. Then everything had gone to shit. He couldn't believe Valder had killed the girl. For nothing. For his mistake. *Fuck!* Eddie felt like crying. He began to rock, a gentle movement that gave him little comfort. It all came back to him in vivid detail.

He sat in the back of the van, watching the building out the rear window. Everything was ready, including the washcloth in his hand. The parking lot was quiet, and only one car pulled in while he waited. The pretty girl came out the door just before ten o'clock as Valder had said she would. Eddie scrambled over to the van's sliding door to get in place. He grabbed the handle and listened for her footsteps. Suddenly she was there, keys jangling.

Eddie threw open the door and stepped out directly behind her. He locked his left arm around her chest and pressed the chloroform washrag over her nose and mouth with his right hand. She made a small startled sound, dug an elbow into his ribs, then went limp as he dragged her backward into the van and slammed the side door. Handcuffs on first, then handkerchief over her eyes. Another cloth around her mouth, then the nylon rope around her ankles. The whole thing took less than three minutes.

Eddie climbed into the driver's seat, glanced around, and started the van. Damn, that had gone smoothly. He pulled out of the parking lot, thinking it shouldn't be that easy to kidnap someone, even if she was expecting it.

After the girl fell out of the van in Valder's garage, Eddie squatted and lifted her onto his right shoulder. She was heavier than he thought she would be. He staggered into the house where Valder was waiting. Eddie kicked the door to the garage closed behind him and followed Valder through the stainless-steel kitchen into a hallway.

By the time they reached Valder's office at the back of the house, overlooking a tennis court, Eddie was winded and his knees hurt from the weight. He dropped the girl on the leather couch just inside the door.

"What was the noise I heard?" Valder picked up something from his desk and headed toward Eddie.

"She got a little feisty and I fell against the car. Your car's fine." Eddie hated the way his voice sounded. Nervous and submissive, like a kid.

Valder looked down at the couch where the girl was sprawled, chest heaving. He turned to Eddie and screamed, "You fucking idiot."

"What?"

Valder grabbed his arm and propelled him away from the couch. "You grabbed the wrong girl."

"What?" It was all he could say. His heart hammered so hard he couldn't think.

"She's not even blonde. How could this happen?" Valder's anger-twisted face was inches from his. Eddie glanced over at the girl, who no longer had a hood over her hair.

"I don't know." He fought the panic rising in his throat. Valder was a businessman, not a thug. He wouldn't hurt him. *Would he?* "She came out of the building where you said she would be. The time was right, the place was right, she looked right."

"She's not even blonde! I gave you a fucking photo."

"She had her hood up over her head, so I didn't see her hair. And she had on sunglasses. Are you sure it's the wrong one? Women color their hair."

Valder's hand came up as if he were about to slap Eddie, then the big man got control of himself. His face went blank and his voice was smooth. "Look at the photo again, then go back out there and kidnap the right girl. None of us get paid until we get it right."

"Where do I find the blonde girl?"

"Tonight at Diego's. It's a nightclub on Pearl Street. Park in front of the building and wait for her to come out."

"What if she's not alone?"

"Follow her until she is."

"What about her?" Eddie nodded in the direction of the couch.

Valder's eyebrows came together. "Did she see you when you picked her up?"

"No." Eddie had been careful, despite assurances that he couldn't get into trouble.

"Don't worry. I'll clean up your mistake."

Eddie's gut flip-flopped. "What do you mean? You're not going to hurt her, are you? This was supposed to be a clean job."

"I'll give her some drugs, then drop her off near the hospital. Don't worry, she'll be fine. Just don't fuck this up again or you won't be."

Eddie didn't tell any of this story to the cop. Instead he said, "I can't believe they're both dead. It wasn't supposed to be like that." He hated to be a rat, but he wasn't going down for a murder charge. "Valder said it was a straightforward adventure kidnapping. It was supposed to be easy money."

* * *

"How much money?" Jackson asked. Eddie was hard to read, but he knew he was holding back.

Eddie hesitated. "Three grand."

"So what happened?"

Eddie massaged his bottom lip some more. "I messed up. It was an honest mistake. I had a short list of places Courtney could be, so I waited in the shrink's parking lot. She came out right on schedule. She had a hood over her head and I didn't see her hair." Eddie's voice tightened. "I thought she was Courtney. I saw the contract she signed. It was a legit job."

"How did you kidnap her? What exactly did you do?"

"I used a little bit of chloroform to knock her out, then dragged her into the van. I cuffed her hands and tied her feet."

"Did she struggle?"

"Not at that point. It went very smoothly. I thought everything was fine." Eddie bit his lower lip. "Until I got to Valder's house."

"What happened then?"

"I carried her in and set her down on the couch in Valder's office. He started freaking out and yelling at me." Eddie's distress was palpable. His eyes blinked rapidly and he worked his lower lip in a rhythmic motion.

Jackson needed the whole story. "Then what?"

"Valder said I had to go out and get the right girl or I wasn't getting paid. He made other threats too. He kinda scared me."

"What about Danette? What happened to the girl on the couch?"

"I don't know." Eddie glanced away. "Valder said not to worry about her. He said she would be fine."

"You accepted that? You left her there?"

"He said he would drop her off at the hospital. I believed him."

Jackson wasn't buying it. "You know Seth Valder has agoraphobia? He doesn't leave the house. How was he going to drop Danette off?"

"He has other people working for him, bringing stuff to his house. I thought she would be okay."

"You were happy to walk away from her. You didn't want to have to deal with the aftermath of your mistake."

Shame flushed over Eddie's face. "I wasn't thinking straight."

"You still went out and kidnapped Courtney that night."

"I needed the money. I was afraid of what Valder would do to me if I didn't."

"You were afraid of what he would do to you, but not worried about what he would do to Danette?" Jackson was disgusted and let it show.

"It's not like that. I thought he might send someone to rough me up or maybe bad-mouth my business. I wasn't worried he would kill me, and I didn't think he would hurt that girl either. I know he used to be rough on his dancers sometimes, but nothing serious. I swear it was an honest mistake. I didn't mean for anyone to get hurt."

"Why did you leave town?"

Eddie let out a mirthless laugh. "I knew I was screwed. Once I heard Courtney was dead, I knew the cops would be after me. I figured the whole thing about the other woman I took by mistake would blow up in my face."

"Do you know what Valder did with Danette?"

"No."

"You saw Valder when you took Courtney to his house that night and then again when you picked her up for the final drop-off. You didn't ask him about Danette?"

"I never knew her name."

"Weren't you curious about what happened to her?"

"I figured he did what he said he was going to do."

"Which is what?"

"I told you. He said he would give her some drugs and drop her off at the hospital."

Jackson began to think the little coward was telling the truth, or mostly the truth. By itself, Eddie's testimony might not be enough to convict Valder, but if they came up with any of Danette's DNA from Valder's house, that would cinch it. Jackson had no idea what kind of deal the DA would make with Lucas, and he didn't care.

"Could I have something to drink?" Eddie whined.

"Sure." Jackson grabbed his recorder and left the room. He asked one of the desk officers to take his suspect something to eat and drink, then he called McCray.

"Eddie Lucas just confessed to abducting Danette from Callahan's parking lot. He says he left her at Valder's house and never saw her again."

"I needed to hear that. Because I'm sitting here at my desk reworking this subpoena because Volcansek turned it down. Cranston is out of town."

"Put it all back. Tell her about the confession. I want Valder's computer and his phone and bank records. I want his DNA. Everything you can think of."

Jackson went to his own desk, sat down, and closed his eyes. On one hand, the who/why of these cases seemed to be wrapping up. Yet he sensed he was still missing something critical. Like Danette's body, and a definitive cause of death for Courtney. He decided to take a moment to empty his mind and not think about anything. It was his own form of meditation. Sometimes after a ten-minute session, he would get new ideas.

Jackson woke twenty minutes later. He glanced around to see if anyone had noticed he'd nodded off. Two other detectives were in the crowded room, but he was relieved to see one was on the phone and the other was staring at his monitor.

An image of Danette sitting in Dr. Callahan's office holding Micah surfaced in his brain. He had dreamed it during his short nap. Jackson closed his eyes again and tried to remember more of the dream, but that one brief image was all he had. That often happened in the morning when he woke rapidly: his dream would dissipate like a puff of smoke.

Jackson headed for the bathroom, where he splashed cold water on his face. He still had a long day ahead. The image of Danette stayed with him. Did it mean anything? Could Danette still be alive? But where? And why? It made no sense. She was a witness to her own mistaken kidnapping. Valder had very likely killed her simply to make the problem go away. He had a lot of property on which to bury her.

Jackson strode down the hall to see Sergeant Lammers. He needed a digging crew and equipment. His boss wasn't in her office, so he called her from the hall and left a request. *Could they convict Valder without a body?* It was unlikely.

Jackson decided it was time to go back to the jail. Valder was the key, and Jackson would keep chipping away at him until he cracked.

The county jail was only six blocks from city hall, and Jackson decided to walk over. It was a warm, blue-sky spring day, and he hadn't been out for his morning run all week. He thought it would feel good to his intestines to stretch out.

Except for the proximity to the police station, the location of the jail made no sense. It sat at the foot of Skinner Butte, only blocks from upscale shopping, dining, and theater. You could see the two-story redbrick building from the glass-walled top floor of the Hilton, the only major hotel in the downtown area. In the morning when they released groups of inmates, a crowd of riffraff spilled out past the surrounding shops and restaurants.

As he walked past the Hult Center for the Performing Arts, his cell phone rang. Jackson didn't recognize the number.

"Mr. Jackson? This is Shelley Ferguson, the vice principal of Kincaid Middle School. We've asked Katie to leave the premises for the day, and it's important you come pick her up."

The knife in his gut gave a little twist. "What happened?"

"It's rather complicated."

Jackson spun around and headed back to the department. Of all the times not to have his car! "Tell me anyway, I think I can manage to process it."

"I'd rather discuss this in person, with Katie here to explain her side of it."

"I'm on my way." Jackson started to run.

Kincaid Middle School was located in a busy south-side neighborhood with a mix of commercial and residential buildings. The building's gray utilitarian look with grass-only landscaping had not changed since Jackson had attended almost thirty years ago. As a kid, what he'd liked best was the school's proximity to the minor-league baseball field, where he'd watched the local team play.

He remembered the secretary from his visit here last fall to question students about the death of one of their peers.

"Hello, Detective Jackson. Ms. Ferguson is waiting for you." She pointed down a narrow hallway.

As Jackson entered the vice principal's office, he felt strangely nervous.

Katie waited in a chair, doing math homework, and the vice-principal was just hanging up the phone. Shelley Ferguson was middle-aged, a little pretty, a little plump.

"Thank you for coming. Katie told us you were very busy with a case, but she wouldn't give us another adult to call."

"What's going on?" He looked at Katie. She met his eyes and he didn't see any trace of contrition.

"I left school to buy something to eat at the little store."

"Leaving the campus during the school day is a serious violation," Ms. Ferguson said.

"Why not eat in the cafeteria? You have a lunch card." Jackson knew there was more to this incident.

"The cafeteria was closed," Katie said, with small flare of drama. "I was late because Ms. Summers kept me after class to talk about Ms. Driscoll."

"Just give me the story, so we can get going."

Katie rolled her eyes. "Almost every time Ms. Driscoll sees me she puts her arm around me and blows a kiss. I don't like it and I've asked her to stop. She did it again today, so I came to the office and said I wanted to file a sexual-harassment complaint."

Oh oh. "That's a pretty serious allegation, Katie."

"It can ruin a teacher's career," the vice principal added.

Katie sighed. "I know that now. Ms. Summers kept me after math class and explained it in detail. She was very upset with me. When I got to the cafeteria it was closed. So I went to the little store and bought lunch. I don't do well in class if I'm hungry."

Jackson turned to the vice principal. "What's the penalty for leaving campus?"

"Two days' suspension."

Jackson rose to leave. "While Katie is out of school, I want you to talk to Ms. Driscoll. Please explain that her behavior is inappropriate and unwanted and it needs to stop. Explain to Ms. Summers that this is not her business and she should not discuss it with Katie further."

He turned to his daughter. "You will not file a sexual-harassment complaint this time. You will never leave campus again without permission, except if there's imminent danger. Grab your backpack and let's go."

He smiled at Ms. Ferguson. "Sorry for your trouble."

Jackson debated his options. His ex-wife was likely at work, and Kera was taking care of her baby grandson. On another day, it would have been fine to simply keep Katie with him and make her sit and read or do homework while he filled out paperwork at his desk. Today was not a paperwork day.

Jackson drove back toward the jail. Katie could sit on the bench in the visitors' waiting room while he interrogated Valder, but he couldn't take her out to Valder's for the search. Maybe he should call Kera.

"I'm still hungry, you know," Katie announced. Earlier she had apologized for interrupting his day, then lapsed into silence.

"I'm hungry too."

They made a quick stop at Taco Bell, Katie's idea, and ate in the car.

When he finished his burrito, Jackson said, "Why didn't you ask the school to call your mother?"

"She can't leave work. There's no one to cover for her."

Jackson knew bullshit when he heard it. Something else was going on, but Katie wasn't ready to tell him. He wiped the salsa off his hands and called Kera. Katie was still picking at her food.

"Jackson, it's good to hear from you."

"We've had a development I can't discuss right now. Are you busy this afternoon? I mean other than taking care of Micah?"

"Not really. I took the week off from work."

"Can I bring Katie over? She was suspended from school."

"Of course."

As they drove west, Katie said, "What happens if Danette never comes back? Will Kera keep the baby?"

"It's quite likely. Micah's her grandson."

"If Kera keeps the baby, and you keep dating Kera, will you be the baby's father?" Katie gestured with her hand. "I mean stepfather, or adopted father, or whatever."

"Good question." Jackson had not let himself think that far ahead. "If we end up getting married and living together…" He looked over at Katie for a reaction, but she didn't give one. "I'll end up helping raise Micah."

"Will he call you Dad?"

The idea knocked the wind out of him. Kids needed commitment. He'd often thought it would be joyful to raise a son. Could he bond with someone else's child? It wouldn't be the same, would it? If he wasn't willing to help Kera raise the child, then he owed it to both of them to get out of the way.

"Is this freaking you out?"

"Maybe." Jackson turned left on Chambers and headed up the hill. "Is it freaking you out?"

"Heck no. I've always wanted a brother. Every baby needs a father."

He glanced over to see her smiling. His daughter was serious. "I appreciate your attitude, Katie." Two weeks ago when he'd brought up the idea of moving in with Kera, Katie had stopped speaking to him for days. *But a baby had changed everything?*

Yes, a baby changed everything.

* * *

With Micah perched on her hip, Kera opened the door. Jackson kissed her quickly on the lips. Katie rushed past them, seeming rather animated for someone who had just been suspended from school. Kera couldn't guess what her troubles were about. Katie was usually a good student and not inclined to make trouble.

"Hi Katie."

"Hey. Can I hold Micah?"

"Sure. I've got a bottle in the kitchen ready to go if you want to feed him."

"In a minute."

Katie took Micah into the living room and sat on the floor with his toys.

"Thanks for taking Katie this afternoon," Jackson said, sneaking another kiss. "I know she's old enough to be home alone during the day, but that would just be a reward for getting suspended."

"What happened?"

"It's a long weird story and I don't have time to repeat it right now. I think Katie will tell you if you ask her. It's nothing serious. I think she may just be trying to get my attention."

"Kids will do that." She wanted to know about the investigation. "Can you tell me about the breakthrough? Does it involve Danette?"

"I think we may be very close to finding out what happened to her."

His deadpan tone and pinched eyes told her to expect the worst. "It's not good, is it?"

"I think the best we can hope for is closure."

His handsome, caring face held so much conflict. Kera sensed that Jackson believed Danette was dead. She put her forehead on his shoulder and fought back sobs. Another young person lost. Another hole in the fabric of her life. Jackson stroked her back for a moment, but she sensed his impatience. He was still working this case.

She pulled away. "I know you need to go."

"Will you be okay?"

"What else is there?" She smiled bravely, warm tears streaming down her face. "Go get the bastard."

CHAPTER 24

Jackson climbed into his cruiser and sat for a moment, trying to visualize his future. He couldn't imagine it without Kera. Yet he didn't know if he could love unconditionally a child he had no biological connection to. Other people seemed capable of it. Foster parents, stepparents, adoptive parents. Maybe he could too.

Jackson started the car and mentally forced himself to shift gears. Finding Danette was the best thing he could do for Kera in the long run. A brief memory of his dream flashed in his head. If by some miracle Danette was still alive out there somewhere, finding her was the best thing he could do for that little boy as well.

He was so close to getting the whole story. If only Valder would talk, slip and say something.

On his way downtown, McCray called. "I've got the search warrant for everything. Valder's property, phone records, bank records, DNA, the works."

"Great. Let's get the phone records first. Pull in another detective for the bank records if you need to. I'm going back to the jail for another session with Valder. We need to keep pressuring the bastard."

Jackson made a quick call to Schak. "We finally got the warrant, so you can go in. Call the crime lab and get some evidence techs out to Valder's place too. I've got a call in to Lammers about getting a digging crew out there."

"We'll do it ourselves if we have to."

"Right." Jackson thought about his stents and how tired he was already. "Call me if you find anything significant. Anything I can use as leverage with Valder."

"Good luck."

Valder, wearing dark-green jail scrubs, was perkier than he had been the night before. He looked up from his chair in the interrogation room and said, "Oh good, you're back."

"Feeling cocky?"

"More like sarcastic."

"I have a videotaped confession from Eddie Lucas saying he dropped Danette Blake at your place Monday morning. Alive and well." Jackson set his tape recorder on the table as he talked.

Valder noticed but made no comment. "Lucas is a liar, a punk, and a lowlife. His testimony isn't worth a damn."

"Detectives and evidence technicians are searching your house right now. The next step is to dig up your property. Just tell us where Danette is buried and you may get out in twenty years."

"You don't have a body? You're wasting your time." Valder shook his head in mock sympathy.

Jackson's hands clenched into fists. He pulled them down into his lap. "I have two kidnapped young women. One dead and the other vanished without a trace. A jury will be hungry to convict someone of something."

"If you ruin my property, I'll sue the department and put you out of a job."

Oh, just once to be the kind of cop who could smack a suspect upside the head.

"Your statement is that you never saw Danette Blake. You had nothing to do with her kidnapping. Is that correct?"

"I'm not saying anything."

"Did Eddie Lucas bring Danette Blake to your house Monday morning or not?"

"I don't know Danette Blake and I'm not answering any more questions."

"Did Eddie Lucas bring a young woman to your house Monday morning?"

Valder was silent.

"This makes you look guilty."

Valder leaned back and crossed his arms.

For a moment, Jackson considered rounding up a couple of deputies and dragging Valder out into the rec yard to continue the conversation. Maybe his agoraphobic suspect was too comfortable here with all the walls and needed a little fresh air and open space to feel like talking. Jackson envisioned the police department's citizen auditor reacting to the news of such treatment. Followed by the newspaper coverage.

He pushed back his chair and stood. "I'll head out to your house and help with the search. Our warrant includes all the files on your computer, so we'll find something to keep you in lockup."

Valder blinked, and Jackson knew he'd hit a nerve. He eased toward the door, wondering what Valder was into. Double sets of books for his business? Child porn? They would nail him for something.

* * *

Sophie's call to ThrillSeekers didn't go as planned. The woman who identified herself as the assistant director said the company no longer offered any high-risk services. She wouldn't even mention a price, let alone discuss how such a service would be carried out. Sophie's call to Kera had confirmed that Danette saw the same psychiatrist as Courtney, and that Danette had disappeared after seeing Dr. Callahan. Brett, the boyfriend, had yet to return her call.

Undeterred, Sophie called Jackson and was surprised when he answered the phone. "Thanks for picking up. I have some information you'll want to hear. Danette Blake and Courtney Durham were both seeing the same psychiatrist, Dr. Stella Callahan."

There was a long silence. "How do you know?"

"I talked to Elle Durham and I talked to Kera. Do you have a lead in Danette's disappearance? Any suspects?"

"We have a suspect in custody."

"Can you name him?" Sophie reached for her tape recorder, just in case.

"You know I can't."

"Was Danette involved with ThrillSeekers too or just Courtney?"

Another silence. "We're looking into that, but it's highly unlikely."

"What do you think happened to Danette?"

"I'm not at liberty to say just yet."

He knows, Sophie realized. *Interesting.* "Any possibility she's still alive?"

"We don't know yet."

"Elle Durham says you won't tell her how Courtney died. Do you know? What are you protecting her from?" Sophie put the recorder down. "Off the record."

"The cause of death is undetermined, and we're still waiting on toxicology reports. I have to go. Thanks for the information."

The phone clicked in her ear. It was more time than Jackson usually spent on the phone with her. *Cause of death was undetermined.* How was that possible?

Sophie grabbed her sweater and headed outside. She needed to think and she did her best thinking when she was walking. She took the little dead-end road that ran parallel to the property the newspaper owned across the street.

Jackson had a suspect in custody who was connected to Danette's disappearance. He thought he knew what had happened to her. Was she dead? Was that what he couldn't say? Better yet, was Danette still alive? Was there someone else involved? Someone who was holding her? Kidnapping an adult would probably require several thugs to pull it off.

It was Friday and she had the weekend off. Sophie decided to keep an eye on Jackson and see if he would lead her to the story.

* * *

Jackson entered the foyer at Seth Valder's home and didn't see or hear anyone moving around the house. He'd expected a swarm of activity, based on the number of vehicles in the driveway. He hustled down the hallway toward the staircase to the basement. The door at the bottom was propped open and he heard Schak's voice. Jackson trotted down the stairs.

He went into the small room on the left and nearly collided with Evans. Beyond her, Schak was inspecting the bare mattress and Jasmine Parker was using a forensic light source to look for fingerprints and/or blood on the walls.

"Hey, I was just going up to call you," Evans said. "There's no cell-phone service down here." Her eyes flashed with excitement. "Guess what I found?"

Jackson raised an eyebrow. He was not expected to answer.

"Check this out." Evans crossed the stubby hall and entered the room on the other side. They hadn't looked at the room yesterday because Valder hadn't offered and they hadn't written the warrant yet.

"What do you suppose all this is for?"

A work space on one side of the room held camera equipment and spotlights, while the long desk on the other side held a computer tower and twenty-six-inch monitors on either side.

"Somebody is making videos." Jackson tried to process how this scenario fit with his two cases. On the surface, it didn't. "My guess is porn."

"That's what I'm thinking," Evans said.

Schak moved into the room. "Did you get anything out of Valder?"

"Not yet." Jackson glanced over at the computers. "We need to take all of this into the lab. Do we have pictures of this room yet?"

"I took some and so did Joe," Evans answered.

"Where is Joe?"

Schak gestured with his thumb. "He's in the bathroom across the way, collecting hair from the drain pipe, floor, and toilet."

"Have we found any trace evidence that could belong to Danette?"

"Specifically, no," Schak said. "The sheets that were on the bed yesterday are not there now. So Valder probably decided to launder them after we left here. Joe says the bathroom has been scrubbed clean, which is why he's looking in the drains for hair."

"All of you started down here?"

"Yes," Evans answered. "Our thinking is that if he kept Courtney down here, then he probably kept Danette here too."

"Were they here at the same time?" Jackson was thinking out loud. "Eddie Lucas picked up Courtney late Monday night and brought her here. Valder wouldn't want Courtney to know about Danette, because Courtney was supposed to walk away from her adventure. So Danette was not likely in this basement for long if she was here at all. Lucas says he carried Danette from the garage into Valder's office and dumped her on the couch." He turned to Evans. "When you're done down here, start with the couch and work your way along the route to the garage. She could have dropped a hair, an earring, fibers from her hooded jacket. I'll head up to Valder's bedroom and see if I can find his cell phone and wallet."

"McCray says we have permission to access the computers. True?" Schak wanted to know.

"I haven't seen the paperwork, but I assume so. Let's load this one into the evidence van and take it to the lab." Jackson didn't want Schak to get sidetracked looking at Valder's porn files. That wouldn't help them find Danette.

"You don't suppose he made a video of Danette while she was here?" Schak's question sounded casual, but it hit Jackson like a blow to the chest.

Evans booted up the computer. "I think Schak should take a look. I'll go upstairs and start in Valder's office."

Jackson left Schak to do the dirty work and followed Evans upstairs. He was anxious to get his hands on Valder's cell phone. The homebound sleazebag would have needed to call in help for dealing with Danette.

Valder's wallet was in a pair of jeans on the bedroom floor. In it was a thousand in cash, a second driver's license issued to Sam Walton, and a credit card in that name as well. It seemed odd for a man who didn't leave the house to carry that much cash and fake ID, but Valder had said the agoraphobia had come on a year ago. Had he lied about it? What the hell had he been up to before he lost his nerve?

Wearing latex gloves, Jackson slid the wallet into a prelabeled evidence bag. He glanced around the room to see if anything struck him as worthy of immediate attention. Other than its twenty-by-twenty size and high-end furniture, the room was not noteworthy.

Jackson moved to the tall dresser, where he found Valder's cell phone on top, plugged in and charging. He flipped it open and clicked around looking for a record of recent calls. The last call Valder had received had come in at ten the night before, about three hours before they'd picked him up. The name associated with the number was Beth. Two hours earlier, Valder received a call from someone named G. Scrolling through the list, Jackson noted three other calls from G, one additional call from Beth, one from A. Sanderson, several from numbers that had no names associated, and a call yesterday morning from ThrillSeekers.

Crap. Mircovitch's assistant must have called Valder and warned him they were coming. No wonder he had been so calm and cooperative. He'd had hours to clean and hide whatever he didn't want them to see.

Jackson clicked over to recently dialed calls and found a similar list. Once he was back at his desk, he would access the database and see who these numbers belonged to. The real day in question was Monday—the day Lucas claimed he had brought Danette to this house—and Jackson wouldn't have access to those calls until McCray brought in the phone records. Jackson bagged the phone and tucked it away before continuing his search.

The two dressers revealed nothing except a collection of nice clothing, but in the nightstand by the bed he found a loaded handgun of a make he didn't recognize. Jackson emptied the chamber and bagged the bullets and the weapon separately. Valder's criminal past meant he most likely was not permitted to own a weapon, but Jackson wouldn't be surprised to find more.

On the floor of the walk-in closet was a two-foot safe. He twisted the handle to see if it had been left unlocked. No luck. They would haul it into the lab as well. With the right tools, anything was penetrable. In a floor-to-ceiling cabinet in the back of the closet, Jackson found a massive collection of porn, shelf after shelf of old videotapes on the top half, with two shelves of slimmer, new DVDs underneath. Had Valder's obsession with porn led him from watching to making his own?

Jackson wondered about the man's intimate life. Did he have a girlfriend who came here to see him and didn't mind that they never went out? Or had his mental condition turned him into a celibate recluse? Except, of course, for the women who made videos in the basement. Who were they? Dancers from his Lucky Numbers club?

Jackson unconsciously stepped back from the cabinet. He hoped there would be no reason to look at any of this. If Valder was making videos with consenting adults and no one got hurt, then the activity was legal.

His next thought made him queasy. What if Valder had made a snuff film? Gotten rid of Danette while creating a high-dollar product at the same time?

CHAPTER 25

Jackson slipped into the conference room, grateful the other detectives weren't there yet. He needed a moment to empty his brain again. His body was beyond tired, running on the caffeine he'd consumed in the form of Vivarin. His nerves and tendons were stretched so tight he felt as if they would snap with any sudden movement.

He sat quietly, not thinking, until his phone rang. The caller ID said Elle Durham. *Damn.* He'd been avoiding her. This was her third call, and the second message she'd left was less pleasant than the first. Jackson picked up. "Hello, Elle. Sorry for not getting back to you. I've been extremely busy with the case."

"Are you making progress? How did the autopsy go this morning? What did the pathologist say?"

The autopsy had been this morning? "The pathologist's report was inconclusive. Courtney may have had an asthma attack. She also had bruising on her neck, but her hyoid bones weren't broken, so it probably didn't kill her."

"What are you saying? Someone strangled her but didn't kill her?" Elle's emotional level was elevated, yet her voice seemed muted. Jackson suspected she was medicated.

"Courtney's boyfriend, Brett Fenton, admits to causing the bruising."

"Brett hurt Courtney?"

"We're not sure." How much should he tell this poor woman? She seemed so desperate to know. "Brett says he choked her during sex because she wanted him to."

Schak walked in and Jackson gave him a nod.

"Why would she want that?"

"It's about pleasure. Look, Elle, I have to go. I have a task-force meeting. What I can tell you is that the men who kidnapped your daughter are both in custody. I believe they will both do time in jail."

She burst into tears. "Thank you. You don't know how hard this has been for Brooke and me. She is just not herself. This news will help."

"I'll call when I know more." Jackson got off the phone. He looked at Schak. "Elle Durham. You heard what I said to her?" Schak nodded. "If Lucas and Valder do time, it will be because of what they did to Danette. If Lucas hadn't screwed up, this case would be over. I don't think Slonecker would have even prosecuted them. Courtney hired someone to kidnap her, then likely died of an asthma attack afterward."

"From what I know about her, it's easy to think she had a death wish."

"Maybe."

Schak slumped into a chair. "She was definitely self-destructive. She set herself up for it."

Jackson couldn't argue. As a parent, he understood that Elle must have wanted to believe Courtney would change and turn out okay.

Evans hustled in, carrying tall coffees.

"You're a goddess," Schak said, reaching for a cup. Jackson reached for his wallet. Their addiction was not cheap, and he wouldn't let her pay for it.

Jackson looked at his watch: 4:45. He needed McCray to get here with the stack of paperwork. He wanted a look at Valder's Monday phone calls before he did anything else. In the meantime, they would catch up. They had all been going in different directions and it was time to get up to date on everything.

"Let's get started." Jackson glanced at his notes.

"Want me to update the board?" Evans reached over and touched his arm.

"Just the highlights. Essentially, we've broken both cases, yet haven't resolved either one. We know most of what happened to Danette, but we haven't found her. The pathologist couldn't make a conclusive ruling on Courtney's death."

"You really think it was just an asthma attack?" Evans asked.

"I don't know." Jackson took a long drink of hot black coffee. "Things about it bother me. Such as why Brett lied about Courtney calling him, and the bruises on her neck. It's so easy to slip from sexual play to lethal pressure. Without any witnesses or evidence, we'll never get a conviction. I'm not saying we're giving up, but we have to find Danette first."

"You say that like she might still be alive," Schak noted.

"It's possible. We'll stay on the case round the clock for now." He watched for his team's reaction to the idea of working through the weekend and thought he saw a flash of distress on Evans' face.

"We may not need everyone, if you have plans, Evans."

She gave him a half smile. "I have a date tomorrow night."

"New guy?" Schak said.

"Yeah. He's an artist. It's good so far."

It'll never last, Jackson thought. Evans would end up with someone in law enforcement or the military. She just hadn't accepted it yet. "Don't break your date yet. We may not need you."

"Anything else from Courtney's autopsy we should know?" Evans wanted to get back on task.

"Not yet. We should have toxicology reports on Monday. They may help explain what happened." McCray came in as Jackson glanced back through his notes from that morning. "Glad you're here. Did you get what we need?"

"Mostly. What were you saying about toxicology?"

"We're waiting on reports. The autopsy was inconclusive. Courtney may have died of an asthma attack."

"Someone that young and healthy? Very rare, if it happened." McCray sounded sure of himself.

Jackson vowed to keep digging. Until he remembered his surgery was Monday. He needed to tell his team, but not yet. "I stopped by the Young Mothers Outreach Center this morning," Jackson reported from his notes. "It's a loose connection point between Courtney and Danette, but I don't know how it's significant." He took another gulp of coffee. "The psychiatrist who was treating both women knows the director of the center, Elias Goodbe. Goodbe referred Danette to Callahan, the psychiatrist, as a pro bono patient. And Elle Durham donates money to the center." He made a connection he hadn't realized before. "Dr. Callahan, Elias Goodbe, and Elle Durham all know each other from the chamber of commerce."

"Goodbe gets cash donations from Elle Durham and free mental-health services from Callahan," Evans said, as she made notes on the board. "What do the women get out of their relationship with Goodbe?"

"A chance to feel good about helping the young women at the center?" Jackson offered.

Evans gave it thought. "I buy that. Did Courtney and Danette know each other?"

"I don't think so. But we know Danette took Courtney's canceled appointment with Callahan and that's how she got sucked into Courtney's little kidnapping adventure."

"Did you talk to Valder today?" Schak asked.

"He was uncooperative. He wouldn't admit or deny that Lucas brought Danette into his house."

"He's counting on us not finding her body or not finding trace evidence in his house." Schak shook his head with frustration. "I didn't see Danette in any of the video clips I scanned briefly, and the technicians didn't find any blood or prints in the basement."

"We have the hair I found on the couch in Valder's office," Evans said. "I dropped it at the crime lab, but we still need a comparison sample."

"We'll get one from Danette's house. I think Kera has a key."

"What's the plan for finding Danette?" McCray spoke up for the first time.

"We'll start digging up Valder's property tomorrow. The lab techs will keep looking at the computer we took from the basement. We'll pore over Valder's phone records and bank statements until we know everyone he has contact with, then we'll prioritize those contacts and question everyone." Jackson paused, still thinking it through. "I think I'll stop in at his club tonight and talk to some of his employees, maybe some of the dancers."

"I'll go with you," Schak said.

Jackson laughed. "Why not?"

Evans rolled her eyes.

"What's your best guess about Danette?" McCray was dead serious. "Assuming Valder doesn't really leave his house, did he get someone to take her away or did he bury her on his property somewhere? Both pose inherent risks."

Jackson had worked this question over. "Having people help him has probably become second nature to Valder by now. You have to go outside to bury someone. So I lean toward the idea that he hired someone to dispose of her." After a moment, he added, "It could have been Eddie Lucas. The Dirty Jobs bastard might be crafty enough to pin the worst of it on Valder and get off with something as light as reckless endangerment."

"Oh shit. Are you serious?" Schak sprayed his last gulp of coffee. "What does the DA say?"

"I'm just speculating. Slonecker is still open about how to prosecute." Jackson checked his watch. "Let's order in some sandwiches and dig into Valder's files."

* * *

Danette woke to the faint smell of cigarette smoke. Just as she oriented herself to the reality of still being in the second small basement, the man rolled her up in a blanket and lifted her from the narrow mattress. He placed her over his shoulders in a fireman's carry and started up the stairs. She vaguely remembered him coming into the room to give her food and water, but it seemed like days ago.

Where was he taking her now? Still gagged, Danette couldn't ask or complain. Her arms ached with the pain of being pressed hard to the front of her body, and her mouth was so dry her tongue felt sticky.

At first, she was relieved to be going somewhere. Even if he raped and killed her, at least it would be over. She couldn't take being bound and gagged and drugged anymore.

At the top of the stairs, he opened a door. For a second, Danette felt warm wind on her face. He dumped her in the trunk of a car and slammed it closed. Minutes later, the car was in motion.

Danette let her mind go blank. It was easier than thinking about how much her body hurt or what might be coming next.

In time, the frequent stops ended, and she thought they might be on a highway. *Was she leaving Eugene?* Danette began to hyperventilate. If she left Eugene, she might never see Micah again. Danette gulped in air as tears soaked the cloth over her eyes. She couldn't believe she'd ever considered giving up her precious baby. Danette had prayed so much in the last few days, she didn't know if there was still any point. Once again she asked God to save her so Micah wouldn't lose his mother. She promised to be the best mother a little boy could have if she ever made it back. *Please*, she begged. *I love my son. Give me a chance.*

The hum of the tires reached a higher pitch as the car picked up speed.

* * *

Valder's banking information made all four detectives feel bad about how little money they had in savings. Valder had four accounts: two business accounts, one personal savings, and a personal checking. Three of the four accounts were with a small credit union, and one of the business accounts was in a national bank. That account had almost a hundred thousand dollars, and the other three together had that much again. Jackson wondered why someone with that much money would carry out a risky adventure kidnapping for ten thousand dollars, minus the three he paid Lucas. Maybe that was why Valder had that kind of cash. He said yes to every moneymaking opportunity that came his way.

Jackson asked Evans and McCray to go through the statements, line by line, while he and Schak started on the phone records. Jackson flipped through the pages until he found the calls for Monday. "I'm taking this page to my desk so I can plug these phone numbers into the database."

"You can use my laptop," Evans offered.

"Thanks, but I'll be more comfortable at my desk."

Jackson pulled a pair of reading glasses out of his top drawer. So far, he only needed them when he was looking at pages of small print like this. Monday's calls started a third of the way down the page. At 8:03 a.m. Valder had received a call from Alice Valder, located in Aurora, Illinois. His mother, Jackson assumed. Calling first thing Monday morning. It was rather typical. Most of the male suspects he encountered fell into two categories: they either hadn't seen their mothers since they left home or they were tightly bonded, sometimes in a life of crime.

The next call, at 10:36, was outgoing, from Valder to a local number. Jackson punched it into LEDS, the law-enforcement data system. The name Robert Napper came up with an address in Springfield. Jackson added the information to his case file.

First he would make a list and check each name for criminal history. Those with records, they would visit in person, and the others he would call just to see who they were and how they reacted. Robert Napper was twenty-three and had a DUI conviction two years earlier. Jackson wondered if he was an employee, someone who worked at the club. In a minute, he'd call him and find out.

At 2:17 p.m. Valder had placed a call to another local number. Jackson keyed it in and waited. *Elias Goodbe, 2255 Wolf Meadows.*

His heart did a tiny tap dance. Goodbe was somehow in the thick of this. The importer-turned-philanthropist not only had associations with both missing women, Goodbe knew Valder, the strip-club owner and porn maker who had held both women in his house. Valder, with a gagged and bound young woman he needed to dispose of, had called Goodbe. Most interesting.

A rush of adrenaline surged through his body and Jackson's fingers flew as he keyed Goodbe into CODIS. He came up with nothing. Goodbe was not a known criminal. Was the name an alias? Without fingerprints or DNA, they had no way to cross-check.

Jackson scanned the other Monday calls. One at 4:47 p.m. came from Goodbe. He keyed the other three Monday calls into LEDS and came up with two that went to Lucky Numbers, Valder's club, and one to a woman named Trisha O'Neil.

Jackson pulled out the small evidence bag with Valder's phone. Jackson slid the cover back and started hitting buttons, looking for a contact file. After a moment, he gave up, grabbed his bag, and headed back to the conference room, signaling Schak at his desk to follow.

Evans made notes on her laptop while McCray read from a list of figures. They both looked up as Jackson announced, "I think we have another solid lead."

He took a seat as Schak came in. "Seth Valder talked to Elias Goodbe twice on Monday. Goodbe knows Elle Durham, who funds his center, so we might assume he knows Courtney too. The question of the moment is: Why does Goodbe, a supposed philanthropist, know someone like Valder? And why did Valder call him when he was dealing with the scenario of having the wrong kidnapped woman in his house?"

"You talked to Goodbe, right?" Schak asked. "What kind of vibe did you get?"

"Sorry to say, I didn't get much of a read." Jackson flipped back through his notes and tried to recall the interview that morning. "Goodbe seemed uncomfortable talking about Courtney." As he remembered something else, he snapped his fingers. "Goodbe lied to me. I asked him if he knew Seth Valder just to see his reaction and he said no."

"I can see why he would want to keep that relationship to himself," Evans noted with a slight sneer.

"Do we bring him in?" Schak cracked his knuckles.

"No, we tail him," McCray said, springing to his feet. "Bringing him in will get us nowhere. We can sweat Valder to roll over on Goodbe, but Goodbe has no reason to tell us anything."

"I like your thinking," Jackson said. "We also need subpoenas, which may take time."

"I'll take the first shift on the tail," McCray offered. "I'm tired of paperwork."

"You've got it. His address is 2255 Wolf Meadows. I think that's in the area between Green Acres and Chad Drive. His business is downtown right next to the center."

"I'll take a shift watching the center," Schak offered.

"Great. We'll get uniform backup if we need it." Jackson turned to Evans. "I need you to create the paperwork for a search of Goodbe's house, import business, and the center. I'll dig into the databases and see if there's anything in Goodbe's background that will help sway the judge."

"What's your working theory about Goodbe's role in this?" Evans wanted to know.

"I haven't had time to formulate one." Jackson's brain scrambled as he tried to generate a hypothesis. "Maybe he's connected to Valder's porno operation or some sex-trade business. If Goodbe picked up Danette from Valder, I'm a little more hopeful she's alive."

Evans asked what everyone was thinking. "But where?"

"We need to determine, then search, every piece of property Goodbe owns." Jackson remembered he had Valder's cell phone in his pocket. He pulled it out. "Does anyone use this type of phone or know how to locate the list of contacts?"

Evans reached for it. "It's a Google One." She clicked a few buttons. "I assume this is Valder's phone and you want me to scroll through his contact list for calls and see if Goodbe is in here."

"Yes." A wave of uncertainty hit Jackson. "What other kind of contact list would he have in the phone?" Jackson hated being behind the times on technology, but he always was.

"Most new phones have e-mail capability. I don't know if it has a standard e-mail address file though." Evans was scrolling as she talked. "Goodbe is in here at contact number twenty-six."

Jackson barely listened. His mind was on Courtney's missing phone. What if Courtney had one of those phones and sent a text to someone Tuesday night after Eddie Lucas dropped her off? He turned to Schak. "When you asked for the records for Courtney Durham's phone, did they say anything about texts?"

Schak looked taken aback. "No. I asked for a record of her calls for the last two weeks." Jackson watched him make the connection. "You think she might have sent a text before she died?"

"We need to find out. Get back to her phone-service provider and see if they track texts. Next head over to Seventeenth and Oak and keep an eye on the outreach center for a while. If you spot Goodbe, call me."

McCray let out a little sigh. "Should I follow up on Valder's phone e-mails?"

"No. Get out to Goodbe's house ASAP. We need to get this guy under surveillance."

CHAPTER 26

Jackson ran Elias Goodbe's name through every database and browser he had access to. What he discovered was that Goodbe had opened Goodbe's Imports in Eugene in 1996, had purchased a house at 2255 Wolf Meadows in 1997, had joined the Eugene Chamber of Commerce the same year, and had started the Young Mothers Outreach Center in 2006. It was almost as if he hadn't existed before 1996.

No vehicles came up associated with Goodbe's name either. It only meant he'd never been pulled over by an Oregon police officer. Jackson would have to check with the Department of Motor Vehicles in the morning.

He felt guilty about giving Evans the impossible job of writing a convincing subpoena to search Goodbe's personal records, home, business, and charity. No judge would sign off on it based on two phone calls between Valder and Goodbe on the day Danette disappeared. The men could have been talking about anything. They needed something more solid.

Jackson remembered Kera had visited the center so he gave her a call. "Quick question. What was your impression of the Young Mothers Outreach? Did you meet the director?"

"I did. Elias Goodbe. He seemed charming at first."

"What happened?"

"I mentioned talking to Sophie Speranza about doing a story to get the center some publicity and he rejected the idea. Then he kind of shut down."

"Did you talk to anyone else or learn anything interesting?"

"Hang on a sec." Jackson heard some shuffling noises, then Kera was back. "I had to put Micah on my other shoulder. He's a solid little chunk. Back to your question. I talked to a volunteer named Gwen who said some of the women who come to the center don't have families, and they place their babies in state care. Sometimes they never come back. It made sense when I first heard it, then it bothered me later and I'm not sure why."

Considering what he suspected about Goodbe, it bothered Jackson too. "It's a little unnerving. Anything else?"

"Not really. Will I see you this weekend?"

"I hope so. I'll call you later. Give Katie a hug for me." Evans walked up with paperwork in her hands. "I have to go see a judge about a search warrant."

"Good luck."

"Bye, babe."

"Oh wait. I just remembered something else Goodbe said I thought was interesting. He said some of the volunteers were at the center as part of their own therapy. He said it right after mentioning Stella Callahan."

"Thanks. Love you." Jackson flipped his phone shut and looked up at Evans, who had a funny smile going. "What?"

"When did you first tell Kera you loved her? How long into the relationship?"

"About four months, I think. I knew long before that Kera was the best thing that ever happened to me." Jackson started back to his desk. "Not that it's any of your business."

Evans had the audacity to wink at him. "I hope you found something on Goodbe, because this subpoena is weak."

"I haven't yet. We'll just have to be very persuasive. I'll start calling and see if I can find a judge who's willing to look at it tonight."

Jackson made calls to three judges and left messages, emphasizing the need to find a missing young woman. He sent Evans home to rest so she could take the next shift in front of Goodbe's house in about five hours. Jackson didn't want to leave McCray out there longer than that. He called Schak. "What's the update?"

"I couldn't get anyone with authority at Verizon on the phone tonight, so we may not get any information about Courtney's texts until Monday," Schak reported. "Now I'm sitting across the street from the Young Mothers center. The lights are off and no one's home."

"What about the import business across the parking lot?"

"Also dark and quiet. Why?"

"It's Goodbe's."

"No kidding? Convenient for him."

"I'm still working on the warrant. I'll get patrol units to keep an eye on the buildings, so you can go home and get some sleep."

Judge Cranston called back around nine thirty. "What's your situation?"

"We have a missing woman. She was kidnapped on Monday in a case of mistaken identity. We're trying to locate her. We know she was delivered to Seth Valder on Monday and Valder called

Elias Goodbe soon after, so I need a search warrant for Elias Goodbe's home, business, and charity."

"Elias Goodbe of Goodbe Imports and Young Mothers Outreach?"

Oh shit. "Yes."

"I know Elias." The judge cleared his throat. "I find it hard to believe he would be involved in kidnapping. What makes you think he is? Other than a phone call?"

"Two women disappeared earlier this week. The other one was Courtney Durham. Goodbe had contact with both of them. He also had contact with Seth Valder, who held both of the women in his house."

"Elle Durham's daughter was kidnapped? When? I was out of town for a while."

The conversation was not going according to plan. "Courtney was kidnapped Monday night. She arranged it for herself with a company called ThrillSeekers. Two things went wrong. First, the company kidnapped the wrong woman, Danette Blake, and no one has seen her since. Second, Courtney died soon after she was released and we're not sure yet how or why."

"Good Lord." A scraping sound followed, as if the judge had pulled out a chair.

"If you knew the family, I'm sorry for your loss."

"I know Elle, and I met Courtney once. I'm a little stunned."

"Courtney had mental-health problems." Jackson wanted to get back to Goodbe, but he needed the judge to come along with him. "Courtney was seeing a psychiatrist named Stella Callahan. Danette Blake was seeing her as well. That's where the mix-up came in."

"What makes you think Elias knows anything about either kidnapping?"

"Seth Valder called Elias Goodbe on Monday after Danette was mistakenly delivered to his house. Two hours later, Goodbe called him back. They spoke twice on the phone while a kidnapped woman was in Valder's house."

"You've searched Seth Valder's property?"

"Yes. Tomorrow we start digging up his backyard, but I have a feeling Danette isn't there. I think Goodbe picked her up."

The judge made an odd noise in his throat. "For god's sake why? Why would a businessman who started a charity for young women get involved in something like this? Have you even asked him?"

"Not yet. If we bring Goodbe in, we can't follow him around and see where he goes. Once we question him, he'll be on guard after that."

"I'm not letting you tear apart Elias Goodbe's home and reputation on such thin speculation. Go question him. Maybe he has a good reason for talking to Seth Valder. Good night." Cranston hung up.

Jackson was disappointed, but the judge had a point. Why would a businessman and philanthropist get involved in kidnapping a young woman?

Porn. It had to be about sex somehow. Some men became so obsessed with pornography it took over their lives and made them irrational. A year ago, a Springfield man had shot and killed his wife after she smashed his computer because she couldn't live with his porn addiction any longer. Their three children were in foster homes now.

McCray answered on the first ring, so he must have had his phone in his hand. Jackson pictured him sitting there on a dark street, watching a dark house, and wishing someone would call.

"What's the report?"

"The house is quiet. A couple of lights are on, but I'm not seeing any movement. No one has come or gone since I've been here.

No cars are parked out front, but there's a big garage, so the cars could be in there."

"I didn't get the warrant to search, so we'll have to bring Goodbe in for questioning. I'm on my way."

Goodbe lived in a new subdivision in the North Delta area, bordered by a golf course and a river. The homes were newer and nicer than in Jackson's neighborhood, but they didn't have mature trees or real backyards. Jackson shut off his engine and checked his watch: 10:52. Anyone in the house was likely sleeping. Too bad. He would have liked to be in bed too, preferably with Kera, but he was trying to find a missing young woman and he was willing to inconvenience anyone in the process.

McCray climbed out of a car across the street and trotted over. They strode up the sidewalk together, and Jackson gave the door a good pounding. His patience had expired hours ago. After ten seconds, he pounded again. Finally, a female voice on the other side said, "Go away, or I'm calling the police."

"We are the police. We want to talk to Elias Goodbe."

After a long pause the woman said, "He's not here."

"What's your name?"

"Doris Goodbe."

"Will you open the door and talk to us please?"

The porch light came on and the door slid open a crack, still secured by a heavy chain lock. "Let me see your badges."

As they held up their badges to her line of sight, Jackson asked, "Where is Elias?"

"He's on a business trip." Through the crack, he saw short iron-gray hair and a thick body; he guessed her age at sixty.

"I just saw him today, so I'm not buying it. Please go get him."

"He left late this afternoon. The trip came up unexpectedly." Doris made no move to open the door more.

"Where did he go?"

"Seattle, I think."

"Did he fly?"

"I assume so."

"Where is he staying?"

"I don't know."

"Give me his cell-phone number."

"I'd rather not."

Jackson tensed. "Your husband may be involved in the kidnapping of a young woman. If you protect him or hinder our investigation, we'll charge you with accessory."

She slammed the door and they heard her footsteps moving away.

"That didn't go well," McCray commented. "Can we believe what she said about Seattle?"

"Maybe. I'll go back to headquarters and start calling airlines. I need you to stay here until Evans relieves you. I told her to be out here by two this morning."

"No problem. I've got my iPod with me. My daughter gave it to me for Christmas. Love the damn thing." Under the porch light, McCray's weather-beaten face looked serene, and Jackson was relieved. He hated making the older man work this late. Although McCray never complained. None of his team did. That's why he chose to work with them again and again.

Back at his desk, Jackson dug out his Vivarin and swallowed one with a long drink of water. He'd started to get sleepy on the drive back, and he couldn't afford that. He wouldn't rest until he had some idea of where to find Elias Goodbe or Danette Blake.

Only five airlines had service out of Eugene. In theory, it wouldn't take long to determine if Goodbe had left town on a plane. If he'd driven to the Portland airport a hundred miles north, there would be many more options. For that matter, Goodbe could have driven to Seattle. Or taken the train to Santa Fe. Or maybe he was pacing his house in the dark trying to figure how to get past the cop parked outside.

Jackson rubbed his eyes and forced himself to focus. He keyed *United Airlines* into Google and quickly found a phone number. Now to convince a low-paid service person to tell him what he needed to know.

After Jackson stated his case, the young female operator said she would help but she insisted on hanging up and calling the department directly to verify he was a police officer. Jackson didn't mind. He respected smart citizens who didn't let themselves get conned. He drummed his desk while he waited for the callback. Only one other detective was still at his desk from the night shift. Michael Quince was also one of his top choices. Jackson considered recruiting him to help make calls, then changed his mind.

In a moment the clerk called back, and Jackson learned United Airlines had not booked a flight for Elias Goodbe for today, tomorrow, or any time in the future.

Four calls and forty minutes later, he knew for certain Goodbe had not booked a flight out of Eugene. His wife had lied. No surprise. Actually, she'd said, "I assume so," when he'd asked about a flight. It was possible Doris didn't know what her husband was up to or exactly where he was.

It occurred to Jackson he might have spooked Goodbe when he'd stopped at the center earlier that day asking questions. *Oh crap.* Was his suspect on his way to the Cayman Islands or some other place where he could assume a new identity, disappear into the population, then pick up where he'd left off? Jackson suspected Goodbe had done that once already when he moved to Eugene. Also the name, Goodbe. The bastard must have gotten a kick out of calling himself that. Or had he really intended to start over and live the good life?

Jackson called the Greyhound station and Amtrak just to cover the bases. Neither had sold Goodbe a ticket recently. Their suspect had packed his car and driven away this evening while they were eating sandwiches and looking at Seth Valder's phone records.

Damn! Jackson smacked his fist against the desktop. In the quiet open space it sounded louder than he'd expected. It also startled Quince, who jumped out of his chair.

"Sorry. Just expressing a little frustration."

Quince, who was ridiculously handsome for a cop, took his hand off his weapon and walked over. "Can I help with anything?"

"Thanks, but I think I'm going home to sleep for a while."

On his way out, Jackson reminded himself that looking at Valder's phone records had led them to Goodbe. He had done everything he could, when he could. He wasn't giving up. In the morning, he would call his contact at the DMV, who worked Saturdays at the branch in the Valley River mall. Once he had Goodbe's vehicles, he'd put out a bulletin for him.

After driving for ten minutes, Jackson realized he was headed toward Kera's instead of Harris Street. Katie was still at Kera's, so there was no reason to go home to his empty house. He needed to wrap his arms around Kera and feel her warm skin on his. He needed to soak in some of her energy and wake up feeling human. Jackson would have liked to make love to her as well, but he was so tired he didn't think he could make it happen.

He would lie there with her and dream about it.

CHAPTER 27

Saturday, April 11, 5:36 a.m.

Jackson woke to the sound of a baby crying and felt disoriented. Where the hell was he? He smelled Kera's fruit-scented hair and remembered coming over. They scurried out of bed simultaneously. Kera grabbed her robe and headed for the crib in the corner, and Jackson grabbed his pants, starting the day feeling guilty. His partners had pulled an overnight surveillance shift while he'd slept with Kera for a few hours. Oh well, he would make Evans take the night off and go on her date with the artist.

As he reached for his shirt, Kera came back with the baby. "It's so good to have you here." She kissed him with Micah squawking in both their ears.

"You know I have to run?"

"Of course." She smiled. "You have a clean shirt in the closet."

Jackson decided to take a quick shower before putting on most of yesterday's clothes. He gulped down a cup of coffee and a piece of toast while Kera gave Micah a bottle.

"Tell me what you know about Danette, please."

Jackson didn't blame her for asking. He trusted Kera more than he'd ever trusted anyone. Still, she wasn't a cop. "This information is completely confidential."

"Of course." Kera nodded and sipped her coffee.

"Courtney Durham paid to have herself kidnapped, just for the thrill. She was seeing the same shrink as Danette. The guy who did the abduction is not very bright and he grabbed Danette by mistake because she had taken Courtney's canceled appointment."

Jackson watched her process the information.

After a moment of stunned silence, Kera said, "Now Courtney is dead and Danette is missing. What happened?"

"That's the part I don't know yet." Jackson hesitated. "I was pretty sure Danette had been murdered just to silence her, but now I have a little hope she might still be alive."

"That would be glorious." Kera bit her lip. "What should I tell Maggie when she calls? She checks in with me every day, asking about the investigation."

"Tell her we found Danette's car and we still hope to find her daughter too."

Kera started to ask another question, but Jackson stood. "I have to get rolling."

"Okay. Go find her."

"Say hi to Katie for me when she gets up. Tell her I'll call her later." Jackson kissed Kera and the baby. "Thanks for letting Katie stay here. Something is going on with Renee, and Katie doesn't seem to want to be over there."

"Do you think Renee's drinking again?"

"Probably." Jackson had been avoiding the thought.

"Poor Katie. It must be hard on her to get her hopes up, then be disappointed again and again."

"It sucks and there's not a damn thing I can do about it."

The early sky was pale blue, and the air smelled of fresh-cut grass. Eugene was warming up for another gorgeous spring day. Jackson wished he could stop and savor the moment. Not this morning.

On the way down the hill, he called Stacy Garrett, a woman who worked for the Department of Motor Vehicles. He'd met her when her brother had been murdered and he'd found and arrested the killer. He knew Stacy wasn't at work yet. Hell, she might not even be up. He checked his cell phone for the time: 6:02. After three rings, he left a message: "Stacy, it's Wade Jackson. Sorry for the wake-up call. I'm looking for a woman who's been kidnapped, and I need you to do me a huge favor. Go into work early and see if you can find Elias Goodbe. I need to know what he's driving ASAP."

As he neared downtown, Jackson called Evans. "Good morning. Everything all right?"

"You sound chipper. Did you get laid?"

"Jesus, Evans. I got some much-needed sleep. I'll send a patrol unit out there so you can go home and do the same."

"What's on the agenda today?"

"Elias Goodbe. I've got a call in to the DMV."

"It's open today?"

"The little office at Valley River Center is."

"Call me when you need me."

While he waited to hear from Stacy, Jackson reworked the warrant for Goodbe, planning to take it to Judge Volcansek, who might be more inclined to sign it. As a woman she might empathize more with an abducted woman's situation. Unless Judge Volcansek also knew Goodbe personally.

Jackson wolfed down a pastry and chugged a tall black coffee. Should he call the judge this early on Saturday? She hadn't
returned his call last night and pissing her off wouldn't work to
his advantage.

Instead, he left a message for Sergeant Lammers, updating
her on the case.

Just as he reached for his desk phone to call the judge, his cell
phone rang.

"It's Stacy Garrett. I've never been to work this early before.
It's kind of weird. The mall cops didn't want to let me in."

"Thanks for doing this. What did you find out?"

"Elias Goodbe has a blue 2005 Chrysler Sebring and a gray
2006 Honda Odyssey. Both cars are registered to him and Doris
Goodbe."

Jackson asked her to repeat the info as he wrote it down.
"Anything interesting in his file?"

"Hmm." There was a pause while she looked. "I don't know if
this is what you mean by interesting, but he also has a boat registered with the state."

"What kind of boat?"

"It's listed as a sixty-foot Altima. I think that's a small yacht."

"That is interesting. Does it say where he keeps it?"

"It's docked at the marina in Florence."

"You don't have a slip number do you?"

"No, you'll have to contact the marina."

"Thank you. You're a lifesaver."

Jackson put out an attempt-to-locate on both vehicles and a
description of Goodbe with instructions to apprehend, then he
called Schak. It took the big man six rings to pick up and grunt
into the phone.

"Ready for a trip to Florence?"

"What's going on?"

"Goodbe didn't get on a plane, train, or bus from Eugene yesterday. At least not using his own name. I found out this morning he owns a boat and keeps it docked at the marina in Florence. So we're going over to check it out."

"Have you called the marina?"

"That's next. I thought I'd give you a few minutes to get ready."

"Will do."

Jackson found the marina's number with a quick Google search. No one answered and there was no option to leave a voice mail. Not surprising. It was early Saturday morning and Florence was a small coastal town with limited resources.

What next? Should he get the Florence police involved? He had so little evidence to go on. If Goodbe was taking a cruise, he was likely leaving this morning. Or had left already.

He googled the Florence police department because it was faster than using the database. When someone finally answered, Jackson identified himself and asked to speak to the highest-ranking person in the office.

"That would be me. In fact, I'm the only person in the office right now."

"Who are you?"

"Officer Janice Miller." She sounded too young to be left alone in a police department.

"I'm trying to locate a man who may have kidnapped a young woman. His name is Elias Goodbe and he has a sixty-foot Altima that may be sitting in your marina. Can you get a uniformed officer over there to look for the boat and stop it if it tries to leave?"

"I'll need a little more information. What slip is it in?"

"I don't know. The marina didn't answer my call this morning." Jackson started for the stairs as he talked.

"What's her name?"

"Who? The missing woman?"

"The boat."

"I don't know that either."

"That'll make it challenging, but I don't suppose there are too many sixty-foot yachts in the harbor, so we'll do our best."

"Please have the uniformed officer call this cell-phone number as soon as he spots the boat."

"Yes, sir."

Schak's face looked puffier than usual, but he was moving with purpose, thermos in hand.

As he climbed into the cruiser, Schak said, "I think Tracy is actually jealous I'm going to the coast with you instead of her. I've been promising her a weekend getaway, but it never seems to happen."

"Gorgeous day for a drive," Jackson said, reaching for his sunglasses. "I hope it's not a colossal waste of time." He thought about asking Schak to drive, then changed his mind. He would put up with the discomfort for an hour. He needed to be in control today.

* * *

Sophie couldn't believe she was tailing a police officer. She'd come down to the department, hoping to catch Jackson and ask him some questions in person. He still owed her a half-day ride-along to go with the brief interview he'd given her. Coming down here had been a long shot, but Jackson was being a little nicer to her these days, so she figured it was worth a try. She hadn't been able to think about anything but the two kidnapped women since Elle Durham had called her the day before. It was such a bizarre case.

Sophie kept coming back to Dr. Stella Callahan and her connection to both Danette and Courtney. She'd called Callahan but hadn't reached her. She'd also considered following the doctor for a while.

This morning, unable to sleep, Sophie had decided to approach Jackson face-to-face and see if he would let her inside this case for her in-depth feature. As she'd pulled into the empty parking lot across from city hall, she'd seen Jackson leaving the underground parking space. She'd followed him on instinct.

She saw him pick up the burly cop while she passed by the house. Now she followed the two of them as they headed out Highway 126. Sophie had no idea where they were going, but it had to be important for them both to be working Saturday morning. She didn't have anything better to do this morning than chase down this bizarre story. The newspaper might be slowly going out of business, but she wasn't giving up on her career yet.

* * *

The streets were nearly deserted, the sun was still low in the horizon, and they sipped their coffee in silence as they drove out of town. Once they passed through Veneta, the road to the coast narrowed and the forest crept in so close he could practically reach out the window and touch it.

Out of nowhere, Schak said, "I looked up that disease online. Retroperitoneal fibrosis. For some people, it's really bad. They have a lot of surgeries, then die anyway."

Jackson had known they would have this conversation sooner or later. He was touched his partner had been concerned enough to do some homework. "The growth is around my aorta but it's only affecting my kidneys. This surgery will take care of it."

"Can it grow into your heart?"

"I've been working this case round the clock since I was diag-
nosed and haven't had time to look into it. If you went online, you
probably know more than I do."

"When is your surgery?"

"Monday."

"Two days from now?"

"Yep. Thank god. These stents are killing me."

"Is that why you keep scowling and standing up?"

Jackson laughed. "Sorry if I've been abrupt or unpleasant."

"Don't worry. You haven't. If it were me, I'd be lying around in
my fatboy chair, making the wife wait on me."

"I'm not that lucky."

Schak was quiet for a moment. "So you're not going to die?"

"Hell no. Not unless I take one of these curves too fast and
put us in the river."

"Not a chance."

Jackson's cell phone rang, so he eased off the gas and popped
in his earpiece before answering it.

"It's Evans. Doris Goodbe just left her house. The officer who
replaced me called and wondered if he should follow her. I said
no, stay with the house. I'm heading out the door now and hope
to pick her up. Was that the right call?"

"Yes. It could be a ruse to pull the watch off the house so
Elias can sneak out. Get on the radio and get some help. Until we
know what's going on, we don't want to lose Doris either." Jackson
turned up the phone's volume to compensate for the traffic noise.
"What's she driving, by the way?"

"A gray Honda Odyssey. Where are you?"

"Schak and I are headed to the coast. I found out from the
DMV that Goodbe has a big boat in Florence. He doesn't have
any travel tickets, so I'm thinking he may plan on slipping out
by sea."

"A boat, huh? Do you suppose he's running drugs?"

"No clue."

"How long do you want me to stay on Doris Goodbe?"

"Long enough for McCray to relieve you. I reworked the Goodbe subpoena and it's on my desk. Take it to Judge Volcansek and play on her female sympathies. Tell her about Valder's pornography setup. Express your concern for what could be happening to Danette and get her to sign it."

"I'm on it. Keep me posted."

"Later."

As Jackson hung up, Schak asked, "What's going on?"

"Doris Goodbe left the house." Jackson talked without turning to look at Schak; they were about to enter a tunnel. "If Doris is driving the Honda, we should probably look for the blue Chrysler Sebring."

"What else should I know?"

"That's it. Goodbe's life seems to have started here in Eugene in 1996. He has the import business and runs the outreach center next to it. Goodbe is probably an alias, and I can't wait to run his prints through—"

The ring of his cell phone cut him off and Jackson answered it.

"Officer Miller with the Florence Police Department. I sent a uniform down to the marina, and he thinks he may have spotted your Altima. There's a white sixty-footer called *Sweet New Hope* in slot fifty-three."

"Great. Is the officer watching the boat?"

"Yes. He's in the parking lot, and he'll keep me informed."

"Give him my cell number and have him call me directly. Please."

"Yes, sir."

Jackson relayed the information to Schak and willed himself to relax. Just because Goodbe had a boat and they had located it didn't mean the suspect would be there. It was more likely he'd driven his car to Seattle. Or Mexico.

Still, he kept pushing their speed despite the increase in traffic as they neared the coastal town. At least the road had straightened out again.

"Do we have a plan if we find him on the boat?" Schak tensed as Jackson passed an old man in a truck.

"Cuff him and bring him in for questioning."

"You have your taser, right?"

"Always."

"Do we know if Goodbe owns weapons?"

"They're not registered if he does. I don't expect a confrontation," Jackson said, trying to reassure both of them. "We'll be prepared for one anyway."

"I gotta quit drinking so much coffee," Schak said, rubbing his chest a little. "It's giving me heartburn."

Jackson's cell phone rang again and he answered, thinking it would be the Florence police.

It was Elle Durham. "Detective Jackson?" She sounded slurred and weepy.

"Elle, I'm right in the middle of something important. I'll call you back later."

"Is it about Courtney? Are you going to get the bastard who killed her?"

Jackson didn't know what to say. Goodbe probably had nothing to do with Courtney, and Courtney might not have been murdered. "I'm doing everything I can. The pathologist's report was inconclusive, but we're still waiting on toxicology."

"Tox-i-col-ogy?" She spoke slowly, as if she had difficulty forming the syllables.

"Are you all right, Elle?" Jackson was thinking he might ask Stella Callahan to counsel the grieving woman.

She let out a gurgled sound. "No, I'm not all right. My husband is dead, my oldest daughter is dead, and I'm dying too."

Jackson slowed his speed. "What are you saying?"

"I have kidney cancer."

"I'm so sorry. I'll do everything I can to resolve Courtney's case as quickly as I can."

"I don't have much time left."

"I'm sorry. I'll be in touch." Jackson clicked off the phone, feeling like a shit. But they were coming into Florence and he had to focus.

"What was that about?"

"Elle Durham is dying of kidney cancer. She wants me to give her closure on Courtney's death."

"Poor woman."

"I know. What a way to spend your last few days on earth, grieving for your child."

"What about the poor sister? What's her name?"

"Brooke. No kidding. Once Elle's gone, she'll have lost her whole family."

They were quiet as they pulled up at the stoplight that signaled the entry to Florence. Jackson again thought of calling Stella Callahan and asking her to get involved. Or maybe Brooke would need someone who specialized in grief counseling. He had to stop thinking about the Durhams. Elias Goodbe was his focus now.

They turned left and headed for the marina. Jackson noticed the blue sky had disappeared, replaced with a thick wet fog. Maybe that was why Goodbe's boat was still in the dock.

"I don't know a damn thing about boats," he realized out loud. "I mean the big ones that go out on the ocean."

"Me neither."

They knew where to find the marina, though, also known as the Port of Siuslaw. Normally, from the turn near the bridge, you could see the docks extending into the bay and the pretty white boats all lined up along the wooden planks. Not today. They drove down through Old Town Florence, where a few shops were just starting to open for the early tourists and breakfast seekers. The fog had kept people home, and the sidewalks were deserted. Jackson smelled the salty tang of the bay before he saw it.

They spotted the Florence patrol unit in the parking lot to the left, and Jackson parked nearby. They hopped out of their cruiser and the officer did the same.

"You must be Jackson. I'm Officer Roy Patroni." His face looked ready to retire, but his conditioned body looked ready for anything.

They shook hands as a strong cold breeze came out of nowhere.

Patroni turned to face the marina, pointing to a large white boat near the end of the first dock. "That's the *Sweet New Hope*, but I haven't seen any movement on the vessel since I've been here."

"Thanks. Will you stay and watch from this vantage point? We don't expect trouble, but I need you here to call for backup if anything gets weird."

"I'm your man. Can you tell me what this is about?"

"A missing young woman and a businessman who is not what he appears to be."

"You think the woman is on the boat?"

Jackson had tried not to let himself hope for that, but the scenario had flashed through his mind a few times. "She could be."

"Better go get her."

Jackson jogged toward the steps leading down to the water, breathing in a mix of seaweed and diesel. Behind him, Schak kept up but his breath was ragged. Instinctively, Jackson touched the Sig Sauer at his waist, then felt for the taser as he pounded down the steps. Goodbe was an unknown quantity. Just because he dressed in a business suit and ran a charity didn't mean he wasn't capable of violence. Almost everyone was capable of violence, especially if their freedom was at stake.

The dock swayed under them as they trotted toward the end. By the time they reached slot fifty-three, droplets of fog dampened Jackson's face, and his chest was wet with sweat. A big engine kicked to life on the next dock over, making Jackson jump a little. The *Sweet New Hope* was deathly still. Was no one here? Had he wasted their time?

With a glance back at Schak, Jackson stepped up on the narrow ramp connecting the dock to the ship. At the top, he reached over the three-foot wall of the boat to feel for the latch. As the entry swung open, it made a loud creaking noise. Jackson paused, waiting to see if the sound would bring someone out of the boat's interior.

Still and silent.

It occurred to him he needed a warrant to board the boat, but he couldn't make himself stop or call out. Danette's life could be at stake.

Jackson crossed the deck with Schak's labored breath right behind him. Weapon in his right hand, he reached for the doorknob with his left. It turned easily. Jackson's heart rate quickened. If the door was unlocked, someone was probably on the vessel. No one would leave his boat open for vagabonds to take up residence in. If Goodbe wasn't here, he was in the marina area. Maybe he'd gone to the little shop for supplies.

They entered the yacht's main living area, which reeked of polishing oil, stale smoke, and spilled bourbon. Jackson glanced around and spotted a woman's white jacket on one of the low-slung couches.

Out of nowhere Goodbe's head and chest appeared on Jackson's left, followed by the rest of his body as he climbed the stairs from the lower part of the ship. Jackson's Sig Sauer came up, aimed at Goodbe's chest.

"What are you doing here and why do you have a gun pointed at me?" Goodbe tried to sound calm and civil while taking rapid breaths. He looked ready for a sea cruise in his jeans and white sweater, but his feet were bare.

"Keep your hands in front of you." Jackson stepped toward Goodbe. "We need to question you about a crime, and we're taking you to police headquarters in Eugene."

"I'm happy to talk with you, but the guns and theatrics aren't necessary." Goodbe gave them a forced half smile. "I'd like to drive my own car back to Eugene, with you following, of course."

Schak moved up next to Jackson, gun drawn. Jackson motioned with his weapon at an area of open wall and said, "Step up to the wall, put your hands on it, and spread your legs wide." He reached to his inside pocket for handcuffs.

"That's really not necessary." Goodbe didn't move.

"This is not open for discussion."

"Do you have a warrant to be on this boat?"

"Move!" Jackson's stent pressure was intense and his patience was gone. He holstered his weapon so he could manipulate Goodbe into the cuffs, while Schak had him covered.

"What's going on?"

A female voice emerged from the stairwell, but the woman was behind Goodbe and Jackson couldn't see her yet.

Schak made a strange noise. Jackson glanced sideways.

His partner's eyes were wide, his face flushed bright red, and his weapon shook in his hands.

Oh shit.

CHAPTER 28

As Goodbe started toward the wall, Schak made a moaning, strangling sound.

The woman emerged from the stairwell. She was young and pretty and wearing the same jeans-and-white-sweater getup as Goodbe. "You again," she said with a sneer.

It was Brooke Durham.

Before Jackson could process what she was doing here, he felt, rather than saw, Schak go down. As his partner hit the floor, Schak's weapon shot out of his hand and slid across the smooth wood planks.

For a surreal moment, they all froze in place.

Brooke lunged for the gun. A split second later, Jackson lunged for Brooke.

He rammed her shoulder with his knee and managed to send her sprawling just as she clutched the gun in her hand. Before she could make a move, Jackson lurched forward again and stomped down on her wrist.

"Oww! You fucker!"

Jackson squatted and pried the weapon from her hand. Once he had it, he looked up to see if Goodbe was barreling down on him.

Goodbe was not in sight and Schak lay unmoving on the floor.

Jackson shoved the weapon in the back of his pants, pivoted, and dropped one knee on Brooke's back. He cuffed her as she stopped struggling and began to sob.

Jackson took stock of the situation. He had the wrong person in custody, his suspect was on the move, and his partner lay dead or dying. Jackson fumbled for his cell phone as he rushed over to Schak. He pressed redial, knowing the call would go to the Florence dispatcher.

"Florence Police."

"Officer down. I need an ambulance and backup now. Get every available unit down to the marina. My suspect is on the run. Male, late fifties, gray hair, six foot one, and lean build. Wearing jeans and a white sweater. Call for the ambulance first. I think my partner had a heart attack. We're on the *Sweet New Hope* in slot fifty-three." Jackson hung up before she could ask questions.

Keeping one eye on Brooke, Jackson knelt down and pressed two fingers against Schak's throat.

He felt nothing.

He pulled Schak's arms to his sides and rolled his partner over on his back. Schak's eyes were closed, his face had lost the red flush, and his chest did not move with the comforting rhythm of life.

Shit. Shit. Shit. What to do first? Lungs or heart? He'd taken a CPR class years ago, but his brain wouldn't locate and recall the information.

Jackson began compressions, thinking he had to rotate and do both. The number thirty popped into his head. Thirty compressions, then mouth-to-mouth, was that it?

"Come on, Schak," Jackson said softly as he worked the man's heart.

Every few pushes, he glanced over at the woman in handcuffs. Brooke now sat cross-legged on the floor, hands cuffed behind her back, silently watching him. After thirty compressions, Jackson scooted left and arched Schak's head so his chin jutted in the air. *Pinch the nose*, he remembered. Jackson breathed into his partner's mouth, counted to three, then breathed again.

Back to compressions. He had no idea if the pattern was right, but he stayed with it. "Come on Schak, you gotta fight for it."

Time stood still. Only the sound of seagulls broke through, reminding him life went on around him.

"You're pounding a dead man," Brooke called out after what seemed like forever.

Jackson ignored her and continued pressing with the heel of his palm.

Finally, the sweet sound of sirens filled the air. *Thank god.* Tears built up behind his eyes. Jackson kept compressing.

A officer came through the door first with her weapon drawn.

"Get this suspect into the back of a locked patrol unit and direct the medics down here," Jackson called out, nodding toward Brooke.

The young officer moved quickly without asking questions and pushed Brooke toward door.

A moment later, two paramedics burst through the door carrying a portable defibrillator. Jackson got out of their way. One of the men ripped open Schak's button-up shirt and pressed the paddles to his chest.

Nobody bothered to yell *clear*.

After the third shock, the medic with the paddles said, "We have a pulse."

A surge of joy flushed through Jackson's chest. The medics lifted Schak from the floor to the carry gurney and started out.

"Where are you taking him?"

"Peace Harbor Hospital, unless they tell us otherwise."

The door slammed closed and Jackson's shoulders unclenched. He wanted to follow them out. He was desperate to get off this hateful boat and anxious to join the search for Goodbe. He needed another minute though. His job here wasn't done.

He headed for the stairwell leading to the lower part of the boat. Brooke's presence here, presumably as Goodbe's lover, left Jackson with little hope of finding Danette. Still, he had to search the ship. There could be a massive shipment of illegal firearms in the cargo hold for all he knew.

Brooke Durham as Goodbe's lover. Jackson tried to make sense of the connection. Goodbe was at least thirty years older than Brook, but Elle Durham knew Elias Goodbe and made contributions to the outreach center. Had Brooke met Goodbe at the center? Had Elle unknowingly introduced her daughter to a predator? Jackson still didn't know what Goodbe was or how he figured into any of this mess.

At the bottom of the stairs was a skinny hallway. To the left, a door stood open and Jackson entered a low-ceilinged bedroom suite. An unmade bed took up much of the space. A narrow door in the corner indicated the presence of a bathroom. Jackson's kidneys responded with urgency. He ignored them and forced himself to keep looking. He glanced into the bathroom, opened a tall wardrobe, and finally stepped back out into the hall.

The second door was locked. Jackson tried his handy credit-card trick, but it didn't work. This room was locked with a key from the outside, instead of from a latch on the inside.

Could he bust the door open? It was much harder than they made it seem in the movies. He needed a sledgehammer. The pressure in his kidneys became unbearable. He bolted for the master bathroom and relieved himself.

He started to make a call to the Florence dispatcher, stopped, clicked the phone shut. On the wall next to the toilet was a seven-foot mirror that reached to the floor. A mirror the size and shape of a door.

Jackson grabbed the edge and tugged. Nothing happened. He tried the other side, and the mirror opened like a medicine cabinet. A dark entry loomed. Jackson automatically pulled his weapon. With his free hand, he felt along the edge of the wall for a light switch. He found one, flipped it, and a dull yellow light filled the next room. Jackson stepped through the opening into a musty ten-by-ten space. A bunk bed against the wall held a person on each mattress. As he rushed forward, it became obvious they were women, each strapped to the bed frame and unconscious.

Jackson holstered his gun, pulled out his cell phone, and hit redial.

"I need another ambulance. I'm still on the boat, and I've got two unconscious women."

"Good Lord. Are they wounded?"

Jackson leaned over the woman on the bottom mattress. Danette's eyes were closed and her face looked thin, but she was breathing. Dressed in gray sweatpants and a T-shirt, she had no apparent wounds.

"I think they might only be drugged."

"Another ambulance will be there shortly."

Jackson clicked off the phone and began to release Danette's bindings. In his mind, he saw the joy on Kera's face when she heard the news.

CHAPTER 29

Danette gained consciousness as paramedics rolled her through the parking lot to the ambulance. She sat up, saw Jackson walking alongside, and began to cry. The medics stopped, ready to respond to her needs.

"Jackson, you found me. Thank god. How is Micah?" Danette wept so hard she could barely get the words out.

Jackson put an arm around her and squeezed. "Your baby's fine. Kera's taking good care of him. You're safe now too."

"I thought I would never see him again."

"You'll see him soon."

"I want to go home." Danette swung her feet down to the wet asphalt and stood up.

One of the medics stepped toward her, ready to catch her if she fell. "You should go to the hospital and get checked out. You're dehydrated."

"I'll drink some water."

The other medic, a woman, said, "If you were assaulted, it's important to be examined."

"I wasn't." Danette turned to Jackson. "Can I ride with you?"

"Of course." Jackson understood her need to get home to her family. Kera was a nurse; she'd take good care of Danette. "Bring the blanket with you."

After helping Danette get settled in the front of his car, Jackson jogged over to the officer who had Brooke in the back of her unit. It would be a little odd to transport a victim in the front seat and a suspect in the back, but it would not be the first time.

"Thanks. I'll take her from here."

The officer popped the locks. Jackson opened the door, stepped back. After Brooke's sudden move on Schak's gun, he was prepared for anything from her. The young woman was subdued as Jackson walked her to the car, hands still cuffed behind her back.

They reached the cruiser and Jackson opened the back door.

"Who is that?" Brooke stared at Danette through the plexiglass that separated the seat compartments.

Jackson nudged her into the vehicle and locked the back doors. *Did she really not know?*

As Jackson pulled out of the marina, he felt a surge of relief. He couldn't believe he was headed home with Danette. He wished he had Goodbe in custody too, but given a choice, this was a better outcome. Schak would pull through. He had to.

Three blocks away, an ambulance and a patrol car blocked a side street. Jackson glanced over and saw a dark-green Scion and next to it a small redheaded woman talking to a police officer. *Was that Sophie Speranza?*

Jackson yanked the cruiser off the street and into a no-parking zone. "Sorry, Danette, but I have to check this out. It'll only take a moment."

He jogged up to the scene as paramedics lifted a man from the pavement onto a gurney. The injured man was wearing jeans and a white sweater. Ignoring the officer who yelled at him to stay back, Jackson rushed up.

Elias Goodbe was unconscious and bleeding from a serious leg injury.

Jackson spun around to the officer who was now right behind him. "I'm with the Eugene Police. This injured man is under arrest for kidnapping. I want him strapped down and a police officer by his side. I want him taken to North McKenzie Hospital in Eugene."

One of the paramedics argued, "Peace Harbor is closer. He needs immediate medical attention."

"Give it to him on the way there. I want him in Eugene."

Jackson looked over to see Sophie standing next to his cruiser. He ran toward her. Danette was not ready for a reporter.

Sophie was just observing and taking notes.

He resisted the urge to grab her arm and spin her away. Instead he stepped between her and the car. Sophie looked a little sheepish, an expression he'd never seen on her before.

"What the hell are you doing here?"

"Following a story. I got a tip this morning."

"You followed me here?"

"I said I got a tip. Don't be mad. I helped you get the bad guy."

"You chased him?"

"I saw him run from the marina with a cop after him, so I followed the action. Then I lost everybody, so I was headed back. As I came around a corner, this guy darted out in front of my car and I couldn't stop in time." Sophie shrugged and gave him the tiniest wink.

Jackson was speechless. Her audacity was unlimited, and her knack for getting to the heart of a case was impressive. It almost shamed him. "Go home, Sophie."

"We'll talk later." She turned, notepad in hand, and trotted back to her car.

Jackson checked to make sure Goodbe was under a watchful eye, then climbed into his cruiser.

For the first few minutes on the road, Jackson kept glancing in the rearview mirror at Brooke. She was locked in a confined space and handcuffed, but he was still a little worried. He had no idea what her role was in any of this, and he suspected she might be just another of Goodbe's victims. Still, Brooke had gone for the gun, forcing him to respond and let Goodbe get away. Would she have shot him to protect her lover? Or had the move just been a diversion?

Jackson kept glancing over at Danette too. She was curled up under the blanket and seemed to be praying. The traffic was heavier now than it had been this morning, and he tried to stay focused on driving. He hoped she would tell him something before he dropped her off at Kera's. Eventually Danette would have to come into the department and make a statement, but he would give her some time.

"I'm going to call Kera and tell her you're okay. Do you want to talk to her?"

"Yes."

Once he had Kera on the phone, Jackson's throat felt tight and he struggled for the right words. Finally, he said, "I have a surprise for you." He handed the phone to Danette. It was cowardly, he knew, but he was afraid Kera would start crying, and he couldn't handle that right now. He had almost lost it over Schak this morning and he couldn't afford to be emotional. Too many questions were still unanswered. Such as who was the other young woman he'd found on the boat? Jackson had taken her picture before she was loaded into the ambulance, and he had to get that photo to the media to help identify her. He had to hear these young women's stories.

Danette's conversation with Kera was short, then she handed him the phone. "Me again," he said. "I love you and I'll see you in a while."

Danette was sitting up now, looking more alert. Finally she said, "They kidnapped me by accident. I heard the big guy scream at the little guy and call him an idiot. Can you believe that? It was all a mistake." Her voice shook.

"I actually figured that part out, but I don't understand why they kept you. Do you know?"

"The big guy sold me. I was drugged most of the time, but I remember that. The buyer talked about me like I wasn't even a person." Danette choked up and had to pause. "Then he moved me to another basement and kept drugging me. I kept thinking I'd heard his voice before, but I don't know where. Eventually, I ended up on the boat with the other woman. She said we were sold as sex slaves to someone in the Netherlands. I think we were on our way to Seattle."

"Do you know the other woman?"

"I saw her at the outreach center once. Her name is Marcella. We didn't get many chances to talk." Danette closed her eyes. "How did you find me?"

Jackson didn't want to tell her about Courtney yet. "We figured out who they were supposed to kidnap and why. That led us to Seth Valder. He's the big guy and owns the first place you were taken. His phone records led us to Elias Goodbe. When we learned Goodbe had a boat in Florence, we decided to check it out."

"Mr. Goodbe! I knew I'd heard that voice somewhere." Danette looked devastated. "He runs a charity. Is that the whole point of it? To find women to sell?"

"We just started investigating him."

Danette reached over and squeezed his arm. "I can't ever thank you enough. My life would have become a nightmare. Once you're in a situation like that, in a foreign country, how do you get out? How do you get home without ID or money?" She shuddered. "I'm not the first, am I? This has happened to other women. They're living that nightmare."

Jackson struggled to find something comforting to say. "We'll find out who you were sold to. We'll shut this operation down."

"Good. That bastard. Pretending to help young women so he could grab them and sell them into a life of hell. For money!" Danette started to cry again, but Jackson couldn't comfort her. He realized she would need some counseling. She might never fully get over this.

After a while, Danette dozed off. He checked on Brooke. She was lying down on the seat, but her eyes were open. Jackson called Evans and filled her in.

Kera ran out to the car, and Katie followed with Micah. Jackson was relieved. He couldn't leave Brooke alone in the back even for a moment. Kera embraced Danette as she climbed out of the car, and the two women cried as they hugged. Jackson rolled down his window, and Katie leaned in and gave him a kiss, still holding Micah.

"I'm so proud of you."

Danette came around the car and took Micah in her arms, silent tears streaming down her face. Jackson wanted to get going before he got caught up in the emotion. He knew Kera needed more, so he got out of the car. She hugged him like he'd been gone for a month.

"Thank you," she whispered against his face.

"My pleasure," Jackson whispered back. "I have to go. I have a suspect in custody."

"I know."

He finally drove off, watching his family embrace in the rearview mirror. Brooke moved and blocked his view. She was mouthing something at him, so he reached back and slid the glass open a little.

"I want to stop and see my mother for a moment before you take me to jail. It's important."

"Sorry. It's not on the agenda."

"She's dying, you know. She could die today and I want a chance to say good-bye."

Jackson gave it some thought. Was Elle that close to death? She had sounded weak when she'd called him that morning, but he hated to be played. "I don't trust you."

"Look, I'll tell you everything, but only if you let me see my mother first."

A full confession? To what? Did Brooke know about Goodbe's sex-slave business? "Will you tell me about the women on the boat?"

"Only if you take me to my mother's first. Please. She's dying. Have a heart." Brooke sounded near tears.

Jackson pulled over, put the car in park, and turned to face her. "Why were you on a boat at the coast with Elias Goodbe instead of at home with your mother?"

"I was running. I thought I couldn't face watching her die." Brooke's eyes pleaded with him. "I love her and I need to tell her."

Jackson decided there was little harm in a five-minute stop. He would do it more for Elle than for Brooke.

The house loomed large as ever, but the wealth it represented no longer made Jackson feel inadequate. The Durhams' money hadn't helped them in the long run. They were still human and still vulnerable to disease and death. He wondered if the money had made the daughters even more vulnerable.

"Hey, my arms hurt," Brooke said, as she climbed from the backseat. "Will you at least move the cuffs to the front so I can change positions?" It was a reasonable request. Most suspects had a much shorter ride to custody than the sixty-mile trip Brooke had experienced. Jackson uncuffed one wrist, spun her around, and quickly recuffed her in the front.

"Thanks. It will still be weird for Mom to see me like this."

Jackson kept Brooke in front of him, and she was able to open the front door and lead them in. The housekeeper was nowhere in sight.

"Mom's probably in bed," Brooke said, heading down the hallway.

Jackson followed, realizing for the first time since Elle had told him she was dying that Brooke would inherit this house, and all the property they owned around town, and all the money in the bank. Depending on what she was convicted of, Brooke was likely to have most of her life to enjoy it.

They entered the largest master bedroom Jackson had ever been in. The suite of connected sitting areas was decorated in beige and peach like Elle's office. Elle Durham seemed tragically tiny in the oversized bed in the oversized room.

"Mom, it's Brooke. Wake up for a minute." With her cuffed hands, Brooke gently nudged her mother's shoulder.

Elle opened her eyes. "Brooke, dear, you're back early. I'm so glad."

"I had to see you. How is the pain today?"

"The same, but more."

Jackson shifted, feeling like an intruder.

Brooke turned to him, and before she could ask, he said, "I'll give you a little privacy." He moved back about ten feet, still blocking the only entrance to the area. Brooke wasn't going anywhere without him.

It wasn't easy to offer comfort with her wrists cuffed, but Brooke tried. She stroked her mother's hair and handed her a glass of water. After a minute, Brooke began to cry. Jackson thought maybe he'd done the right thing in letting her come here. Losing a parent at twenty was a shock to the system, like having your roots yanked out of the ground. Jackson had never had that chance to say good-bye to his folks. He'd learned from his supervisor at work that their names were on a crime report and he would never see them again.

He watched as Brooke leaned over and hugged her mother. He wanted to believe she hadn't known about the captive women in the bowels of the yacht, but it seemed unlikely. What had Brooke been doing with Goodbe? Looking for Daddy love? Either way, they would have a hard time prosecuting her as an accomplice unless Goodbe turned against her. He remembered Goodbe was in the hospital. So was Schak. Was it time to call and ask how his partner was doing?

Jackson moved toward Brooke. "Let's go."

She gave her mother a final kiss, then slipped away from the bed.

At the department, Jackson put Brooke in the interrogation room. He went to his desk to call the Florence hospital. He learned Schak was still in critical condition.

He jumped up as Evans approached his desk. "I got the warrant," she said, waving the thick stack of papers. Then she frowned. "What do you hear about Schak?"

"Still critical."

"I hate it that he's in Florence."

"We'll go see him tomorrow. Right now, we have a suspect to interrogate."

"Let's do it."

Brooke, being young, female, and well-groomed, seemed out of place in the dingy room. The women who ended up here had usually lived much harder lives. Brooke also seemed strangely serene. She smiled softly as they sat across from her.

"This interview is being recorded," Jackson said, getting the legalities out of the way. "State your name, please."

"Brooke Ashley Durham." Jackson studied her face. She had the same features as Courtney, only subtly bigger. Her cheeks were wider, her nose a little longer, her chin a little more pronounced. She was still attractive, but not in the head-turning way Courtney had been. He felt guilty for comparing them. Brooke had probably spent her whole life feeling like the not-so-pretty sister.

"I'm Detective Jackson and this is Detective Evans. What were you doing on that boat this morning?"

"Having sex; right up until you showed up, that is." She grinned, amused at herself.

"How long has Elias Goodbe been your lover?"

"About eight months."

"Why did you help him hold those women hostage?"

She stopped smiling. "I really don't know what you're talking about."

"There were two women in a small room downstairs in the boat. They were drugged and bound."

"I didn't know." Her eyes flashed with anger. "The bastard!"

"In the car, you said you'd tell me all about them."

"I just wanted to go see my mom. I didn't know about the women, I swear. Did Elias kidnap them?" She looked puzzled and hurt.

"What do you know about Elias Goodbe?"

"Apparently, not much."

Evans spoke up. "You'll likely be charged with accessory to kidnapping unless you tell us what you know about Goodbe's sex-slave operation."

"I don't care what you charge me with. I don't know about any sex slaves. I mean, I knew Elias financed local porno films, but that's legal as far as I know."

"Do you know Seth Valder?"

"Nope."

"How did you meet Goodbe?"

"At the center. I volunteered there for a while to make my mother happy."

Jackson was impatient. "You said you would tell me everything. Remember?"

"I will. You're just not asking the right questions."

Evans leaned in. "Did Goodbe know Courtney?"

Brooke winked at her. "Of course, the woman gets it."

Jackson's brain spun, trying to make the connections. He'd been seeing Goodbe as an opportunist who took Danette off Valder's hands, thinking he could make some easy money. Was Goodbe involved with Courtney too?

Brooke looked at Evans. "He wasn't fucking her if that's what you're asking. Not that Courtney didn't try. I mean, once she knew Elias and I were lovers, she made a play for him, but it was too late."

"How did you feel about that? Courtney going after your guy?" Evans kept up the questions while Jackson reeled.

Brooke gave a little shrug. "I'm used to it. But Elias didn't go for it. Courtney repulsed him."

It hit Jackson like a baseball bat to the chest. Brooke was intensely jealous of her sister and repulsed at the same time. *How deep was the resentment?*

"Where were you the night Courtney died?"

"Home, with Mom." She waited, then said, "For a while."

"Then what happened?"

"I got a text from Courtney asking me to pick her up. Her stupid little kidnapping adventure was over and Brett had refused to play taxi."

"You knew about the kidnapping in advance?"

"Of course. I'm the one who told her about ThrillSeekers." A small smile played on Brooke's lips.

"Where did you hear about them?" Jackson was laying the foundation for what was coming next. It felt like a freight train shaking the ground, even though he couldn't see all of it yet.

"Elias, of course. He's very well connected in a variety of circles. My mother only knew of the one though." Brooke's tone was so flat and serene it was unnerving.

"Why would you tell Courtney about a company like ThrillSeekers?"

"It was fun to watch her bounce from one freaky thing to another. She was so easy to manipulate. It was a like a game for me."

"Did you expect Courtney to get hurt during the kidnapping?"

"It was certainly a possibility." Brooke smiled slyly, and Jackson felt a shiver of disgust.

"After Courtney texted you, you went to pick her up, didn't you?"

"Of course."

"Tell us what happened."

"I'd like some water first, please."

Evans moved without being asked. While she was gone, Jackson said, "Did Elias Goodbe ever discuss Danette Blake with you?"

"No."

"What about someone named Marcella?"

"No. Listen." Brooke shifted forward, a little more intent. "I didn't know he was holding women on the boat. It disgusts me, and I would never participate in forcing other women into sexual slavery. I'm a mess, I know that, but I'm not a sociopath, and I'm not heartless." She flopped back. "I can't believe I fell for someone who would do something like that."

At the end of her spiel, Jackson thought her words had begun to slow a little. She was probably exhausted.

Evans came back with a paper cup of water and set it down in front of Brooke. With one of her cuffed hands, Brooke reached for the water. Both hands came up together as she took a long drink. She set the cup down slowly.

"Where were we?" Brooke stared straight at Jackson.

"You were going to tell us what happened when you went down to pick up Courtney."

"When I got there, she was having trouble breathing. She gets like that when she goes outside sometimes." Brooke's eyes shifted away. "It was hard to see her like that. I mean, I knew it would happen, but still, to stand there and watch."

"How did you know it would happen?"

A sad little smile. "I emptied her inhaler."

Jesus. What was wrong with these Durham girls?

"You wanted her to have an asthma attack?" Evans was surprised and forgot to hide it.

"Oh, come on." Brooke rolled her eyes. "That's why we're here, right?"

There was a moment of silence, and a creepy dread filled Jackson's stomach. *Dear god. Brooke had murdered her sister.*

Brooke kept talking, her voice flat. "I loved Courtney. And I hated Courtney. She got all the attention, yet she still had to steal my boyfriends. She also broke my mother's heart over and over. Courtney was so selfish."

"Tell us what happened that night."

"She was having a serious asthma attack, but she wouldn't die. Courtney started walking for the car, carrying that empty inhaler and gasping like an old emphysema patient in her last throes." Brooke gave her head a little shake, as if to ward off sleepiness. "I really hoped I wouldn't have to get involved, but it was taking too long. So I came up behind her, put my hands over the little love bruises Brett left on her neck, and squeezed. She went down fast after that."

Jackson struggled to keep his voice neutral. "What happened next?"

"I took her cell phone so no one would know she texted me. Then I drove away and tossed it in a dumpster." Brooke's speech seemed slower, more slurred than before.

Oh shit. "Brooke, did you take something when you were in your mother's room?"

"I'm just tired. So let's finish up."

Jackson didn't believe her. "What did you take?"

"One little pain pill. To make this easier. Can you blame me? What else do you want to know?"

Jackson wanted to hear every piece of her confession, but what was the protocol here? For one little pain pill, there was nothing he could or should do. She was not the first suspect to come into this room under the influence.

"Did you plan to kill Courtney when you emptied her inhaler?" Evans asked, filling the silence.

"Of course." Brooke sighed. "It was Elias' idea. As soon as he heard my mother was dying, he started thinking about the money. We all did. Courtney would have wasted her half of it." Brooke's head fell forward, but she caught herself and pulled back. "I didn't know until I got down there if I could go through with it. But I did." Brooke closed her eyes. "Now I'm sorry 'cause I've got no one left."

"Brooke!" Jackson raised his voice.

She popped her eyes back open. "I'm fine. I want to tell you about Daddy too."

"Your father? Dean Durham?"

"I killed him, you know."

Jackson's heart missed a beat. He'd been so clueless. He glanced up at the camera, grateful the city had finally approved the expenditure. "You took more than one pill, didn't you?"

She gave him a sloppy smile, like only a drunk or a druggie could. "Yep."

"What was it and how many did you take?"

Brooke struggled to get the words out. "Ox-y-contin. I took three at home. And…three more…here."

Jackson leapt up. "Call an ambulance."

He rushed around the table as Evans dialed 911. Jackson grabbed Brooke by the hair and tried to get his hand into her mouth. He thought he would stick a finger down her throat and make her puke. He didn't know what else to do.

Brooke bit him hard and he instinctively pulled his hand back. "Help me hold her mouth open."

"Daddy…molested…us. For years. Courtney…and…me." Brooke was still trying to get everything said. "No…one…ever…knew."

Evans rushed to their side of the table. "That'll never work. We just have to keep her up and moving until the paramedics get here." She put her arm around Brooke's shoulder.

Jackson took the other side. "We might as well walk her out to the street."

They shuffled down the hall, through the empty detectives' area, and toward the front.

"Need any help?" the desk officer called out as they passed.

"Not unless you've got a stomach pump."

Out the door and down the covered walkway. On a Saturday, city hall was quiet and no one was around to witness the drama. At intervals, Jackson grabbed Brooke's chin and shook her head, trying to keep her conscious. It was a losing battle. By the time the ambulance pulled up in front of the wide cement stairs, Brooke was no longer breathing.

CHAPTER 30

A quiche-and-fried-sausage aroma filled the air. Jackson's stomach growled as he kissed Kera in the kitchen and held her close. "Oh man, that smells good. I feel like I haven't eaten in days."

The night before, he'd gone from the hospital to Elle Durham's house to tell her about Brooke's suicide. He'd found Elle dead too. Jackson had come home to Kera's, drunk a beer, then crawled into bed and slept like the dead for twelve hours.

This morning he'd woken to the sound of women laughing in the kitchen. A joyful noise that filled his heavy heart. He'd stayed in bed, listening for as long as he could. The smell of coffee and sausage had finally driven him into the kitchen. This would be his last meal before his surgery the next morning.

"I've missed you," Kera whispered.

Jackson squeezed her again, too choked up to speak. It was so easy to lose people. Often without any warning. "The best thing about this surgery is that I'll get to see you every day for a while."

Kera stepped back and put her hands on her hips. "Are you and Katie going to stay here with me, or do I have run back and forth for three weeks?"

Jackson poured himself a cup of coffee. Kera sat, waiting for an answer. "Don't tell me you don't need my help."

"I won't need help for that long, but it would be easier for Katie if you stayed with us." Jackson looked around. He could smell the food but couldn't see it. Maybe it was in the oven staying warm.

Katie stuck her head into the kitchen. "Morning, Dad. It's about time." To Kera, she said, "Where are Danette and the baby?"

"In the guest bedroom getting changed."

His daughter grabbed a cinnamon roll off the counter. "I wouldn't mind staying here. I've been here since Thursday already." Katie popped back out of the kitchen.

Kera and Jackson stared at each other in disbelief. "That's quite a change of heart," Kera said, stepping in close.

"Maybe we should move in together." It came out in an unplanned rush.

Kera chewed her lip.

"Forget it. I'm rushing this. I'm sorry."

"No. Don't be." She kissed him on the mouth. "I've wanted you to move in here since our second date. It's just that I told Danette she could stay with me. I don't want her to go back to that duplex and be alone. Not yet. Not after what she's been through. Her mother can't handle having the baby around all the time, so Danette can't go back to Corvallis."

"You're a wonderful person." Jackson loved her generosity. The two of them would get their time together eventually.

"I'm not saying you can't move in too. I just wanted you to know that it will be a full house." Kera grinned. "It could be fun."

"Let's see how it goes. Still up for our trip to Florence this afternoon?" They were planning to see Schak, who was out of intensive care, still weak but recovering from his heart attack.

"Oh yes. I've reserved a hotel room for afterward." She lowered her voice to a whisper. "You and I are going to be naked and alone for an hour while we have a chance. I'm already deprived, and once you have surgery…"

"I like the way you think."

Jackson's cell phone rang and he silently cursed it. "I have to get this."

Kera made a face and left the kitchen so he could talk in private.

He flipped open the phone. It was Evans. "What have you got?"

"Two things. There's a rumor that Lammers is thinking of suspending you for letting Brooke see her mother. I think it's only an ass-covering formality since you'll be on medical leave anyway. More important, Goodbe is conscious and recovering well enough to be questioned. Do you want to meet me at North McKenzie?"

"I'm having breakfast with my family right now, but I'll see you there in an hour."

"How's Danette doing?"

"She's fine. You know what? We should go talk to Seth Valder again first. Tell him we have Goodbe in custody and see if Valder wants to make a deal in exchange for testimony against Goodbe. I want to bust his sex-slave ring wide-open. We'll never convict him of plotting to kill Courtney."

Jackson looked up to see Kera standing in the doorway. Her disappointment was palpable. He assessed his situation and made a decision. "Change of plans, Evans. Take McCray with you. I'm having surgery tomorrow, and I'm under doctor's orders to rest."

"That's right. Don't worry, we'll handle it. Good luck tomorrow. I'll call you in a couple days and update you."

"Thanks." Jackson hung up the phone, feeling relieved.

"Good man," Kera said, coming in for another hug.

"I'm learning."

ABOUT THE AUTHOR

L.J. Sellers is a native of Eugene, Oregon, the setting of her thrillers. She's an award-winning journalist and bestselling novelist, as well as a cyclist, social networker, and thrill-seeking fanatic. A long-standing fan of police procedurals, she counts John Sandford, Michael Connelly, Ridley Pearson, and Lawrence Sanders among her favorites. Her own novels, featuring Detective Jackson, include *The Sex Club, Secrets to Die For, Thrilled to Death, Passions of the Dead, Dying for Justice, Liars, Cheaters & Thieves,* and *Rules of Crime*. In addition, she's penned three standalone thrillers: *The Baby Thief, The Gauntlet Assassin,* and *The Lethal Effect*. When not plotting crime, she's also been known to perform standup comedy and occasionally jump out of airplanes.

Made in the USA
Middletown, DE
09 January 2017